HOW

BEAUTIFUL

THEY

WERE

HOW

BEAUTIFUL

THEY

WERE

BOSTON TERAN

HIGH TOP
PUBLISHING LLC

Copyright 2018 by Brutus Productions, Inc.

ISBN: 978-1-56703-065-5
Library of Congress Control Number: 1-7543135581

Published in the United States by High Top Publications LLC, Los Angeles, CA and simultaneously in Canada by High Top Publications LLC.

Special Thanks to A TALE OF MYSTERY by Thomas Holcroft... THE RAVEN by Edgar Allen Poe...Hamlet, Othello, and Romeo and Juliet by William Shakespeare...Frankenstein by Mary Shelley... Tippecanoe and Tyler Too...Oh Come, All Ye Faithful...Just As I Am by Charlotte Elliot

Interior Design by Alan Barnett

Printed in the United States of America

To actors everywhere...who make art out of insanity

ACKNOWLEDGMENTS

To Deirdre Stephanie sand the late, great Brutarian…To G.G. and L.S.… Mz. El and Roxomania…the kids…our wonderful and enduring agent, Natasha Kern…Janice Hussein, for her fine work…Charlene Crandall, for her brains and loyalty…The Drakes at Wildbound, for their deft decisions…And finally, to my steadfast friend and ally, and a master at navigating the madness, Donald V. Allen.

PROLOGUE

CHAPTER 1

IT APPEARS THAT I, JEREMIAH FIELDS, have been cast to portray the character who steps from the shadows of the stage and into the footlights to talk directly to the audience.

A simple youth rising quietly from my work desk and stacks of ledgers to introduce the play.

I am not an actor. I have neither the talent nor the vanity. I am what is called in the theatre — the stage manager. My job is to keep the machinery of a play running smoothly. I work behind the scenes. I am unsung and unnoticed, but essential. And I might say, that in my era, there was not another like me.

Colonel Tearwood's American Theatre Company was my youth, my home, my family. And I was part of the company from its volatile beginnings in 1848 to its much written about final act.

Of course, I am here because of Nathaniel Luck. He was my mentor, my teacher, a reluctant father figure, a man driven, joyous. He was the reason newspaper reporters dogged me for his story. Why publishers tried to seduce me with their promises if I could sell the truth of him. Was he the violent murderer from London known as John James Beaufort as was alleged, or a tragic actor that life conspired against? Was he something else altogether?

If you are familiar with the theatre of those times, you might well recognize the term *la piece bien faite*. Translated, it reads — the well-made play.

La piece bien faite was a popular genre and offered to entertain its audience with a tight plot and pacing, reversals of fortune that created suspense, while

constantly building to a climactic resolution. And…
most importantly, a central part of the action takes
place before the story begins and is not known to all
the characters…but is to the audience. Such is what
follows.

ACT I

CHAPTER 2

THE SCENE IS LONDON, the theatre district, the taverns and boarding houses where the beggarly of entertainment repose. The year is 1836. It is the era before birth of the greatest theatres and the rise of spectacles. An actor not quite twenty by the name of John James Beaufort is garnering heady reviews as a talent to be reckoned with. Be it drama or comedy, he performs either with equal dexterity. He can be dashing and handsome, or unassuming and inward. He slips from playing the fool to a dangerous adversary in the space of a throwaway line.

For him being on stage was the ultimate act of freedom. Freedom from the constraints of the present as well as one's past. A chance to escape inner demons and torments by channeling their fury and creating a complete masterpiece of the self, when that self is someone else, and that self can be shed when the lights draw down.

There is a kind of freedom in the unreal world. There are no actual ghosts in that world, no all too human adversaries, no loneliness, no despair. In life man is disconnected, a fragment here, a fragment there, a lost feeling, an isolated thought, like disparate needs far flung on a map. On stage, man is a landscape, a mural with the sunrise in one hand and sunset in the other. He is darkness and light and all shadows in between. He is what no human can achieve in life.

John James sat on the brick ledge of the roof to the rooming house where he lived, looking down upon the nightstreet and its dark ranks of social insecurity. This is where it would all rise and fall, where the blackness of life becomes a grave cancer or the genesis of creation.

Inside of him he knew, as well as he knew the lines of a play, that wealth and success were within his reach. But in and of themselves, these meant nothing, except for the freedom they would give him to act upon the world, creating performances out of his willful soul that would match the great characters of literature. Foolish, maybe…but as necessary as air to distinguish the *me* from *them*.

It was while having this private dialogue with himself that the stairwell door opened. Light spilled out upon the darkness and a lantern rose and there was a girl near about his own age, caught off guard at picking up a presence there in the shadows, a slip of air rushing out of her, her free hand suddenly flat and open against her chest.

"I'm sorry, sir. I didn't know anyone was up here."

"Why should you?" he said.

"I came up here…" She pointed back toward the stairwell doorway. "It's so unbearably hot downstairs. I thought to escape it."

She came forward holding the lantern high up.

That kind of light can deceive you about someone's looks, it can cheat you with its shadows, just as it does on stage. But there was no denying the girl had singular features, a high forehead where the light glistened, and a long straight nose that seemed befitting European royalty, with black rich hair and eyes to match. She was neatly dressed and appointed, surely a step up in class from the likes of this rooming house.

"Is it all right, my being here?" she said. "Or would you prefer to be alone?"

"There's room for both of us at the ledge."

"I'm not partial to ledges," she said, handing him the lantern. "Although I've had my share of them on rooftops…and off." There was a touch of amusement in her expression and she turned away and he wasn't sure if she were being shy or coy.

He heard shouting now coming up through the well of the stairway. Two men arguing, their voices growing louder, angrier, their tone crass and vulgar.

"I wanted to escape that also." She pointed to the stairway with a look of embarrassment, if not outright shame.

"The louder and more antagonistic of the two voices is my father. He's having it out with one of the actors in his troupe."

John James recognized one of the voices as belonging to an arrogant half talent by the name of Taversham.

"Your father is no Falstaff, I gather," said John James.

"On stage…absolutely, yes. But as for the rest…" She whispered, "He's closer in kind to a Cassius."

"Might you give me your name?" he said.

"Lucretia McCarthy," she said.

"The Dyer McCarthy Troupe." He looked toward the stairwell. "Is that your father?"

"He's not the whole troupe. He only believes he is. Some of us are foot soldiers, or other interesting background."

John James began to introduce himself when Lucretia softly interrupted, "I saw you in Liverpool. In *A Tale of Mystery*."

"Talk about a showpiece of tired passions."

"The audience didn't feel that way. I found them wildly animated."

The shouting got worse. Her father sounded like a man who could easily turn violent. She walked to the ledge, the lantern guiding her steps. She took to studying the street, watching the strangers below. It was the same comings and goings as yesterday, and probably the same as tomorrow, but she watched nonetheless, as if seeking to escape somewhere in all that foot traffic and be freed of a father's intolerable voice that echoed up that funnel of a stairwell.

"Did you ever just feel like running away?" she said.

Her voice spoke with such unhappiness.

"I have run away," he said.

"Really?" How alive her eyes suddenly were. "Was it a wise decision? No...don't answer. If you say it was, I will be distraught that I have not run away. And if you say it wasn't wise, I will be dismayed I have devoted so much emotion to the idea."

Her father's voice now could be heard up through the rough dark.

"Lucretia...where are you girl?"

"I could quote the lines from many plays here, but I will not." She started back toward the doorway. "Come meet my father. He will want to know you. Fine actors are his life."

CHAPTER 3

DYER MCCARTHY STOOD ON THE SECOND FLOOR LANDING searching the hallway and unpleasantly calling out to his daughter when a light descended through the board work of the stairwell.

"I'm here, Father."

"Where have you been?"

"On the roof. It was too warm down here."

McCarthy made note of the young man who seemed to be shadowing along behind his daughter. "And what is this?" he said.

She held the lantern up near John James' face. "Do you recognize him, father?"

John James got his first real look at this Dyer McCarthy. He dressed like your self-serving gent, with a velvet coat and hat to match and a starched collar that his neck looked to have been squeezed into. He was taller and broader than John James and with a nose that had looked to have been broken years before and etched cheeklines, and eyes that were even blacker than his daughter's. And there was no masking the aura of disdain in the way he cocked his head.

"Hold the lantern closer," he said.

The girl obeyed and after one look McCarthy raised a twitchy finger and started in. "I was coming home. It was dark, everything was still. I was winding along the dale, and the rocks were all, as it was turning black. Of a sudden I heard cries! A man was murdering. I shook from head to foot. Presently the cries died away, and I beheld two bloody men with their daggers in their hands steal off——"

He was running dialogue from the play *A Tale of Mystery*. He had a scratchy, baritone's voice, but his acting was too broad and overwrought for John James' tastes.

"I saw you in that play." He put out his hand and introductions were made. McCarthy asked John James to walk with them to where a carriage waited.

"You know the old Saint Paul's church in Liverpool?" said McCarthy. "The auditorium. I'll be there tomorrow working out new troupe members.

Money has come to me, and I'll be staging *The Pickwick Papers*. Be there at wretched noon and let's see what you're made of."

He started for the carriage and there was a moment, as Lucretia blew out the lantern and she and John James were in darkness and alone, for her to safely whisper, "For your sake…don't come tomorrow."

• • •

The Low and the Mighty was a gin hole where theatre people congregated to trade news, spread gossip, and indulge in prior glories. It had a low roof and a loud piano, and the air was ripe from tanning bins across the alley. There was a notion there that was "bible" — one actor will pat another on the back to get a feel for where to put the knife.

A drunken Colonel Tearwood was at his usual post at the far end of the bar to be close to the door that led to an alley where gents went to piss. He was an aging lifewrecked performer who maintained his good will toward the world even as it turned its back on him. John James eased in beside him.

"Colonel, can you go another round?"

"Break my wrists and watch me."

John James called to the barkeep for two gins.

"And how does the world look from where you're sitting?" said the Colonel.

"What's your opinion of Dyer McCarthy?"

"The man travels with a dark cloud over him. Why?"

"He's asked me about possibly joining his troupe."

"*The Pickwick Papers*."

"How did you know?"

Tearwood jutted his chin out. And there in a smoky corner a loud and drunken Taversham was parading his anger over a table full of fellow players.

The drinks came. Reaching for their glasses, John James saw the Colonel was without his prized gold dice cufflinks.

"You pawned them again, didn't you?"

"Needed money for lodging." He raised his glass. "To Lord Eldon… who gave pawnshops a good name!"

They drank away. "Tell me about McCarthy."

"There's whispers among the Peelers," said the Colonel, "he's got some kind of business relationship with that madam down on Hellum Street with her flogging rack."

"The Barkeley woman?"

"He's got at least one Bow Street runner who does dirty work for him. It wouldn't surprise me that's where he gets his money."

"And his daughter?"

"Promising actress…I've heard rumors she's his mistress."

"You can see from their resemblance they're related."

"There's been many a father who ransacks their own."

While they talked, someone back in the bar was shouting, "Hey you… Beaufort. You hear me, you god damn coquette."

John James and the Colonel both heard him, but they paid no attention until a glass whistled past their heads and caromed off the wall before shattering.

"I believe you're being paged," said Tearwood.

John James now turned his attention to Taversham who stood off a half-dozen paces, his tall frame shrouded in bar smoke.

"I don't believe we've ever talked," said John James.

"You don't act like you're better than the next man, you just do it with a look or an expression. And I saw you tonight."

"You saw me what?"

"Playing the coquette with McCarthy. You're not gonna steal my livelihood from me without me exercising my right to kick your guts out. What do you have to say about that?"

John James said, "I steal no man's livelihood. I know my lines and wait like the rest of us. And I play the coquette only on stage and when I'm dressed for it."

There was a ripple of laughter among the murky faces that only made Taversham feel outsmarted and slighted and he started forward and John James was quick to pull a pocket pistol he kept tucked away inside his vest.

"You better hope I'm not as good a shot as I am an actor," said John James.

Some of Taversham's friends were up by now and gathering around him, trying to console and quiet him enough to get him out of that shoddy drinking hole. "This ain't a play…coquette. Understand?"

As the patrons settled out, the Colonel said to John James, "We've been friends about two years now. And I have no idea still where you're from or if you've family. And I had no idea you carried a weapon."

"Silence is better than lying, isn't it?"

"Stay away from McCarthy and his daughter. Find another part of the street to stake your fame."

"But he puts on successful plays."

"All actors suffer the same sin."

"And what is that?"

"They'll sell their souls to the devil for the right part."

John James began to laugh and slapped old Colonel Tearwood on the back. "Maybe that's because good parts are a lot harder to come by than souls."

CHAPTER 4

THE MCCARTHYS LIVED OFF DRURY LANE on Craven. They had a series of well-appointed apartments above a spirits shop that catered to the carriage trade. The neighborhood beggars knew enough to keep clear of the McCarthys except when the daughter was alone. The girl climbed the stairs ahead of her father, so she might draw up the light. She had navigated his moods enough to know silence was her only ally.

His grey white face walked through the doorway and past her as if she did not exist. She closed the door behind him and hoped there was no white hot rage to come.

He set his hat down on the entry sideboard and took off his coat, passing on her help with the dismissive brush of a hand. He gave her the coat and started to undo his cravat as he walked down the hall to the bedroom.

She carried the coat like a servant and passed a mirror above the sideboard to see a seventeen-year-old stranger staring desperately back at her. Lucretia McCarthy was a frightened creature whose youth had been poisoned and her dreams stolen, who was desperate to escape her circumstances, but helpless to do so, and who went about the streets of the world smiling and polite, living out these lies to hide a private sickness of anger and shame at her plight. She wondered if there were other girls like herself living out the desperate helplessness she endured.

The light was golden in the glass and it made her beautiful, and it made her skin shine and her coal black eyes lustrous. She could have been a girl in a painting. But she did not feel like a girl in a painting and her skin did not shine in her heart and her coal black hair and coal black eyes were not lustrous but bleak and desolate. She was not a girl in any painting she knew.

She prayed he would not come, and she prayed that he would come, and she hated herself for either prayer because they spoke to her helplessness.

"Insignificant footsteps."

His voice was suddenly there in the darkness of the hallway.

"Excuse me, Father?"

She saw him now in the mirror at the edge of the light, his eyes squinting with their incurable malice.

"Some of us leave insignificant footsteps."

He took a step forward. She saw now his hands were behind his back. She wished he were dead.

"When you were alone with that boy for a few moments by the carriage, you told him something. What did you tell him?"

"Tell him, Father?"

"What—did—you—tell—him?"

"I said...I...we hoped to see him tomorrow."

He moved a step closer. His boots caused the floorboards to creak. She saw now that he carried the leather strap.

"You will not willfully ruin my plans. What did you tell him?"

"I——"

"Your trembling gives you away. What did you tell him?"

• • •

"Had my instinct about people failed me that night? Was I being drawn and quartered without my knowledge for some nefarious purpose, and I did not appreciate the tensions at work?"

John James was already known on the American stage as Nathaniel Luck when we first had this conversation. It took place in his dressing room long after the theatre was empty, and one could hear it creak with the ghosts of age.

"What about Lucretia?" I said.

Just her name caused hints of shadow around his green eyes. Eyes that when still seemed to open like the sea when the sun was upon it.

"You did go to Saint Charles Auditorium to meet with McCarthy?"

"Yes, Jeremiah...When she whispered to me to not come the next day...Her face...It was always so utterly human and expressive. She could convey any number of emotions in the turn of a look. Innocent

victim…consummate actress. She was both."

It had begun to rain. It had been threatening all that day and all that evening. You could hear the first trace of it high up in the theatre rafters. And that is where he had taken to staring. I imagined he was remembering some intimate moment with her. His expression spoke of suffering and loss.

"Jeremiah, I had a tintype of Lucretia. But it was lost to me while I was being hunted for her murder."

"Why did you go to St. Charles the next day? Truly?"

He took to rubbing the tips of his long fingers slowly down his rouged cheek. He was somewhere in the depths of a thought.

"Good old Colonel Tearwood," he said. "He once told me, 'The eyes of reason are blind to what one sees through emotion.' I assumed he stole that line from a play. Now I know better."

• • •

The church was up in Saint Giles rookery off Great Russell Street. It was a slum of Irish immigrants. A tome to squalor and overcrowding. Born of affluence a century before, it had become a warren of misery and decay, courtesy of man's lesser angels. The church was in a state of distress and disrepair thanks to fire. The auditorium still stood and was used on Sundays for Mass, but during the week the priests rented it out to help feed the poor. Dyer McCarthy was notorious for finding places in the worst neighborhoods to rent for cheap. The surroundings to him were nothing more than a fiction.

When John James entered the auditorium the high sun commanded light down through the stained glass windows and cast colored images of divinity and sainthood across the sets and upon the stage and the pulpit placed there. While on the other side of the auditorium the windows had been smashed to the sashboards and partly boarded up with slatwood. It was a scene befitting a night at the theatre.

McCarthy was on stage rehearsing a trio of pantomimists while a handful of actors sat together over by the boarded up windows waiting on their turn to be ordered about like prisoners to be flogged or carted off to the guillotine. The curse of the actor — always victim to the gnawing insecurity they are not good enough.

And adding to the scene, a dozen set of eyes and partial faces peering through slivery openings in the board work. A gang of street children giving out their unfettered and saucy opinions of the performers and the awaiting actors. A humorous and heartless ragtag chorus of opinionaters.

But it was her that had his attention, sitting alone at a table below the stage, taking down on writing paper whatever her father stormed on about.

McCarthy paused when he saw John James with his hands in his pockets back up the aisle. His eyes narrowed under heavy brows and this sudden change caused his daughter to turn.

"You're late," said McCarthy.

"Noon is five minutes yet," said John James.

"Five minutes early for everyone else is five minutes late for me."

"I'll take that as bible for later."

"Later…is now."

"Let's save our disagreements for after I'm with the troupe."

John James now came forward. The players taking him under consideration, and McCarthy noting John James may have been answering him, but the young man's attention was clearly on his daughter.

"Good noon to you," he said to the girl.

She tried to smile through a look of anguish, but she turned away to hide her feelings.

John James had lived with that expression. Off stage and on. It still wandered his memory in all its shadowy fragments. Terrible sorrow knows terrible sorrow when it sees it.

There were figs in a bowl on the table and he reached out. "Might I take one?" he said.

"Do you think management is here to feed the actors?" said McCarthy.

"No sir," said John James, popping a fig into his mouth. "It is the actor who is here to feed management."

John James saw now there was another man in the theatre sitting off alone. He was no performer, that was sure. He had the look and feel of a man whose business was threats and blunt force. He was well dressed but the clothes seemed to wear him clumsily. Too snug or loose in the wrong places. He couldn't be over thirty by John James' estimation, but the bald head did his youth no justice.

"Well," said McCarthy, "show off your talents. But let's not turn it into a crucifixion scene."

John James thrashed about a few thoughts and looked over his surroundings. He reached out and took Lucretia by the hand. "Favor me. I'll need an assist."

She had no idea and was reticent and looked to her father. John James grabbed a handful of figs as her father watched silently and stone faced as John James led her up the steps to the stage. She followed, the hesitant soul, till they were at the pulpit steps.

Here is where he spoke to her quietly, "I'm sorry for coming, but the thought of you was too much to resist."

No one had taken her hand like that before, ever. Was it the actor talking, or the youth with the spearing eyes and combed back fine hair? Everything in her life had been manipulative or mean spirited, that's what she knew.

This moment was pure physical sensation. The warm sun through painted glass, the unwashed peering children's faces, the curious pantomimists in their baroque costumes silent in the half shadows. She was alive to it all, and the dishonesty and violence around her life, the strap wounds down her body. Alive...free of it all, for those moments.

John James leaned over and whispered in her ear, and as he did, she saw her father nod to that soulless creature sitting off alone. Then as he asked, she slipped down and sat on the pulpit steps.

John James crossed the stage from the pulpit to where the windows were boarded up. The three pantomimists began to stalk along behind him, hands to their chins, comically thoughtful until John James turned on them and they scattered, stumbling over each other to escape his faux ire. Children's laughter through the window boards.

John James yelled to them. "Get back from the windows for a moment. Go on now. Keep clear." And then with his hobnail boots he kicked at the slats until they broke apart and dust filled light poured in the huge opening. "Now you can see," he said.

There was a flurry of faces and shoulders fighting, arguing for position. And John James right there in the mad scramble handing out figs. Then when he had their attention, he put a finger to his lips for them to quiet.

He pointed to the pulpit across the stage. "What light through yonder window breaks."

On that cue, Lucretia stood. The light from the stained glass window gracing her.

He was not dramatizing for an audience of seats. He was speaking quietly, in little more than a whisper, really, to the unwashed urchins squeezed into the opening beside him. He'd made them the world and they were all huddled together secretly in the shadows and his voice was all their voice.

"It is the east, and Juliet is the sun. Arise, fair sun, and kill the envious moon…"

As she experienced the lines she reached up and took the pins from her hair and shook it loose and the hair fell about her face, black and sweeping. The gesture so refined and straight from the heart. He had not cued her to do this. This was the actor in her reaching down into the soul of who she was to capture a moment of freedom.

CHAPTER 5

THERE WAS LOUD, ARROGANT APPLAUSE that stole the moment. Attention turned to the back of the auditorium where Taversham stood clapping. As he came down the aisle, he said, "So this is what you're replacing me with? Some itinerant strolling player. Ascending to the ordinary, are you?"

McCarthy stepped to the edge of the stage, arms folded. "The audience doesn't want you anymore. They haven't for a while. Whether it's because you're getting older, or your performances lazier and obviously stolen from other performers. Or that the paying customer has just grown tired of your look. It doesn't matter. An actor is a suit of clothes, or a dress. When they're too worn, or out of style, they are cast aside. Because there is always a new suit of clothes, or another dress."

There was a cautionary silence about the auditorium, for as performers they were all well aware such a fate may await them. No matter how much they dreamed, or hoped, or prayed.

Taversham looked John James over. Him in the loose fitting trousers and hobnail boots of a workman, with the comfortable shirt and sartorial vest of a showman. Was this strange sketch of a character the future? It left him infuriated and revenge driven.

"You think you're going to survive this?" he said to John James. He scanned a litany of silent, troubled faces he had lived and performed with. "Or you…or you…or you?" Then he turned his spite on McCarthy. "And you. The consummate liar and fraud."

"Mister Jonah," said McCarthy.

The man who had been sitting alone now stood. The hat he had been holding in his lap, he now set neatly on the seat. John James watched as he clasped his hands together behind his back and walked to the aisle where he took up a place between Taversham and McCarthy.

This certainly informed Taversham to end his march to the stage. "The truth about you will come out," said Taversham. "Someone will see to it."

He clearly meant himself. And to this, McCarthy said, "You'd be best served to maintain a tender indifference. I hope you understand my meaning."

• • •

There was a mist that evening along the Thames. John James liked to walk in that kind of weather, as it stirred the imagination. He had made his decision. There is no substitute in the world for daring. It is the only defense man has against the condemned existence that is mediocrity.

John James entered the Low and the Mighty tavern from the alley where a couple of drunks were aiming their pizzle at the brick wall to see who could write their names the grandest.

Tearwood was leaning drunkenly into the bar and knew, as only an actor who is tuned to know, what someone is saying in the way they inhabit space or how they physically dominate a moment, knew. So, when John James slid in beside him with an airy confidence, how he got the barkeep's attention with this perfect little drama of a move with his hand, the old man said, "You're in business with the devil."

"The devil puts on successful plays."

"But he's still the devil."

"If it wasn't for the devil, there would be no need for a Bible. And the Bible is the most successful play of all time."

The barkeep brought a mug of gin and brusquely scooped up his change.

As he drank, John James glanced at the old man's shirt sleeves. "I see you got your cufflinks back."

"Heavenly intervention."

They tapped glasses and Tearwood held up his loose wrist. The cufflink there such a beautiful and only slightly tarnished solid gold dice.

"I'll be doing scenes from *Romeo and Juliet*," said John James. "And *Hamlet*...McCarthy has a contract to put on *Fedora*."

"You've made an error in judgment with that man," said Tearwood.

"As an actor, greatness demands daring...taking risks."

"On stage...not off."

"That...is cheating."

"So says the voice of youthful passion."

John James knew the old man thought him a little mad.

"I got a part myself today," said the Colonel.

"Enlighten me."

"I'll be playing the night watchman at the Thames Theatre. My performance is between midnight and six. The part isn't challenging. It does not demand being daring...or taking risks. But it comes with a dry attic bed."

John James swung an arm over Tearwood's shoulder. "No one can dress up a warning like you do."

• • •

He walked home in a deepening mist, down streets crowded with ill fitting structures, the rosettes of light from the windows growing more unearthly block by block.

He always felt that existence was what he carried around inside him, that he was a citizen of that country. And now this other existence, the one harbored in the world he passed through was coming to him, not only to measure his talent, but to test his resolve and purpose.

He did not take notice of the carriage parked across from his rooming house or the door swing open and a hooded figure quietly rush toward him.

"John James."

He turned at the sound of his name to find an inkblack shadow reaching toward him. "I need to talk to you," she said.

He looked toward the carriage.

"No," said Lucretia. "I'm here alone."

CHAPTER 6

John James unlocked the door to his room, and she waited in the dimly lit hallway as he tuned up a kerosene lamp. She entered, hesitant, looking about, and when she heard footsteps on the shabby stairwell, she shut the door quickly behind her. She stood with her back against the wall and pointed. "The windows," she said.

He understood, and he closed the cheap muslin curtains.

The light trembled from air stealing through the loose fitting window boards. She looked about. It was a small room and surprisingly neat, with a brass bed and paltry armoire and a table with two cushioned chairs by the bay window. And there were folios of plays and books, used worn books, piled in stacks along the wall, by the bed, beside the table.

"Is this all right?" he said.

"All right? How do you mean?"

"Do you want to sit?"

She shook her head. "Not yet."

He was by the table and he opened a music box he'd set there. It ran off a few notes, and from it he took tobacco and rolling paper. "Do you mind?"

"No," she said.

Her breathing was shallow and frightened.

"You should never have agreed to perform for my father."

"I perform for the audience. I am only employed by your father."

"You understand what I'm saying?"

"Do you understand what I'm saying?"

She pressed her hand against her cheek. "I feel terribly uneasy tying to talk like this."

She crossed the room and sat in a chair at the table in the bay window that looked down on the street.

He lit the cigarette he had rolled. "What is at the heart of this?" he said.

Her eyes were sad suddenly.

"It's an immoral world you've entered."

"It's an immoral world we were born into."

"What I speak to you now about, you must exercise caution and silence. My life would be at risk."

"You have my silence."

She looked like someone who knew what it was to have been robbed of their existence, but who was holding on to any remnant of hope. "Trust is terrifying, if it fails you."

He pulled a chair closer to her and sat. "This is what you came for, isn't it?"

She looked at the curtains. She reached out as if she were going to part them and peek out. But she didn't.

"Are you worried that your father might——"

"No. He's gone to Stratford for two days with Mister Jonah. He's the man at the auditorium today. But even knowing that, doesn't make me any less——"

"Yes. I see it in your face."

"My father," she said finally, "he finances his plays through extortion and blackmail. He exploits human failings, heartbreak, personal weaknesses, foibles. Mister Jonah. He used to be with the Bow Street runners."

"The police?"

"Runners pass him information about certain citizens…information that can be used against them. My father makes the approach. He feigns being an intermediary sent there to negotiate a deal and keep their indiscretion from going public. Mister Jonah is there if stronger tactics are necessary. If a deal is consummated, the runner is paid a stipend for the information."

She finished. He inhaled on his cigarette then set it down on a small plate. "I never realized the theatre could be so…interesting…off stage."

"I hope your humor isn't a sign you will misjudge the seriousness of this."

"Quite the opposite. I can find humor in a hanging. After all, it is only a momentary fall from grace. But I assure you I still realize it's a hanging."

"My father will use any means to exploit someone. He did this with Taversham. He found something out about the man. Brought him into the troupe. At his most popular, the troupe hired out for private performances and parties for the wealthy. Not long after, something from the household was missing. Jewelry…silver. He will ruin your life to control you. I know all about this. He has ruined my life, and he means to force me to help ruin yours."

When she offered that, she voiced such personal pain and humiliation. It was a fact and confession, and the shame of it had her leaning forward and staring down at the floor.

He reached for his cigarette and smoked to give her privacy and time. He was looking into a wounded soul, and her suffering was suddenly his suffering.

She had begun to cry. He had not noticed at first. She'd made no sound. John James only realized when her face lifted, and he saw in the trembling light how liquid the pupils had become.

He put the cigarette down and went to her. He kneeled down to be close.

"You're a talented actor, you know that?" he said. "I saw when you loosed your hair and later when we read lines. You have a gift."

"For a little while," she said, "when I act, I am freed of him. And I escape my shame."

He could smell the damp on her cape and traces of perfume in her hair. He was possessed of her already. He knew this instinctively and immediately. And the anguish and pain. They only made her all the more desirable.

"You don't want me gone," he said, "do you?"

She wiped at her tears. She was so hopelessly young. "When it comes to this…my heart is my worst enemy."

CHAPTER 7

JOHN JAMES LOVED NIGHTS LIKE THIS from the roof when the mist so thickened it turned the city into a great black well where you can dream and think and settle accounts to your liking and change the invisible balance of the universe unto your favor.

"He's Lord Ruthven, you know."

John James was caught off guard and his head shot up and his features stiffened. It was Taversham, with a heavy cape around his shoulders coming slowly out of the grey and milky night. He was slightly drunk and disillusioned and fully wearing his fall from professional grace.

"McCarthy, the bastard…He's the Lord Ruthven character in the play. Do you know the play?"

"*The Vampire* by Planché. I know it."

John James reached into his vest pocket and Taversham hesitated. He thought the youth might be retrieving his pistol, but instead it was tobacco and rolling papers he wanted.

"McCarthy is the Vampire…don't you think?" Taversham took the wing of his cape and swept it across the lower part of his face so he was only a set of eyes. He then whispered, "Only this vampire doesn't drink just the blood of the women he marries to keep alive."

Taversham let the cape fall away from his face. "That was the part that brought him notoriety. It made his career. It was also the first play he produced."

John James spread tobacco on the rolling paper. He paid Taversham meagre attention.

"There is one rumor I particularly like," said Taversham. "That he raised the money for that play by murdering a Romanian woman. She was a widow who had become his lover. This took place in Germany. That should say it all, of course."

John James tightly rolled the smokings.

"The real play should be about McCarthy's life as an actor and troupe manager who murders to finance the productions. They are the victims of his professional bloodsucking. Along with the actors, of course. The blood is always sucked out of the actors."

John James licked the edge of the rolling paper and slid a long finger down the length of it, then slipped the cigarette into his mouth.

Taversham had grown angrier, more acidic. "Was she honest with you when she came to you? With heart in hand, I'm sure. Did she play the wounded sparrow?"

"I have no idea who or what you're talking about."

"Very nice line reading. The perfect blend of questioning and honesty. But I saw her leaving in a carriage."

John James struck a match. There was an eyelet of flame he held up.

"Did she tell you how he finances his plays? And that he uses her? And you should escape all this? She's played that little drama before."

He put cigarette to flame and drew in and that slight eyelet of fire flushed up in the mist.

"You know what the best part is?" said Taversham. "You won't listen to me. You won't take any of this to heart. Because you're too proud, too vain and damn defiant. And that…pleases me to no end."

John James stood there watching the match burn.

"Nothing to say?"

"Yeah…parting is such sweet sorrow. Isn't it?"

He blew out the match.

• • •

"Three times in one night, I was warned. One after the other after the other, as if they were the three fates issuing upon my destiny. One spins the thread, one measures the thread, one cuts the thread. Taversham had been right. I was too proud, too vain, too defiant.

"I found myself one day in this world, and I was shocked to learn I meant to take myself wherever being found in this world demanded of me.

"And besides that," Nathaniel had said. "I was twenty and life was suddenly pouring into me from the very soul of things. Everything before that night had been ordinary. And here was this girl, this opportunity, and this challenge."

Reading this, I thought, I could be writing about my own life. I'd met Nathaniel when I was seventeen years old. My existence could have been easily described as empty of purpose. Nathaniel had changed all that with Colonel Tearwood's Theatre Company, and suddenly life was pouring in through the very souls of things. And one of those was a girl who arrived courtesy of misfortune—Rosina Swain. She wasn't yet twenty herself and looked to be born from little fragments of heaven. But that's for later.

CHAPTER 8

McCARTHY WAS A HARD TASKMASTER who made an art form out of insults and bad temper. He was a talented actor, and even more so when it came to preparing and producing plays. Living deceitfully as he did, gave him rare insights into the states of high drama onstage that would be beyond the grasp of less hideous human beings.

His ability to tighten the grip on an actor's performance was second to none. Maybe that's because he believed in Old Testament style fear as a means of bringing the best out in an actor. He would tell his people before a show, "With every performance you put your head in the guillotine... and that is where it belongs." Those in his troupe were known to light candles in church and pray for his swift and terrible demise.

Rehearsals on *The Pickwick Papers* began. McCarthy brought his wrath down the hardest on John James. He plumbed professionalism to its darkest depths. John James defended himself with the one weapon God had given him——his talent.

They argued over stage directions, interpreting lines of dialogue, how to portray Dickens' grotesqueries of character. But these were not, in fact, what they were fighting about. Their war was over existence. Over which will would survive, which will have sway over the future? And central to that future was Lucretia McCarthy, as woman, as actress, and as a living soul.

McCarthy meant to destroy John James even as he worked to make him and the play a success. And in that fact would lie his ultimate alibi for a murder being planned. During rehearsals, McCarthy had Mister Jonah secret himself into John James' apartment and go through his belongings and papers, his books, to search for any hidden cache, hunting for that which could be used against him. In the sanctity of their apartments, Lucretia would often hear her father call John James "that unburied corpse." She warned John James of this, telling him, "He means to build you up, so the fall is that much more devastating."

"And why do I arouse such a passionate reaction?"

"Because you are defiant. And he knows I love you."

John James seemed to thrive during states of unease. The play was a success. John James unleashed little creative changes during each performance. One night he stepped from the stage carrying a jug of gin and offered it to one of the patrons. Thinking it probably water, the patron was joyously shocked to get a swallowful of lethal Blue Ruin. On another night during a monologue, John James marched out of the theatre only to return with a fiddler who had been busking out front before the show and had him spontaneously play while the scene continued.

• • •

McCarthy remained muted, after all, his *Pickwick Papers* was well received and making money. And besides, he was waiting for Mister Jonah to let him know when he was ready to exact a murder.

At home in their apartments, McCarthy was moody and quietly watchful. Lucretia now lived in the growing shadow of crisis. Her despair at home mirrored against the joy she had being with John James.

They stole little ecstasies wherever and whenever they could. Moments that might otherwise seem mundane were now charged with emotion. The shackles of loneliness and worthlessness cast off as an improbable universe showered them with favor. The colors of heaven bled through the blacks and whites of everyday grief, and the touch of the person's hand and the rest of the world was just fictitious air, gone with the first good breeze. If she weren't so fearful of her father she would have written it all down in a journal, but she knew nothing was safe from his unrelenting eye.

McCarthy sat in the dimly lit drawing room, reading. The curtains were drawn to keep out the rabble noises of the street. Lucretia entered, and she knelt on the carpet before him and in her most humbled and deferential voice said, "Could you see your way at letting me go?"

She had rehearsed this endless times, practicing to hide any hint in her voice of embitterment or rage. But to win this fight she had to lose another, and that being, she began to cry. She was crying at the shameful transformation of herself, a young and talented woman, into some pathetic cur.

He didn't even bother to look up from his book, and to get an answer from him she clutched at his pant leg.

"It's impossible," he said.

Her voice trailed off into what seemed the desperate forever. "Why…

can't you allow me this?"

"Because," he said, "I am not finished with you."

She walked from the room trying to gather up her shattered pride. She grabbed a cape and against her father's orders left the apartments. Fleeing down the stairs she came upon Mister Jonah who just then had entered the building. He took off his hat. "Miss McCarthy."

She did not answer. She thought only of getting by him as quickly and painlessly as possible.

"May I say your work on stage has been…a miracle. And that it brings me personal joy to watch you…blossom."

"Thank you," she said, trying not to sound dismissive. She went to pass him, but he edged toward her, so she could not quite get by. He was unpleasantly close to her. He had an unexpressive face, though harshly featured. Privately, she called it "a stagnant pool."

"I only wish," he said. "I had a small part in your flowering. Maybe in the future."

She looked away. "You need to excuse me."

He stepped back politely and let her pass. "Is the good man in?"

She turned. Her look unsettled him. Her eyes were black and violent. "He's not good. And neither are you. Nor am I."

She continued down the stairs.

"Be careful," he said.

She opened the door and noise from the nightstreet poured in.

"It's not wise," he said, "to amuse oneself with insults."

CHAPTER 9

IN HER CAPE, SHE WAS A FIGURE OF ANGUISH trying to escape the knowledge her father would not even let a single seed of love survive within her. She intended to go to John James and confess to him the truth about her life, that so far, she had not. What her father had done to her, and with her. She would plead with John James to escape with her to somewhere actors like themselves could grow and survive. And maybe they could create their own acting troupe with adventurous and passionate——

Standing there in the gritty London daylight she was struck by a terrifying thought — could she kill her father and be done with him?

Under the spell of this ruthlessly simple question she walked among the trading stalls and food sellers and up through vacant lots where destitute travelers camped their wagons and cooked over open fires, and past secondhand shops and cloth vendors and faires and sellers of quack nostrums and imitation jewelry stolen from the realms of the dead while she plotted a violent scheme the likes of which she'd only performed on stage. She wandered through a ramshackle world of paupers and itinerants, bootblacks and beggars and hardened workmen lazing out front of the pubs, their skin like ravaged oilcloth, when she felt the moral hand of God around her throat.

Like the evil witches in *Macbeth* who had risen up out of the swamp that was Macbeth's soul, her father had risen out of her own soul, with all his irredeemable acts, in fact, to possess her.

She took to walking down a busy street of merchants where clowns and jugglers and musicians were known to peddle their talents to pay for bread or lodging. She wanted to be among artists and entertainers, and rid herself of murder.

Among the food sellers and games of chance was a girl playing a battered harp. She could not have been more than ten or twelve, and she wore a ratty coat and railroad cap and looked to be a foreigner. Spanish maybe, or even a gypsy. And sitting alongside her on a wooden crate was her mother with an infant and a tin cup.

Lucretia leaned against a brick wall off alone and listened to this waif musician and the plaintive strings of *Barbara Allen*, the old Scottish ballad rising up through the clattering of carriage wheels and harness metal and merchants hustling. And Lucretia felt this was God reminding her through the music that art and beauty transcend the trappings of human poison.

• • •

She told John James about the confrontation with her father, and his cold blooded rejection of her pleas. They stood together in the alley behind the theatre as the long shadows of evening closed in. She confessed how she had wanted to kill him and how the incident with the little girl caused her to come to see how wrong it would have been. She was ashamed of such a thought, and he held her tightly and she cried against his shoulder. They did not know that her father was watching them from a filthy theatre window high above.

They began to plot the leaving, the escaping somewhere to act and live and find joy. But they knew they could not let themselves be betrayed by loose talk or the foolish missteps of earnestness. She hated the way her father watched them from the wings, like a character drawn from the pages of literary contempt. This made her all the more defiant. And the defiance made her bolder and more determined on stage, enhanced her work, and this only caused her father to hate all the more.

Applause does not lie. And the applause at the end of each show told her that she and John James were growing more popular and that they might be able at some point to put together a troupe of their own. At least that was the dream they secretly told themselves.

The nights when the show went particularly well, her father would take her violently, and afterward, he would seem acutely satisfied. She never confessed to John James about this for fear of what he might do. She only wished the courage she showed on stage, she could steal for her own being and so confront her father face to face on the battlefield he had made of existence, because she realized more and more, if they did not separate from him and soon, this would come to no good end, even after it ended. For as far as her father was concerned, revenge was forever.

CHAPTER 10

A HANDFUL OF ACTORS WERE GATHERED UP on the stoop of the rooming house when John James returned. With their pies and tins of ale they spent the evening pontificating on their miseries and frustrations, when one of them whispered, "The son of a bitch is back."

John James was never much for stoop talk or passing time soaking up stupidities. "Good evening, gentlemen," is all he said. "And if you'll excuse me…"

He meant to go to his room, but the men didn't seem inclined to make it easy for him to pass.

"I don't expect the parting of the Red Sea in my honor, but——"

"There'll be a Red Sea all right," said one of them, "but not one he might expect."

There was a little burlesque laughter. John James edged his way up the steps, keeping to the handrail, when one of the men spit on his boots and got part of John James' trousers.

"I didn't notice you there," said the man.

The whole manner of the men had grown a little more insidious.

"This is all a mystery to me," said John James. "And not one I'm interested in unraveling."

Another of the men had risen up and run inside and could be heard yelling, "Taversham…McCarthy's boy is back."

Another gent sitting on the stoop, but now standing, said to John James, "What you've done is rotten business."

"If it's a rotten business, I haven't done it."

He entered the rooming house with the men from the stoop up and trudging in behind him. A poor cartoon of a mob if ever there was one. And here came Taversham down the stairs with a copy of *The Spectator* in one hand and slapping it across the palm of the other, with two of his drinking friends wearing their best henchman looks behind him. They'd be a joke if they weren't so pathetic. And they all were in the middle of that worn out atrium with John James trapped on the stairs between them. He knew from seeing *The Spectator* what this was going to turn into.

"Well," he said, looking about him, "the only things missing are costumes, a little makeup and the soothsayer warning me about *The Ides of March*."

Taversham held out the newspaper until it was inches from John James' face. He pushed it away without ceremony. He knew. *The Spectator* had put out a review of the play. It had been particularly enthusiastic about John James, calling him a promising presence who knew how to turn a phrase. And, almost as an afterthought, the review had added — "the troupe benefits from not having the frequent hysterics of Byron Taversham to distract from the good work of fellow actors."

All the anger in the world cannot disguise the personal humiliation that Taversham was suffering. John James actually felt bad for him, even as he had first read the review, because he knew this kind of venal dressing down was something that is all actors' nightmare.

"It's bad enough I have to face this kind of badly written rubbish," said Taversham, "but to have the newspaper slipped under my door. To rub my face in the mud of it."

"Then all this drama is about someone slipping that newspaper under your door, and you thought———"

"Not someone, you, ratbag."

A meaty faced sod pressed through the crowd. "Give it up, foozler. Cause we're gonna get the truth out of you."

In no uncertain terms, John James said, "I don't prey upon other people's anguish."

He knew it wasn't going to matter whatever he said. He could smell the meanness in the crowd, that futile, weary anger and pent dissatisfaction they didn't know what to do with. Then here came John James to take out a little misery on.

John James took a step to start upstairs to his room when Taversham lunged at him, shouting, "Watch out. He may be reaching for a pistol."

The men that were close enough charged John James. They were a crowded heap tearing open his vest and shirt, grabbing up through the balustrade at his back, putting their fists and boots to him. When they found he had no weapon, Taversham had the men stand back.

John James reached out with his hand, bobbing as it searched for the handrail. When he had a grip on it, he pulled himself to his feet, blood coming from his nose and mouth.

He looked at the men about him. "Geniuses...one and all." He was unsteady on his feet, but willing for a go at what he knew was coming. "You spend too much time on the stoop," he said. "Basking in all your petty slights and grievances. Crying over bad reviews and resentful of the parts you didn't get. Instead of clinging to your craft and busking on the street if you have to, to keep you lucid and your talents sharp, so you don't sink into the monotonous squalor of your rejections. That not only makes you cowards, it makes you an insult to actual cowards." He wiped at the blood running from his nose into his mouth. And with that, John James thrust himself into Taversham's chest.

CHAPTER 11

TEARWOOD EMBRACED THE HOURS IN THE THEATRE alone with his memories. The quiet, empty seats there in the dark. He would sometimes wander out to where the lights would be, his boots echoing on the worn stage boards, breathing in the musty silence to relive scenes that had been so much a part of his life's journey. He hated the thought that age is married to sorrow, and that sorrow is born of regret. He would never succumb to sorrow or regret, because they diminish oneself in their own eyes. And besides, he still had the hunger he knew as a boy to costume and makeup, then reach out into the dark as a stranger, embracing moments of love or hate, madness and jealousy, murder, the more vile or beautiful the better. To live where art and life are impossible to separate.

There was the sudden pounding of a fist on the stage door. A dark and distant thudding that felt of desperation.

As he pulled the latch bolt and swung open the heavy door John James had been leaning against to keep upright, he collapsed there on the floor. The old man knelt down beside him. The youth's vest and shirt were torn and bloody.

"Dear God, son…What's happened?"

Not one to surrender his sense of humor so easily, he said, "I just gave the performance of my life…but it didn't seem to go over so well with the critics."

• • •

John James sat at a prop table on the stage, the flats of castle walls about him. Here was a basin of water on the table and cloth strips to clean his wounds. He squeezed the blood from the wet rags and the basin turned scummy with red.

Colonel Tearwood came down from the attic with a pocket bottle of whiskey. "It could have been anyone in the rooming house to put that newspaper under the door. There's always plenty of spite afoot. Taversham might have done it himself to set the dogs on you."

John James looked down at his side, his ribs were discolored from where hell had been kicked out of them. "It was McCarthy."

"How can you be sure?"

"Someone's been in my room."

"And what tells you this?"

He drank and he drank. He looked out at the well of dark seats. He would like to lay with her right here, in the dark, looking up at the roof and pretending it was the stellar depths.

"Did you hear me, son?"

"I know someone has been in my room because my pistol is missing."

• • •

When John James entered the theatre the next day for their performance, McCarthy was raining down temper on his troupe that their manner had become complacent and their performance did not shine. The players knew these threats inside out so well that when the master felt stress of any kind, he loaded misery on the troupe. One of the pantomimists who McCarthy could not see during his tirade was mimicking the master in broad gestures, feigning use of a whip, his face contorted, his tongue lolling about his jaw then bending over and gyrating as if being buggered.

This too all turned the moment John James stepped up on the stage and the players saw his cut and battered face and how he carefully walked because of the kicking his ribs had endured. Even McCarthy drew up silent at the sight of him, and then his daughter pushed past the others and how she held John James. There was no contending with that kind of impassioned closeness.

She knew exactly what had happened when John James told the others. "Someone tried to rob me...nothing more." She looked at her father, her mother of pearl skin flushed around her cheeks. Such rage there. She brought her hands up to John James' face and touched softly with her fingers around the edges of such marked violence. "It must end," she whispered.

"It will," he said.

That night during the play, when John James was to introduce another episode from *The Pickwick Papers,* he stepped out of the scene and into life, leaving the actors like stranded islands for the next two minutes. The audience though, they did not know John James had loosed himself from the moorings of the plot.

"I'm going to tell you a story," he said, "about a boy who was a tosher. You all know that is one of the filthiest means of survival God has ever permitted to exist on this earth."

He moved to the edge of the stage, he was just beyond the lights——a man lit from below and behind. A stark shadow just come from another world.

"You ladies and gentlemen be thankful to never know what life is to haunt the foul sewers of London searching through miles of human waste, and worse, for anything of value to sell, so you may eat…shards of metal, silver cutlery, human bones, the rare coin that was dropped in the gutter and lost to the hole of man's leavings. And the tosher, always in fear of the Thames rising or the flooding waters from a sudden rain.

"And during one such storm the sewers flooded over by the fish market, and the boy was washed up on the muddy banks of the river with his life, but two broken legs, to die or to survive according to God's will.

"Well…he crawled up endless steps in agony to the road where he almost went under the wheels of a carriage.

"God must have been watching, for in the carriage were Christian ministers who ran an orphanage…The William Elias House…I'm sure you've heard of it. The boy was gotten well there and then leased out to a bookkeeper of records who taught him to read and write and so work for him. And more than that, for the bookkeeper had a secret…He was going blind. So, for a time the boy was his eyes.

"That boy…He grew up to be, of all things, an actor, like the ones here you see on stage.

"Now," he said, starting to move about as if with a secret. "This particular actor was in love with a maiden who was an actor like himself, only better, and who had a father who was a master with his own troupe, and how he hated the youth, even more than he hated most everyone, for hating was his nature."

He glanced at McCarthy, who was an actor himself, on stage bearing his fury as he looked for a moment to end this witch hunt without disquieting the audience.

John James then said, "Would you like to know what ruinous game the master tried to play on this youth?"

Lucretia stepped out from the waiting cast on stage. "I want to know what trick the master played. Tell us, please——"

• • •

"She was the essence of lurid curiosity," said Nathaniel. "The way she drew the audience into the scene was beautiful to watch."

He was back there in the theatre that night with the pure joy of the moment, and then he drew in on himself.

"You told them about the rooming house?" I said.

He nodded.

"Did they suspect you were talking about yourself?"

"What kind of actor would I be if I didn't at least tease them with the possibility?"

"The story about the boy. Was that your story?"

He gave me a look that was impossible to discern.

"An actor's life is a little piece of everything he's lived and seen and read and heard...*and played.* The actor should never be tied to one story for too long. Think how limiting life would be for a person to be Edward the Second, or Faust, or Romeo or Joan of Arc...every day!"

CHAPTER 12

BEFORE THE CURTAIN HAD FULLY CLOSED, before McCarthy could turn on John James and have him fired then violently removed from the theatre the young actor flung his costume coat and hat in the older man's face.

"I'm going to begin a campaign to see you never work in London again," said McCarthy.

"Better you were born indifferent than immoral *and* intolerable. Faust, at least, sold his soul to the devil. You are the devil."

McCarthy turned his rage upon his fellow actors who had been standing there in fear and watching and they immediately scattered like sheep.

John James took Lucretia by the arm. Her father shouted for her to get away from him. Mister Jonah had by this time come backstage. John James was talking quickly and quietly with Lucretia with the little time they had before events turned.

McCarthy had ordered Mister Jonah to have done with John James. As the former policeman approached them, John James rose up a fisted hand and told dear Mister Jonah, "This won't be as easy as sneaking into a man's room. And before we're done occupying each other's time, I will have torn your sex out with my bare hands."

• • •

There was no fight, though not because either man was wanting, but because Lucretia had so confronted her father with veiled threats that spoke to his possible undoing, he just let John James go.

John James had had his belongings moved from the rooming house to the theatre where the Colonel now took up his attic residence.

"An old trunk and suitcase," said John James. "My whole life."

"That's a trunk more than I have."

"But you've got gold dice cufflinks."

Tearwood sat on the edge of his bed, shoes off, unwashed toes protruding through thankless socks. He fiddled with a cufflink. "My one valuable possession. Besides a dream or two I chased and caught. My family in

New York still has an attic filled with the *precious cargo* of my previous life. What are your intentions, John James?"

He had been kneeling beside his trunk. He had taken out a tin packed there. He set it on the suitcase and opened it. He began to finger through what the Colonel saw were passports, marriage certificates, death certificates, letters of identification.

"Curious," said Tearwood.

John James looked up. The old man's eyes flitted toward the tin. "I won't ask."

• • •

He could slip into a fluted shadow or disappear into the murk of a doorway as if he were made of liquid. There was nothing about Mister Jonah that would tell you this upon looking at him. He seemed to be too blocky a man, too stiff and slow for such surreptitious doings, but he was drawn to this kind of work with unmatched earnestness. The weather, the endless hours, even if he were ill, did not cause his dispatch to waiver. The slow and methodical hunting of human beings, that was his true life calling.

He waited in the squalid refuse of crates and barrels between buildings, squatted down on his haunches, his black coat buttoned tight, his white collar pulled off and put in his pocket, his arms crossed watching the pub entry across the way. Lanterns on posts decorated the façade and made it easier to see the drinkers come and go.

He slid upright with his back against the wall as a drunken Taversham stepped out into the night air with a few of his fellow pub mates. The men talked a few moments, shook hands, shared a laugh and then Taversham started up the street alone.

Mister Jonah glanced about furtively. He had in his pocket a hand on the grip of John James pistol as he slipped past lights, keeping close to the opaque and locked up storefronts.

The best laid plans, as they say, are sometimes exactly that, as Taversham stopped and looked about and then disappeared into an alley to urinate.

He was standing there with his trousers unbuttoned and his piss steaming hot against a brick wall when Mister Jonah put a bullet into the back of Taversham's skull.

CHAPTER 13

THE BODY OF TAVERSHAM WAS DISCOVERED by a watchman checking lamp-lights and calling out the time when he thought what looked like a man to be lying among the trash in a pitched alley. Upon closer inspection the fellow's trousers were seen to be partway down and his sex dangling there for all to see. He prodded the miscreant hard with his cane and when the head rolled a bit to one side, the watchman was presented with a violent reality.

The watchman ordered a beadle who kept check on the neighborhood to summon the police. A small crowd had gathered at the grisly site where the constables went about their business, disliked and mistrusted as they were among the citizenry, asking questions, knocking on doors, conducting interviews at the nearby pubs.

It wasn't long before a streetwalker was made to look down at the body against her will there in the light of a handheld lantern. She recognized the man and she pointed out for them the rooming house where he lived with the rest of those "rude and thankless actors."

The investigation proceeded quickly after that. There was no shortage of actors in the rooming house happy to empty the vault, so to speak, with their opinions and observations. A profile of John James Beaufort emerged: the young arrogant actor——defiant, selfish, aloof——put a review under Taversham's door meant to mock and insult the actor—— instigated a fight on the stairwell——his sudden moving out the day just before the shooting——the fact that he sometimes carried a gun——the fact that he'd threatened Taversham with that gun during an argument at a pub.

• • •

A pair of constables arrived at the McCarthy apartments the following morning. Mister Jonah was there with his employer. They knew if they plotted right, this would happen. The only surprise was how swiftly it happened. The best laid plans——

It was Mister Jonah who answered the door, and when Lucretia heard

43

John James' name brought up in connection to the murder of an actor named Taversham, she threw question after question at the police officer until McCarthy asked Mister Jonah to usher his daughter away, so that he might talk with the constables more amiably.

Mister Jonah took her forcibly by the arm and got her out of there without incident then dragged her up a flight of stairs to what had been servants' quarters. He closed the door and told her to sit on the daybed and he folded his hands and blocked the doorway.

"What have you and my father done?"

She stood and started for the door.

"Please, don't," he said.

She charged him, but he withstood her easily. She screamed, but he covered her mouth until her face drew in desperate for a breath. "Please," he said, pleading. He let her go and shoved her back toward the daybed.

"Do you know who Iago is?" said Lucretia.

Mister Jonah preferred to keep silent but could not for fear of seeming ignorant. "I have seen enough of your father's plays to know———"

"That's who you are. Iago…But a steerage Iago…A second hand, second rate Iago…A sweat shop Iago…an Iago not great enough to be the standard bearer of a king, but just enough to clear the gutter and serve the likes of my father."

"Well, miss…No Iago to end up close to a king had to climb as far as I did to clear the gutter is the essence of it, isn't it now?"

• • •

"A couple of raw lobsters were in here this morning questioning us," said the shopkeeper, "looking for your friend."

The Colonel had gone out for his morning ration of whiskey. "I don't understand. What would the constables want with John James?"

"To question him. Taversham is dead. Shot through the skull not five streets from here. Poor soul has done his last pontificating."

Tearwood hustled back to the theatre, running on tired legs when he could, his stomach jostling, a foolish looking thing, if ever there was one, trying to make time.

John James had finished packing the one suitcase he'd take until he and Lucretia were settled somewhere. He was about the business of moving on, of setting his sights on the dreams and desires that had swept through him. He was feeling an unquenchable excitement when the Colonel returned to the attic out of breath and pale as alabaster.

"You look like you've been in a footrace," said John James.

"And so I have."

The old man crossed the room wagging a finger at the outside world.

"What's the matter?" said John James.

"The devil's been unloosed."

CHAPTER 14

ONCE THE CONSTABLE HAD GONE, McCarthy called up to Mister Jonah who opened the door to the sunless little room where he had kept the girl. Lucretia was now allowed to go. A new chapter in humiliation, she thought. She walked past her father with a look of pure disgust.

"Go to your room. Mister Jonah and I have to talk."

"You'll kill one wretch too many, Father."

He backhanded her across the mouth.

She winced.

"Your strikes carry less weight than they used to. Soon they won't carry any at all."

He would have hit her again but for Mister Jonah's timely passing between them. In her room alone, Lucretia sat in a chair by the window watching the street. He would be coming soon and then this would all be done. But her intuition told her to get out now. She glanced at the bed. The suitcase underneath it. A creeping dread came over her. It caused her to feel ill, numb. It was what she imagined death would feel like.

She made quick work of getting out. One suitcase, a few absolute needs, a few precious mementos.

When her father entered the room unexpectedly he was astonished at what he saw. The closed suitcase on the bed. A simple coat beside it. His daughter standing by the window, her back rigid with the light on her face, she was going to fight for her future.

"You have one of two choices," he said. "Melodrama or tragedy."

"You will not groom me to be your servant any longer. He's coming for me. And I am leaving."

He would not accept her freedom. She was his by right. He was in the grip of a terrible bondage he could not understand, could not live without. That propelled him forward with clenched fury and compelled him to beat her mercilessly. There was hatred and need in his blows.

It was her scream that stopped Mister Jonah on the entry stairs. He looked up at the shadowed doorway. Everything in his body was warning him to leave, but he was an expert at keeping extreme reactions in check.

He went back up to the apartment. He entered without bothering to shut the door.

He stopped in the foyer. There was no one in the drawing room. From down the hallway he heard this stuttery kind of sound, but he had no idea what it was. He came to the door of the girl's room. He could see McCarthy standing with his back against the wall, his hands fisted and kept close to his chest. He was staring at something as yet not in Mister Jonah's line of vision, until he entered and glanced to his side.

A table had been knocked over, so too a chair, amidst that melee was Lucretia. She sat on the floor with her back against the wall, her legs stretched out, her arms hanging powerlessly at her side. This awful hideous birdlike scraw was coming out of her with each struggling breath.

"She's dying," said McCarthy. He was trenched with fear. Mister Jonah went to the child. He knelt before this beautiful, ruined thing. He could see from the way her head was angled her neck or spine had been broken. He glared at that filthy coward of a man he served. "You've killed her."

"I can't hear that sound." He pressed his hands to his ears. "Do something."

"What?"

"Suffocate her."

For all his crimes and sins, Mister Jonah was appalled at the awful fate of strangling a girl. He shook his head.

McCarthy stepped away from the wall and tossed him a bed pillow. "Suffocate her."

Even as death closed in, Lucretia was aware of what was going on. Though she could not move her arms or legs, her eyes were like black enamel stricken with the fear of what she saw was to come.

"Lucretia———"

Both men were shocked by the sound of John James' voice. They stared at each other, a decision had to be made on how to confront him. For a moment Lucretia gathered herself. The sound coming from her throat louder, more plaintive.

"The gun," whispered McCarthy.

Mister Jonah pointed toward the parlor. "In my coat," he said.

"Lucretia———"

John James could be heard moving about.

"Stay here," said McCarthy.

He went out to find and confront John James. At the far end of a gloomy hallway, there he was looking into a cryptlike room used as a library.

"What are you doing in my home?" said McCarthy.

John James came about. "Where is Lucretia?"

"She's not here. Now get out."

"Where I go…she goes."

McCarthy had no patience for this. He was slightly hunched. His long hands gripped each other. He looked as if he meant to forcibly evict John James. But John James grabbed McCarthy by his coat and flung him back into the foyer where he landed hard on the rugged floor.

John James continued down the hallway, wary something lay ahead, lest why would McCarthy call out, "He's coming." Mister Jonah tossed the pillow aside. He knew this would come to a complete and awful end. He charged out of the bedroom. He had no way of knowing John James had slipped the fingers of each hand through the brass loops of a duster.

Mister Jonah hit him first, and he hit hard. But John James' blow squared it. The heavy brass bar with the fanged edges caught the gentle-man under the chin. It not only tore flesh but it broke jaw and shattered teeth. Mister Jonah's eyes rolled back in his head and he staggerfooted and was out cold when he hit the floor.

When John James entered the room, life as he knew it ended. The small private kingdom that they both had dreamed now lay on the floor with her back against the wall among the debris of a knocked over table. A look of terrible desperation in her eyes, the helpless knowing. He could feel the claws of the earth rising up to take the only person he had truly loved.

He knelt down. She tried to speak through a broken airway. He saw suffering there that only death could ease. He took her lifeless hand and her eyes fixed on him and only him, the jewel like brilliance had only moments left.

She did not want to die now, when she had just reached the doorway of happiness. He leaned in and kissed her small curved mouth. She tried to speak to tell him that she loved him. "I know," he whispered. "We've always known, haven't we?"

He was going to cry, but he fought not to because he had later to cry. Her body began to tremor. Her consciousness was being taken by the terror of life. He held her tightly. He wanted her to know she was loved. "Sleep now," he whispered. "We have later."

He could hear her breathing struggle and subside, struggle and subside. All her dreams were leaving her. Everything that made her tender and wonderful, that was a presence of joy and kindness and hope, was being carried away on the winds of death. Her breaths became fewer, the struggle lessened...and then Lucretia McCarthy was no more.

CHAPTER 15

HE CAME OUT OF THE BEDROOM ALL SET FOR WAR. Mister Jonah lay where he'd fallen. Barely conscious, moaning. He was not the object of John James' fury. When he reached the foyer, there was a gunshot and an explosion of wood from the wall just near him. John James had to cover his face because of the fragments. Through the parlor doorway the smoky figure of Dyer McCarthy with John James' own gun in hand. He was already past the laws of man, and he charged the hulky and panicked figure.

Before the old actor could get off a mortal shot, John James hit him across the side of the head with the brass duster. McCarthy went to the floor like a slain ox, his legs buckling beneath him.

It was a black and insane minute that followed. He kneeled over the brute beating him with both hands. The brass dusters crushing bone and tearing flesh. The troupe manager and lord of players was long dead before the beating ended and the beating ended only when Mister Jonah got his arm around John James' neck and began to strangle him.

There on the carpet beside the body was the pistol that John James reached for. He held the barrel against Mister Jonah's elbow where it viced the youth's throat.

He fired, and the grip loosed, and Mister Jonah lay on the floor all curled up and writhing. John James stood, the universe around him swimming with disorder. He was panting. He leaned over and grabbed Mister Jonah by the coat. He could have shot him but didn't. His sense of reason was beginning to return. He said nothing, he did nothing. He flung his gun across the room and was gone.

• • •

As he walked the streets he did not realize he was being stared at by a pack of streetboys skatting along behind him. Their eyes on his hands and the forearms of his shirt. All covered with blood were his shirtsleeves, and his hands and the brass dusters were streaked with blood and threads of flesh. It quite simply shocked him, as much as it did those in the street whose stares were drawn to this violent sight.

"Get away," he shouted, and the urchins scattered like alley cats. He removed the dusters and they clanked in his hand until he reached a high wooden fence and tossed them into the empty lot beyond.

He came around the theatre, but carefully, like a man on the dodge, to see if any officers from the municipality were looking to find him through the Colonel, over the Taversham murder. And now, with that horrifying scene at the McCarthy house…he would be as hunted as supper would be for a pauper.

He made his way through an alley of rag shops to the back of the theatre. The cargo door was open. He kept to the shadows along the seats and well back from the stage where actors rehearsed. He recognized the play as *The Inspector General*. And if ever there was a story about human greed and stupidity done with the absolute wrinkle of an eye, this was it. But that world of costumes and wit was falling away, and it could not be undone.

A voice behind him whispered, "They were here."

He turned. It was the Colonel.

"What's happened?" said Tearwood. "You're shaking all over."

"I found I am capable of terrible things when I'm confronted with terrible things."

John James took him back into the darkness. The Colonel listened and had to believe what he could not believe. He held the boy's arms as he talked like a father to the son he'd never had. John James just stood there staring at that troupe on the stage in dusty light like a dream just out of reach.

"She's gone," he said, his voice quivering. "Everything she was, everything she hoped to be. And the world will go on as if it was nothing."

"There's no hope for you here right now," Tearwood said.

"But where to go?"

"America."

"America…?"

"They've got theatre there. And I have family in New York. I'll write you a letter of introduction. And give you one for my sister. I still write them, you know. This way I'll have a place to reach you. Keep you apprised of what goes on here. I'll even try to make a case for——"

"She's gone," said John James, as if he had not heard a word the Colonel said.

The Colonel took off his cufflinks and pressed them into John James' hand. "For luck."

ACT II

CHAPTER 16

THE FIRST THING NATHANIEL TOLD ME about the trip from Liverpool to New York City was, "That's how I got my name…Nathaniel Luck."

I had not even known up to that point Nathaniel Luck wasn't his name.

He'd made the trip in steerage, on a packet boat stripped down for cargo. He and one hundred and fifty others cramped in below deck from half the countries of Europe and others you never heard of.

"It was a godforsaken crossing," he said. "Days below deck in darkness. And there was a run of diphtheria that took one in four. A dozen children died. There were fevers, lice, rats…and tuberculosis. The name of the boat was the PERSEVERENCE. Ironic, don't you think? I was consumed with sorrow and grief, and below deck resembled my very being. Of course, at the time, I had no idea how much I was clinging to life itself."

He had hidden out at a Liverpool inn until the boat was to sail. He'd kept up with the newspapers. His story was front page news. Because of the play they coined it The Pickwick Club Murders…to gin up readership. *The Spectator* had even done up a portrait of the Sam Weller character. That was the part John James had played onstage. The character was quite a hit. The newspapers had taken the illustration right from the Dickens book. Nathaniel had shown me the picture. The character had a gaudy vest and bandana and a hat pitched at a cocky angle. "That's supposed to be me," said Nathaniel.

"When the time came to sign the ship's manifest I gave them the name James Luck. Why the name Luck? The Colonel giving me the cufflinks...for luck.

"The crossing took almost eight weeks. I spent my time alone, in my berth, or on deck. I cried privately many times. I was with her there below deck, but she wasn't there. I read a lot to keep sorrow at bay. They had magazines on board for the wiping of our asses. Stacks of American annuals with short stories, essays. I learned about American writers. How the people talked and thought...Nathaniel Hawthorne...I liked the name Nathaniel.

"When we landed we had to pass through Castle Gardens...The immigrant line. They used the ship's manifest to confirm our identities. I saw they sometimes got a name or fact wrong, so when it was my turn, I said my first name wasn't James...but Nathaniel. And that's how I came to be Nathaniel Luck."

Listening to Nathaniel, I thought to myself...if it were only as simple as changing one's name. What a comfort that would be.

• • •

Nathaniel was suddenly in the grasp of the New York City sunlight with the whole of life ahead of him. What comes tomorrow will be different, but that day, he found himself succumbing to tears. Standing there alone in the Manhattan harbor without a friend in the world told him in no uncertain terms that the past was dead, the dream destroyed. John James Beaufort——meet Nathaniel Luck, your heir apparent, chosen by the unanimous vote of one, to carry on. But what am I carrying, he wondered, the burdens of destiny?

Standing there and suffering, the world still came flooding in like that bountiful light through the church doorway, with its harbor, and fish market, its drays and wagons and the clippers all docked and in neat order, the composite of humanity all along the wharves and streets. It was London——but with an accent.

Nathaniel made his way to the street amidst the swindlers and con men, the hoodwinkers and thugs that worked the immigrant boats trying to scam money from the poor for transportation that would never come, or rooming houses that didn't exist, employment agents promising work for upfront fees, and money traders who exchanged currency for American silver at deft rates. A parade of charlatans and liars, cleaned up criminals and white collar scum——they were all actors in their own way tragically. Welcome to America.

CHAPTER 17

Missus Millicent Harrison lived on Lafayette Place. It was a new development carved out of the upper Manhattan countryside. Two blocks of gorgeous rowhouses fronted by monolithic Greek columns carved from white marble and quarried by the inmates of Sing Sing Prison.

It was the talk of the city and reminded Nathaniel of European luxury. Tearwood had never mentioned there was such money in his family.

He knocked on the door and in short order a neatly attired black maid answered. She looked over this rather bedraggled creature carrying an old suitcase.

"I have a letter here for Missus Harrison," said Nathaniel. "From her brother in England. And also, a note by way of introduction."

The maid took the envelopes, asked he please wait and closed the door. All this happening with a quiet gentility. He stood there with his suitcase at his side looking out over the cobblestone street of this elegant cul de sac. It dawned on him suddenly, he seemed to have covered the full arc of an American city in just one clipped afternoon.

The door opened, and the maid invited him in. The rowhouse was supremely quiet and beautifully furnished. The maid asked he set his luggage down and he was led up a flight of mahogany stairs through an atrium with a fountain and then a parlor to a sunroom. Here was silverwork everywhere and silk tapestries on the walls. The delicacy to the furnishings and drapes was born of artistry as much as wealth. Missus Harrison was on a settee with her hands folded in her lap, and the light coming through the tall windows was golden with the coming dusk. It was a painterly moment that he could not imagine ever having a place for the Colonel.

"I want to thank you for bringing the letter."

"You're very welcome."

"My brother's introduction...James Luck. I may let you read it sometime. Very touching."

"Nathaniel. I prefer to be called Nathaniel."

"Well then...Nathaniel Luck. Would you..." with the gesture of a hand she offered him the chair facing her. As he sat, she said, "Would you care for refreshments? Tea...something cool? Though being a friend *and* protege of my brother's, I assume you would prefer ale...or whiskey."

"A whiskey would go nicely."

She asked the maid to fill the young man's request.

"And, how is my brother? Is he still the wild eccentric?"

"I would say that describes him very well."

The maid brought a silver tray with a decanter of whiskey and a glass. She set the tray down on a sideboard and poured Nathaniel a whiskey.

Missus Harrison watched Nathaniel with an unerring eye as the young black girl went about the business at hand. Nathaniel noted Missus Harrison was younger than her brother. He was a ground down fifty. One of those racehorse to carthorse in record time gents. His sister, on the other hand, could not have been forty. She was not a stout woman, on the contrary. She had a comely face and a charming manner. Her eyes were warm and her lips full, and when she spoke her voice was quite expressive. In that, she was much like her brother.

Once the girl had left the room, Missus Harrison said to Nathaniel, "Is my brother still drinking way more than he should?"

Nathaniel had been sipping his drink. He took a few moments.

"The hesitation of a true friend," she said. "So...he's still a hopeless drunk."

"I don't believe your brother would embrace that description of himself as *hopeless*."

"Braveau."

She got up and walked to the sideboard. She took the decanter in hand. Nathaniel just realized there was a second glass on the tray which meant the servant anticipated her employer would be drinking. Missus Harrison poured herself a neat whisky that would match Nathaniel's. She went and sat.

"My brother wrote me about a year ago that he gave a performance of King Lear that was quite well received."

He'd given a performance all right, thought Nathaniel. Only it did not take place on some reputable stage, but rather in the raunchy confines of a notorious drinking hole where actors came to show off or debase themselves and sometimes both at the same time, as is the custom with certain actors.

It happened on the Colonel's birthday, and he showed up late, the dramatic entrance being his absolute addiction. He was drunk and wearing a castoff prop crown and cape and a fake beard a foot long. His gnarled voice shouting out as soon as he hit the doorway, "Blow winds and crack your cheeks! Rage, blow!"

He was going into the King Lear scene in the woods. Only he was intent on portraying the monarch as a degenerated merrymaker who didn't have two daughters who'd like to gain a kingdom and a third he'd disowned for honesty. He came flanked with a trio of concubines, gaudy young things. Just as drunk as he was. And he put his hands up between their scrawny legs and railed as Lear about being sinned against more than sinning.

At his most profoundly enraged this Lear rubbed his member as if it were attacked by mice. He rumbled on about spitting fire and spouting rain and he ripped off his boots and then his trousers and there he stood, naked but for a crown and cape, as he had left his drawers at home for drama's sake.

"Yes, ma'am," Nathaniel said. "His performance was quite well received."

"Please, call me Millicent." She stood. "You'll stay for dinner, of course. You can tell me stories about my brother. Lies if you need to, though I'd prefer the truth. And why a young and aspiring actor would leave London and come to America."

The dining room walls were covered with silk. The table was Chinese and a thing of rare beauty with inlaid pearl. The dinner silver, Millicent pointed out, had been bequeathed to their family from Paul Revere. And this building had been the brainchild of the millionaire John Jacob Astor, who had sat at that very table a few weeks ago. She took great joy in telling Nathaniel all this. He had no idea who the famous Astor was.

"By the way," said Millicent, "I won't force you to lie about my brother. We grew up together, after all. Even though he is a dozen years older. He was a great soldier. A colonel. He fought in the 1812 War and against Napoleon. I still have a room upstairs filled with the mementoes of his life. His courage knew no boundaries." She turned thoughtful. "Like everything else about him...no boundaries. It's a failing that seems to run in the family." She puffed up a smile. "Tell me about yourself. Where you grew up...what your life was like."

He set his drink down. "Do you know what a tosher is?"

She leaned forward. She did not.

He told her the story of the boy from the sewers just as he had on stage.

After dinner, Millicent ushered Nathaniel into the library. She then excused herself. The young black lady who worked for her was named Sarah. She was in the kitchen cleaning up when Millicent entered with a vial of powder in her hand. Without a word, Sarah went to the pantry and came back with a snifter and brandy which she set on the counter. Millicent opened the vial and topped one of her prized Paul Revere spoons with the chalky powder. She emptied the spoon into the snifter and added brandy. She stirred and stirred until the granular substance had completely dissolved.

"When I call you," said Millicent.

"Yes, ma'am."

"Then go get Sam."

CHAPTER 18

THERE WAS AN OIL PAINTING OF MILLICENT'S FATHER on the library wall. He certainly didn't seem to have the clear passion of the Colonel or the cool vivacity of the daughter. Like so many of these upper-class family portraits, he seems to have had the stale stare of someone recently shot and stuffed. Nathaniel noticed the gold name plate at the bottom of the frame——William Yearwood Sr.

When Millicent returned, Nathaniel pointed to the name plate. "Yearwood?"

"That's the family name. Not Tearwood. Sometime I'll tell you how it came to change for my brother, since he obviously hasn't."

Sarah had lit the room with candles, and Millicent went and sat on the couch. She asked Nathaniel to join her.

"May I see your hand?" she said, offering her own.

"You're not a gypsy fortune teller, are you?"

"Let's find out."

She took his hand and flattened it out, then turned it over slowly. She ran her fingers across the breadth of his palm and the knotty back of his hand. Her movements were slow and gentle, as if there was something unsaid between them. She nodded once at some private thought, then smiled at him. She asked for the other hand. She took his pinky and ran her fingers along the length of it pressing in the flesh below the middle joint. She then let that hand go and sat back. She seemed satisfied with her observations.

Millicent called to Sarah. When she appeared in the doorway, Millicent said, "Be so kind as to bring Nathaniel some brandy."

"Yes, ma'am."

"I realize," she said to him, "it's probably more advantageous and accepting, and better for his career, if an actor has a dramatic and exciting past. It reads well in the newspapers."

Her eyes twinkled as she gave him a sidelong smile.

"I feel like the unknown traveler in the undiscovered country," he said.

"You're not a boy from the sewer."

"No?"

Sarah came with the brandy. He took the glass and set it down.

"Boys who worked like you claim you did had hands that were scarred and beaten up. And your pinky. The way the flesh is pinched below the knuckle. Boys who wore a ring for a long time have fingers like that. And poor boys from the sewer don't wear rings. And if they find one or steal one they don't wear it for long because someone will beat them for it. And that's not all…"

"No?"

He reached for the brandy glass. She watched him drink. She encouraged him to continue drinking with her ladylike silence.

"And your English," she said finally.

"What about it?"

"It's too good. It doesn't lapse into grammatical sloppiness or become the grimy way the poor speak. In essence… I believe you're from good breeding. And that you wore a family ring of some kind on that pinky, one that you outgrew. And it reshaped the finger. Like I've seen on other boys from good families who wore rings. School rings, signet rings."

She sat there like the courteous host while he drank until the glass was empty. He assumed she was waiting on his answer. She was waiting all right, but not for an answer.

• • •

He did not remember keeling over. There was just this unclear nausea that turned into a swimmy darkness that washed over him. He stood, trying to shake himself loose of it. He saw Millicent's face sweep past him as he staggered, and her saying, "Are you all right?" and then her calling out to Sarah. Her voice sounded as if it were coming from somewhere at the end of a steep fall. He tried to get hold of anything to keep himself upright, but his flesh began to feel like cold ashes and for a moment he flashed on Lucretia, there in the bedroom, on the floor, at the unbearable moment of death, and then he felt nothing at all.

The women were kneeling over the body when Millicent called out to Sam. He entered from the kitchen. He was Sarah's husband and a scrappy bastard whose allegiance to Missus Harrison was unquestioned. "Carry him up to the top room."

He grabbed the unconscious youth by his vest and hoisted the limp body over his shoulder. Millicent had Sarah bring along the boy's suitcase and Millicent led her slow entourage up three flights of stairs guiding them with a candle.

There were two rooms on the top floor. A storage room and a bedroom with a skylight. She had Sam lay the boy on the bed.

"Undress him," she said.

She set the candle on the bureau that had once been her son's. She had Sarah put the suitcase down on a pine chest and open it, as Sam stripped the boy, tossing his clothes upon a chair and then covering his naked body with a blanket.

"You two can go now," said Millicent. "And thank you, Sam."

He glanced at the boy. "You be all right?"

She nodded she would. "He's harmless enough."

Once they were gone, she sat on the pine chest beside the suitcase, her dress rustling. She began to pick through it. The clothes were uninspiring to say the least, except for a flashy vest. An actor's trophy, she thought. Then she came upon a beat up tin. After she managed to get the top off, things became a little more interesting.

There were a handful of English BT's——certificates of marriage, certificates of birth and death. Different names, different church parishes. None with the name Luck. She set them aside when she noticed two envelopes.

In the first there was what looked to be a dozen articles torn from the newspapers. She held them up to the light so as to be more easily read. They were reviews of plays. Nothing extraordinary or telling about that, except for one common denominator——an actor named John James Beaufort.

The last articles had nothing to do with play reviews but were certainly more telling, and chilling, as they detailed a grisly murder that had taken place in London two months prior. And there was that name again—— John James Beaufort——an actor they were looking for in connection to the crime. One of the articles ended with a description of this John James Beaufort, which bore a striking resemblance to the boy lying there in the bed. She put the articles neatly back where they belonged. There was one envelope left. On the back of this was the name——John James Beaufort——in rather delicate handwriting. Opening the envelope, she discovered a letter in the same delicate handwriting. It had to be a woman's hand. Men, she believed, were incapable of such flourishes.

> *Dear John James,*
>
> *I did not know this kind of feeling was alive in me. I did not know the love I feel for you could exist in me. I thought those emotions could only exist in the realm of plays, not life.*
>
> *When you are near me, you change the light, the air, the sky. I breathe now and take in a beautiful world, not the sorrow or any of the terrible things I have endured.*
>
> *I feel as if we have been touched by the grand hand of fate.*

The letter went on, but she read no further. Except for the name at the end of the letter——*Lucretia.*

She put the letter back in the envelope. She went back to the first envelope because of the name——*Lucretia.* She searched through the articles about the murder. Yes——there it was. One of the victims of the crime. An aspiring actress and daughter of the troupe manager, himself a victim. She put the envelopes in the tin as they were and closed the tin and put it in the suitcase where it was before and closed the suitcase.

She sat there in the shadowy presence of ghosts. She glanced at a small portrait above the bureau. A father flanked by two sons——one ten and the other not quite eighteen and lost to the wrongs of the world in the dead of winter. Christmas now a mournful blight on her life. The portrait never did capture the love or the joy, nothing of the humor. They are just images there, not souls. Her shadow rose over the portrait as she stood. The loss and longing of mother and woman gripped her.

She went to the bed and looked down at this youth. He was about the same age as her oldest. She carefully pulled back the sheet and looked over this naked body. The flesh was clear. There were no signs of disease or disfigurement. His skin was creamy where the sun had not colored it.

She was surprised at how little he looked like how a murderer is supposed to look.

CHAPTER 19

HE WOKE TO A BLAZING SUN burning down from on high through the skylight. He tried to understand where he was and how he got there. His mouth felt like used woolen drawers and there was a grim drumbeat in his head that made him wish he were dead. He sat up shakily and realized he was naked. He suddenly scrambled about with his hands looking for his clothes, wondering if he'd been robbed.

Once he remembered where he was and pathetically righted himself, he slipped on his trousers. He looked about. He was in someone's bedroom, that was for sure. There was a writing desk against one wall, and a portrait above a bureau against another. He noticed one boy in the painting that looked very much like Millicent Harrison.

There was an open door and he peered in, thinking it might be to the hall. He was astonished to find a tub and a sink in there…and a toilet.

He went and fidgeted with the sink handles. He ran water across his face then slurped from cupped hands. There was a knock at the door that caught him off guard and he jumped a little. "One minute," he said, and he hustled to get a shirt on. "Come in."

He stood there sheepishly as Sarah entered. "What happened?"

"You passed out. Missus Harrison is waiting."

"Before you leave, may I ask you…?" Nathaniel pointed above the bureau.

"That's the late Mister Harrison and his sons."

"I thought the young boy looked like his mother."

"They're gone now. Father and son. Died in the big Wall Street fire that burned down part of the city."

"I'm sorry. What about the other boy?"

"He's gone…missing."

• • •

Millicent sat at a table in the sunroom looking over correspondence and having coffee when Nathan walked in. She asked if he were all right and would he please sit and have coffee and breakfast if he had any appetite. He apologized for passing out, and she dismissed it with the slightest gesture of femininity.

As he sat, she called for Sarah to bring coffee.

"What are your intentions now?"

"To find a place."

"When actors aren't acting, what do they do? My brother would drink and brood..."

"They work. Coming off the boat I was given a flier. They're looking for day laborers to help build a reservoir up on Fifth...Street or Avenue."

"Fifth Avenue. It's at the edge of uptown. Would you rather have more gentlemen's work? A men's shop or a merchandizing office. I know many people——"

"Thank you...But I need to be where I can hear all kinds of everyday Americans speak...So I learn the patter, the phrases...How they sound. So I can be one of them." He felt awkward suddenly. "I guess it's the actor in me."

"Very industrious."

"I asked Sarah about the picture on the bedroom wall."

"Did you? Why?"

"The young boy looked so much like you."

He saw in her face now something he had not noticed the night before. There was a sadness about the eyes. An expression that pulled with longing and loss.

"Do you know," she said, "what it's like to have a loved one unexpectedly and tragically taken from you?"

"I do."

"Well, then you and I have something profound in common, don't we? Something to build our relationship on."

She took a sip of coffee. He was watching her closely. The way she had said that spoke to much more than just what she'd said. He felt it in the pit of his stomach.

"You never did get to tell me why an aspiring actor such as yourself decides to come to America."

"No. I didn't." He finished his coffee and stood. "I've got to get to this Fifth Street——"

"Avenue...Fifth Avenue. You can stay in the room upstairs. It has its own entrance. You can save money that way. Get yourself a foothold."

"That's...kind of you."

On the way out, she mentioned one more thing. "I get the London papers sometimes. On the chance there's word about my brother...he writes so infrequently. Shall I save them for you? The newspapers?"

He felt a paleness coming up through his insides. "Yes..."

CHAPTER 20

HE ASKED HIS WAY UP TO FIFTH AVENUE and Forty Second Street where they were digging the four-acre foundation of the reservoir. He was put on one of the ragged day gangs that were to trench out the tunnel that would carry water from the Croton River forty miles north down into Manhattan. It was a hard, long and filthy job. You spent the day in darkness with mucked air and soggy ground water.

But there he could disappear into the lives of the workmen around him. Their daily struggles, their frustrated home lives and unquenchable dreams, their personal war with government and class, with day wages and the recession, their vulgarities and slang and their cadence, their beautiful, gritty cadence. Down in that murky tunnel, he was no longer an actor wanted for murder in London, he was just another poor immigrant soul shoveling his way through the confused depths and burying his British accent one day at a time.

Walking home at night, he had to pass a theatre and a music hall, and the old life came back to him. The lost life. He suffered the purgatory of feeling and thinking. She was there holding his arm, her head against his shoulder, but he could not hear her voice. The sound of her beautiful voice was slipping from his senses. He stopped in the street and looked at the theatre, the lights out front burning white hot against the stone. She was being taken from him again and again by time. He could not hurt like this and bear it. He hated the theatre for the pain it had caused him, yet he could not live without it. The need was everything.

He lay in the dark many nights, tortured and alone, and the world downstairs began to drift up through the silence. Men would sometimes arrive late at night in their carriages. There would be muffled conversation from beyond shut drawing room doors. After a half hour or so they would leave in their carriages. Sometimes after these meetings he could hear Millicent crying up though the bones of the house. He considered going to her, then thought the better of it. One night, he noticed through the slit across the bottom of the door, a light ascending the stairs. It stopped outside his door and flickered there gently for the longest time. It went finally as it had come, and in the morning, there were copies of the London newspapers on his doorstep. He rifled through them with a desperate urgency but there was no mention of the murders and it took him that whole long walk to work to quit his hands from shaking.

. . .

At dinner Millicent said, "I have to go to the Park Theatre. An opera for charity. I usually went with my family as we have a box there. I am uncomfortable going alone. Can I ask you to accompany me?"

"I would make a disreputable companion," he said, "as I brought no such clothes with me upon the crossing."

Millicent nodded to Sarah who was standing in the doorway and who brought a box over that had been on a chair. She set it in front of Nathaniel. He opened it to find a tailored suit.

"It belonged to my older son," said Millicent. "I hope he will get to wear it again sometime."

"If it doesn't quite fit," said Sarah, "I can fix that."

He closed the box and thanked Millicent and then took it upon himself to question her. "Your older son...What happened to him?"

She fixed her eyes on Nathaniel. "He's missing. That's why you hear men coming and going at night."

When dinner was finished, she stood and asked Nathaniel to follow her. "Now I get to fulfill my promise...or maybe it sounded like a threat." She led him upstairs without a word, humming surprisingly, to the storage room beside where he slept. It was stacked with trunks and suitcases, an armoire and a chest of drawers. It smelled of dust and decades old air and the sunset upon the skylight made it seem ancient as a tomb. She stood by what looked to be a large painting covered with a tarp. "Pull the tarp away," she said.

He came up alongside her. She stayed close to him. He pulled away the tarp. A great full grin settled across his face and his eyes filled with delight.

It was a theatrical poster and painted there on the wood was the Colonel himself, when he was young and trim, in a dapper suit and suave looking at that. He sat in a kingly chair with one arm slung over the back, and a banner painted with rich colored lettering fanned over him——the colors faded regrettably somewhat with time——that read: COLONEL TEARWOOD'S AMERICAN THEATRE COMPANY.

"Tearwood," said Nathaniel. "Even back then."

"I promised to tell you. Well…the first real part he played on stage was Falstaff. He was too young and too thin but when they made him up, was he the image. Well…the show was in Boston and the reviews could not have been more sterling. But there was one flaw…They misprinted his name. They had him as Tearwood and not Yearwood.

"He was a raging mess. Thinking his career was ruined. Actors are so ridiculously vain. After a few days of misery and sulking he came to think it was a sign of good luck, so he kept the name. And our father promptly disowned him."

Nathaniel couldn't take his eyes from the poster. It had always been a dream to have his own theatrical company. He'd talked about it with Tearwood. But the Colonel had never mentioned the poster. Maybe it brought up his own failed expectations.

"What was her name?" said Millicent.

Nathaniel looked up. "Excuse me?"

"The person you lost unexpectedly."

He blinked, confused, surprised at the turn the conversation had made. "I never said it was…a girl."

"It's the woman in me that just…surmised."

"Her name…was Lucretia."

"What a lovely name. How did you lose her?"

He felt a strange disquiet coming over him. A nerve touched. "She was killed of a broken neck."

"Murdered, you mean."

"Yes," he said, his breathing had shallowed. "I'm afraid so."

She saw him suffering there and she came up to him and gently took his face in her hands and she kissed him on the cheek. He could feel her hesitant breathing on his neck and she leaned up a bit and she kissed him on the mouth. The kiss lingered and when she stepped back, she said, "I may have a favor to ask of you soon…with regards to my missing son."

CHAPTER 21

You wouldn't think digging tunnels and drinking in shabby bars would give you a good education on how the theatre worked in New York, but you'd be surprised. Theatre is ideas, and ideas can change the flow of power, and the flow of power affects who has the money, and everyone has a dog in that fight. And besides, there's nothing that juices a poor man like walking into a rich man's theatre and having a taste. Or better yet, having a theatre of their own.

The Park had been the jewel of Manhattan theatres. It catered to money and elitism and prided itself on the finest imported actors and sold them to the bon ton like you would a good wine.

But the last decade had been heir to a recession and the great Wall Street fire and the Flour Strike and a rabbit influx of immigrants. A mere six blocks south of the Park were the Bowery and the Garden theatres by Five Points. But those half dozen blocks gave Nathaniel a hell of a portrait on the ignoble unfairness that was America. Those two downtown theatres catered to what was despicably termed the "middle class" or more aptly described as the "aspiring poor."

The Park had an extended stage and tiers of private booths, with a gallery above. A couple of panhandlers out front informed the patrons that the Park even had a higher class of rats than the downtown theatres as they were better fed.

Nathaniel was introduced to the likes of the Delano's and the Vanderbilt's and John Jacob Astor, as the actor friend of her brother just over from London and looking to settle here. She did not mention that at present he was digging tunnels for the new reservoir.

Before they were ushered to their seats, Astor had a private conversation with Millicent. He was seventy and very Germanic. He had risen up from his father's butcher shop to become the first American multi-millionaire, trading in furs, and some say opium. Nathaniel overhead him tell Millicent, "I have a promising lead on your son. I'll know by tomorrow."

Nathaniel had not been inside a theatre since that last day in London. But as he sat alone with Millicent in her private booth, he was taken away by the sounds and the smells, the dry old timbers, the soft movement of the ladies' dresses, that mysterious glow of lighting that ringed the stage, the anticipation of the people talking among themselves. These were all polished to a brilliance in his consciousness, but they left him now a well of conflicts. He loved this time, lived for it, but now it reminded him of all he lost. It touched upon his suffering so thoroughly. There was a beautiful innocence that had been ripped from him. An innocence he had never really appreciated or understood, or even knew existed. He'd suffered a heartbreak he could not, as yet, come to grips with.

He felt a hand on his leg. It settled there almost imperceptibly. He looked at Millicent.

"Are you, all right? You seem———?"

"I was just…remembering."

The opera that night was *Norma*. He had seen a performance of the Bellini work in London. It was known for its tragic beauty and the challenging bel canto. The delicate art of love and torment that tested not only the limits of the artists' voices, but their emotions as well.

He had always been a good audience because the stage was real and true to him. It was there to immerse oneself, to experience, feel, to be. And that night, Norma's tragedy———that she had stepped outside the bounds of society, and born two illicit children with a man who now not only no longer loved her but wanted to be done with her———became his tragedy.

Not the facts of it, but the fated impossibility of her situation.

He began to cry. They were slight tears and silent and he sat back as if to hide in the dark tied as he was to the music by heartstrings. And Millicent, she had been stealing glances at him and she saw and realized. She leaned over, then taking his hand, whispered, "My dear…what is it?"

He pulled his hand loose, eyes moist, saddened. "I have to leave," he said, "I'm sorry."

• • •

He talked about how he walked that night till the streets turned to shoddy tenements. Prostitutes, wastrels and bars. Families huddled behind sackcloth curtains. He needed something to pour himself into to drive back the demon memories.

"You had no idea?" I asked, "that Millicent knew

about London…the murder? Not a suspicion?"

"Not an inkling, Jeremiah. That's how naïve I truly was. I saw this woman who was beautiful and sensitive. And she had this stillness that was utterly sensual. She could have been a fine actress possessed with that kind of stillness."

"In a way she was an actress…wasn't she?"

Nathaniel slapped me on the back as he got up and went and poured himself a drink. "Yes…she might have been the most gifted of us all."

I was surprised the years had not worn him down more. That having a murder strapped to your back had not broken him.

He looked at me. I knew that pensive smile.

"The play The Monster was born that night," he said, "when she came up those stairs."

CHAPTER 22

HE WAS SITTING IN BED IN THE DARK with his back against the headboard. He smoked, the sheets twisted around him, when he saw through the slit along the bottom of the door the same slow light ascending the stairs, that stopped on the landing for a long few moments, only this time there came a gentle knocking.

He put out his cigarette.

"Nathaniel," said Millicent.

He wrapped the sheets around him even tighter. "Yes."

She opened the door without being asked. The light from her candle moving toward him. She closed the door behind her. She stood there lit from below. She was barefoot and wearing a white linen peignoir.

"I came to see if you were all right."

"I'm sorry for leaving like that."

"Do you want to tell me?"

He shook his head, no.

She looked past the light to the portrait of her husband and sons hidden there in the shadows. "I may hear about my older boy, Robert, tomorrow."

She went and set the candle down on the bureau. "We have a lot in common, you and I."

She licked the tips of her thumb and index finger. "It is treacherous to feel so much. It leaves the soul nowhere to hide."

She snuffed out the light. A strand of smoke from the wick rose up through the darkness like a rope. She came toward the bed. She began to take off her sleeping gown. Through the roof window a perfect moonlight upon her skin. She undressed before him with a practiced nuance.

"Downstairs, tomorrow. It will be as if nothing happened." She then took the sheet from his hand and slid into bed beside him.

• • •

75

He returned from work the next day in a sheeting rain. No sooner had he stripped off his wet and mucked clothing than there was a knock at the door.

Sarah called to him. "Missus Harrison wants you to get cleaned up and be downstairs quick as you can. Robbie has been found...and you're needed."

John Jacob Astor was sitting at a writing table in the sunroom with his hands folded, talking to Millicent quietly, calmly, as she paced about. She, all nervous anticipation. She reintroduced Nathaniel, but that was not necessary, the old German made it his stock and trade to remember names.

"Son," he said, "I'm here tonight as a friend to this family. I don't know if you're aware, but Millicent's late husband did work for me over twenty years, so I feel I have a responsibility to see Robbie is home and safe."

Nathaniel looked from one to the other. The rain was hard against the windows now. The Greek columns across the front terrazzo were grey with wet. "How could I be of assistance?" said Nathaniel.

"Millicent," said Astor, "does he know the whole story?"

"I didn't believe it fair to burden him with it."

"Well...now is the time."

Millicent took to wringing her hands. She stood by the window looking out. There was no sky, just a wash of gloom. "The night of the Wall Street fire," she said, "Robbie took his younger brother downtown to surprise their father. They were in a building when the one next door exploded. Robbie was badly burned. Disfigured and——"

She stopped. She looked the wounded mother.

Astor took over. "We believe this episode affected his mind. If not his reason. Too sensitive," said Astor, standing. "Alcohol and opium. It has him thinking crazy."

Millicent came to him. She took his hands in hers. "Try to befriend him. Watch out for him. Write me how he is. And if chance prevails, convince him to come home. Do this and I will be here for you always...so you may embrace your career."

"We will both see you rewarded," said Astor.

• • •

He was packed and ready within the hour. Sarah had brought him a cape to keep him warm and dry that had belonged to Millicent's husband. For a few moments he and Millicent were alone on the second floor landing. She took him by the hand and led him to the darkened entry of her bedroom. "Be careful," she whispered. And then they kissed as only lovers would.

A carriage waited in the rain. Two men were sheltered in the doorway. They introduced themselves as Jack Foxworth and Gideon Katt.

"We're your chaperones, lad, to Philadelphia," Foxworth said.

The carriage took them to the docks. A private boat powered by a small boiler ferried them down river to New Jersey. Since working in the tunnels, Nathaniel had taken to wearing a forage cap that he'd found among the Colonel's possessions. He stood with his two chaperones, well-dressed thugs was more like it, crowded together on deck under a tarp, the engine chugging away, the tide black and nasty. Lightning broke over the city. The tall ship masts, the squat grey and brick buildings that loomed up beyond——all there for a moment in a pure blue light, then gone with a cutting shock of thunder.

There was another carriage waiting at the dock when they landed to shepherd them to Amboy where they would board the train for Camden. It was still raining, a hard, beaded rain. The roads had turned to slop, the carriage trundled along, pitching unpleasantly.

It had all been so perfectly arranged by Astor, as if he knew without reserve the boy would take on the task. Nathaniel considered, was it the promise of reward, the advancement of career that assured Astor of the boy's compliance? And from that thought, he became victim to another. Had Millicent's actual reason for coming to his room the night before been so tactfully concealed behind a play of emotions? He'd never lived out such questions before what happened in London. Had that so tainted the course of his thoughts that he must now take under consideration the darker prophecies behind people's motives? It would be hardly surprising, but regrettably hateful.

And what about his own motives? He was now a rich source of questions. And the first——do I have the right to question others if I do not have the courage to question myself? What if I had not been offered the promise of profit and career, would I do this? What if she and I had not slept together? What if I were not living in such a fine house? Would I be here?

CHAPTER 23

"ARE YOU A MARMALADE MAN?"

Nathaniel looked up from his thoughts to the two men who sat across from him in the carriage. It was Gideon who'd spoken.

"What is that?"

"A limey, for Christ's sake."

"Yes…I guess I am."

"You don't talk much like a limey. You ashamed?"

"Leave the boy be," said Foxworth.

This Gideon was a slight soul with narrow eyes widely set in a skull that rested on a chin which looked to have been smashed in by a brick. Nathaniel guessed his age at about thirty. Foxworth might have been a shade older, or at least acted that way. He had a long narrow face that drooped at the edges. Gideon eyed Nathaniel with disdain. Foxworth just eyed him.

"So, is it true?" said Gideon. "That you're an actor?"

"Yes, it is."

Gideon sat there tapping his front teeth with the tip of his finger staring at Nathaniel, "Let me ask you…seriously now."

"Hardly," said Foxworth.

"No, I mean it. I've never got to ask an actor this question. But since I have you here. Could you explain…What does an upright looking fellow like yourself want to be an actor for?"

"For actresses, you fool," said Nathaniel.

At such earnestness, Foxworth let out a "Ha!"

• • •

Come morning the rain had eased down to a steady drizzle, but you still could not see the one room clapboard depot there at the edge of a wood, or the waiting train for that matter, because of the ground mist that just oozed out of the trees and along the tracks. And that simple John Bull engine was nothing more than the tip of a skinny black smoke stack pulling three rickety coach roofs.

Nathaniel had never been on a train. The seats were bare plank, the coach cold and wet and gloomy and when that John Bull pulled out of the station the train jerked so violently in fits and spurts, the passengers were thrown about. The train clinked and rattled and shot forward and then hitched and from the engine came this horrid high pitched hissing.

When the rain finally stopped, and the mist had cleared, Nathaniel got glimpses of the American countryside as it swept past his rattling window. The wonder of deep and tangled woods turned into sudden open glades where the earth steamed.

He sat there watching and listening to the clacking of the train wheels and could only wonder——was this the beginnings of home? Was this the road my human soul would walk? Where my dreams would take physical shape?

"I hear it's just you and Missus Harrison livin' in that great big beautiful rowhouse," said Gideon. "I'm not countin' the nigger servants. Is it?"

"Is it what?"

"Is it just you and Missus Harrison livin' in——?"

"Leave it be," said Foxworth.

"I'm just asking."

Nathaniel took out his tobacco and paper.

"I hear Missus Harrison is up at all hours. Roamin' around at night. Beautiful woman like that. Left to roamin' around like that…Like she was lookin' for Hamlet's ghost."

Nathaniel licked the smoking paper and smoothed it out and slipped the cigarette in his mouth. "It was Hamlet's father's ghost. Not Hamlet's ghost."

"Ha," said Foxworth.

CHAPTER 24

THEY DISEMBARKED AT CAMDEN ALL WRINKLED, bleary eyed and worse for the wear then ferried across the river. Nathaniel saw pretty quickly Philadelphia was a workingman's town, a labor town, with flat bottoms loaded down with coal and packet boats stacked with cotton from the South. The sky was dotted with filthy smoke from the foundries and mills. It was rough men and rough language and unadorned women and it all reminded Nathaniel of Liverpool.

Foxworth ordered Gideon to bring the luggage from the hold and they'd take the boy where he needed to be. "Remember what I told you," Gideon warned the youth. "Bring that *monster* home."

There was a carriage waiting. Foxworth told the driver, "Moyomensing. Seventh Street."

"You know that neighborhood?" the driver warned.

Foxworth repeated, "Seventh Street."

Once they were underway, Foxworth explained, "Moyomensing is nigger country. Free slaves, runaways. And Irish immigrants. They're basically niggers anyway. Things get pretty rough down there. They had a riot not long ago. And street fights."

"Robbie's living in a little hotel," said Gideon. "The Joseph. I got you a room there."

Surprised, Nathaniel said, "When did you do this?"

"Two days ago…Yeah…Astor knew you'd be persuaded. One way or the other."

"What do you mean by that?"

"What do you think Gideon's expertise is in…"

Through the carriage windows, they passed this castellated monstrosity of a grim Egyptian looking structure with iron gates and mastaba walls topped with, of all things, a battle tower.

"The Moyomensing prison," said Foxworth. "Built right down here in the neighborhood. So, it's a short walk for the niggers and their mick brothers. Something to keep in mind, don't you think?"

Nothing like being in the grasp of a new reality. They drove on without circumstance until the carriage slowed and finally stopped, and the driver shouted down. "We're here, sirs."

As Nathaniel went to get out of the carriage, Foxworth took hold of the youth's cape. "After the fire, when he was still in the hospital with his face half burned off, the Harrison boy was writing letters to the newspapers insinuating the fire was arson. And he suspected Astor of being behind it. And that his own father might have been coerced into starting it. Fancied himself a writer... Good thing the editors had a different impression. Can't have it. Can't.

"His mother has faith in you. Astor has faith in you. Sending you, I thought a mistake. But who listens to the likes of me? The hotel is down the street." He pressed a folded piece of writing paper into Nathaniel's hand and a packet of money. "That's where we'll be waiting. Now...go and do whatever it is an actor would do to see this fixed."

● ● ●

There he stood with his scored up suitcase, a tasked stranger in a strange town. He took his cape off and tossed it over a shoulder. There were mostly black people in the street, a few whites shuttled along, and he was being stared over, with that forage hat pulled down low on his head.

He went looking for the hotel. The block wasn't anything like his two persecutors had led him to believe. The shops were well appointed and clean. There was a tobacconist and barber, a tailor and butcher. Through the front windows he could see they were run by neatly dressed blacks, and there were signs above doorways...PENNSYLVANIA ANTI-SLAVERY SOCIETY... AFRICAN BENEVOLENT SOCIETY UNION...YOUNG MEN'S LIBRARY ASSOCIATION...And that doorway opened to a bookshop. It could have been any sturdy workingman's London street. He took it all in. The only thing he could say thus far about America——everything was unexpected.

The entrance to The Joseph was at the corner of an alley. A few black men sat on chairs out front, talking up a storm. Their silence when Nathaniel walked by them and into the hotel was telling. A bespectacled black woman stood behind a counter licking the tip of a pencil and writing in a ledger. She looked up over the rim of her glasses.

"I believe there's a room held in my name...Nathaniel Luck."

She looked him over and silently reached up and took a key from a rack. The lobby was little more than a hallway and there was a mural painted on the far wall of the Biblical Joseph himself walking out of the lion's den and into a doorway of holy light.

She came around the counter and reached to take Nathaniel's luggage.

"Oh, no," he said. "You don't need to be carrying that for me."

He followed her upstairs. Slightly hunched, she had to hold onto the railing as she went. His room was at the head of the second floor stairs. It was a simple room. Above the bed was a small mural of a young Joseph being sold into slavery.

"I guess each room has a scene from Joseph's story."

"It does at that. And meant to remind us that God is always watching out for us…and that righteousness be rewarded, and goodness be done."

CHAPTER 25

ONCE ALONE, he peeked out the drawn curtains. The window faced the street. He could hear the men out front of the hotel. From there, he smoked and he watched, he watched and he smoked. And he listened.

Every city has its own rhythm, its own language. And it's that language that creates the largess of the soul, the people's soul. The actor is born of that creation, he grows and thrives through it. America seemed more raw to him than England, less staid. As if it were still discovering itself, which it clearly was.

He glanced at the mural above his plain covered bed. A young Joseph with his hands bound behind his back. The twenty shekels of silver he was sold for there in the dust at his feet. The road to Egypt and slavery before him. Yet there was a blueness to the sky and one white cloud that stood in contrast to the scene.

He went back to watching out the window and was soon rewarded. A young white man in a black suit and hat strode across the street and entered the hotel. Nathaniel creaked open his door just enough to see the hallway. He could hear footfalls climbing the stairs. A shadow first on the wall rising then a figure with his collar up and his head bowed. But even in the faulted light, Nathaniel could still see the youth's face was scarred.

Around dusk, Robert Harrison left his room carrying a book. Nathaniel followed him to a small restaurant with a bar and a rinky piano. Robert took up a table in the corner. Nathaniel studied him from across the room. As for the boy's face, it was worse, even in such tame light. One side from cheek to jaw looked like rubble, the eye narrowed down to nothing. Patches of hair had been burned away from the scalp and there was nothing but ruined skin. His hands were no better.

• • •

"You want to hear one of the great barroom drunk questions ever asked?"

Robert Harrison looked up from his book. Was shocked suddenly to be playing host to a wobbly drunk who dropped down in the chair facing him.

Before Robert could tell him in unnerved terms that he did not, the drunk said, "*Is it better to think...or to live?*"

The drunk held up his mug as if it were an exclamation point to the statement. He repeated the question. "Is it better to think...or to live?" His eyes widened, brightened. He swilled his beer. Thin streams of brew spilled down his chin. "Hey," said the drunk, wiping at his mouth, "if you don't mind, I'm gonna change the subject for a minute. Anyone ever ask you?" The drunk pointed to the youth's face and hands. "Do they ever?"

Robert drew in on himself.

"Not that I am..." said the drunk.

"No, of course not," said Robert. He closed his book.

"What you reading there?" said the drunk.

Robert slid the book away.

The drunk went right on. "I heard people answer...thinking is better. Now, thinking always ends up raising questions in your mind. And questions demand answers. And how do you get those answers? You get them by going out into the world and living. Vesting yourself in some true living to find an answer to those questions you've been thinking about."

The drunk was using his fingers like a pointer, poking at those invisible thoughts in the air above the table.

"Of course," said the drunk, "others said it's better to live than think... Funny thing, to live, really live, you have to have a reason to live. That only stands to reason, right? And where do you get that reason?" He tapped the side of his head. "That's right. It comes from thinking."

The drunk slugged down more beer. Cricked his jaw a bit. Grinned. "Would you rather think...or live?"

There was a strained look on that scarred face, as if its owner were in contest with a private torment.

"The book," said the drunk, snaking his hand across the table. Robert slid the volume toward him. The drunk lifted the cover to see——

FRANKENSTEIN

or

THE MODERN PROMETHEUS

The drunk slowly closed the cover and looked at the youth sitting across from him.

"That about says it all…doesn't it?" said Robert.

The drunk stood and nodded. He suffered the boy's reality. "That question——the first time I heard it I was in London…in a pub."

The drunk seemed a lot less so suddenly. Robert grew suspicious, unsettled.

"I'm an actor," said Nathaniel. "I practice my craft sometimes. As far as the question…I heard it from an actor friend of mine. You might have heard of him. His name is Colonel Tearwood."

CHAPTER 26

NATHANIEL ESCAPED INTO THE BUSY NIGHTSTREETS of that black neighborhood alive with small bands of music and laughter and sidewalk vendors, before Robert could pay the bill and be after him.

Frankenstein thought Nathaniel. Here was a truly lost soul in a little Philadelphia restaurant reading *Frankenstein*. Existing in a kind of exiled turmoil and isolation reading about this creation being called *monster...creature...abortion*. Names that Nathaniel was sure the youth had had hurled at him from vile time to time.

There were few whites on the street and Nathaniel picked up the sidelong glances and the way people seemed to ease away from him as if they were liquid. Nathaniel went back to the hotel. He left the door to his room open. He sat at a table by the window where he had a bottle of whiskey and two glasses. He rolled a cigarette and waited as he knew Robert would eventually return. And so he did.

He came up the dim stairwell with his hat in one hand and that volume in the other and he walked straight for the room and stopped in the doorway. He was cautious to say the least.

"What's going on?" he said.

"Come in...have a drink."

Robert leaned his head forward and glanced about, but he did not enter. "Who are you?"

"Nathaniel Luck is my name."

"What was all that back at the bar?"

Nathan poured a glass of whiskey. He spoke in a much more relaxed, off handed manner. "You know it's hard to play a drunk effectively. It takes real work, genuine concentration. People think it's easy. That all an actor has to do is act like a person when they are actually drunk. But that's where you can get to really ham it up. Now you might get away with it in a bad burlesque or overly broad farce *or* when the audience is actually drunk. Then hamming it up might be——

"What—was—that—all—about—back—at—the—bar?"

Nathan offered him the glass of whiskey. Robert declined. Nathaniel set it back down on the table.

"I wanted to come up with a less threatening way for us to meet."

Nathaniel went and began to pour a second glass of whiskey.

"Astor," said Robert.

"Astor," said Nathaniel. "And your mother."

"So…you're the latest field hand I'm to contend with."

Nathaniel set his glass down. He reached for his cigarette. "I'm here because your mother befriended me. She has been kind to me. She asked me. And I felt sorry for her."

"And Astor will pay you well."

"And…I will be paid well."

"What about the rat and his keeper?"

Nathaniel blew smoke out his nostrils. His eyes peaked at the description of whom he could guess. "You're speaking of Foxworth and Gideon Katt…thugs extraordinaire. They're in a hotel. Waiting on word from me."

Robert looked despondent and angry. He entered the room. He set his hat and book down on the bed. He looked about as if needing to make sure of his safety. He took up the glass that had been meant for him.

He drank, and he studied Nathaniel and he drank some more, and he looked at the mural on the wall of another of Joseph's trials from Genesis. Robert Harrison, as disfigured as he was, had a sensitive face, and it was telling Nathaniel something. Fine actors learn the art of reading expressions, to understand and complement that expression, to become a mirror for that expression. Robert was plotting.

"You know my uncle?"

"The Colonel was my mentor in London. And the truest friend I ever had. That's how I came to meet your mother. I was given a letter of introduction by him."

"Is he still a drunk?"

"As fine a drunk as you'll ever find."

Robert pointed his glass at the mural. "I have one in my room. Joseph rising above the prison walls on a dream cloud and floating toward the king of Egypt…You don't seem like the sort for this kind of work," he said.

"I'm an actor. I should be able to play any kind of part. I guess they felt that was qualification enough to try and help convince you to come home."

"What if I paid you to convince them I disappeared?"

"You can disappear for free."

"But if I hired you to convince them."

"The rat and his keeper seem intent on having you come home."

"They are intent on my silence. You know about the fire? And my claims."

"I know some…from what they say."

"I can't prove Astor was behind it. But I won't be silent. I don't know what my father's involvement was. But he was. There was some criminal act to it all. It wouldn't surprise me if the rat and his keeper were up to their necks in it.

"Well, actor. Try this scenario. You convince me to go home. We are on the way. Everything is sunny and bright. Then I end up in the Delaware River. And the blame is put squarely on your shoulders. Things like that happen."

Nathaniel need only look at his own life to answer, "Things like that happen…You're not at all like how they described you."

"And how was that?"

"Alcohol…opium."

"Sordid and mind troubled. Making up crackpot stories."

"Precisely."

"I drink. And I take opium sometimes because of the pain from these burns."

Robert emptied his glass in one throwback, then he set the glass down. Nathaniel watched him cross the room, unfazed, take up his hat and the copy of *Frankenstein*.

"How old are you?" said Robert.

"I'm twenty-one."

"I'm twenty." He put his hat on. "I have a question for you, actor."

Nathaniel smoked, and nodded for Robert to have at it.

"Do you think," Robert said, "either of us will live long enough to see our next birthday?"

CHAPTER 27

NATHANIEL SAT AT THE TABLE smoking and asking himself——why didn't Robert Harrison want to go home? He'd never really nailed down his reason. He'd never explained himself when they'd talked. Was it fear of Astor for his own life? That would certainly be an honest reaction. Was it because of his father's possible involvement in what might have been a nefarious act? Most certainly possible. Could he not bear to face his mother as he now was, or the world he had been raised in, for that matter? Was there just an overriding sense of helplessness or hopelessness to his situation that he could not overcome? Absolutely understandable.

He replayed the conversation with Robert in his head, trying to piece together the answer to that question. He took to playing both parts, himself and Robert, imagining a conversation between them. Going back and forth, and at some point, as Robert, he asked himself, "Why are you so plagued by this?" And then Nathaniel as himself, got to the truth. He had been moved by the youth and he told him so, then, "I might consider helping you disappear…If…If…I thought it was in your best interest."

· · ·

Nathaniel knocked on Robert's door, but there was no answer. He waited, and he knocked again and there was still no answer. He panicked. Had Robert slipped out of the hotel somehow? Nathaniel had been sitting at the table in his room those last few hours with the door open and he could see the length of the hallway. If Robert went to leave he'd have to pass Nathaniel's room, unless he exacted some reckless escape, jumping from out the window or shimmying down the roof. Nathaniel reached for the doorknob and reconsidered, cursed privately then turned away when came this weary half voice, "That you, Candy? Door's open."

Nathaniel entered a darkened room but for the moonlight through the uncurtained window that framed the vague outline of the youth bundled under sheets, one bare arm hanging out from the bed listlessly, and a bedside table, a mess with empty bottles and dirty plates.

"It's not Candy," said Nathaniel, closing the door behind him.

There was some movement in the bed. "Who is it?"

"Nathaniel Luck."

"The actor," said the groggy voiced youth. "How am I looking, actor?"

Nathaniel came forward. He stood over Robert. That marked face was pale and sweating. "You look pretty bad."

"That's honesty for you...Do you think it presumptuous of me to ask a favor of someone who means to do me ill?"

"What do you want?" said Nathaniel.

"Go downstairs and ask the lady who runs this place to have Candy go get Doctor McMumm. She'll understand."

"Doctor McMumm."

"Just tell her I asked for Candy to get Doctor McMumm."

Nathaniel came down into the tiny lobby. A handful of men were in conversation at the counter where the woman who ran the hotel worked. Her eyes fixed on Nathaniel as he approached. He excused himself and the men quieted and stood back. Nathaniel pointed upstairs. "Robert Harrison asked for Candy to get Doctor McMumm. Said you'd understand."

CHAPTER 28

NATHANIEL RETURNED TO THE ROOM. "They're getting the doctor."

Robert gave out with a suffering laugh. "Thanks."

"Can we have some light in here?"

"Candle...on the bureau."

Nathaniel crossed the darkened room with care. Felt for the candle. Lit it. A small blush of light and shadows. He could see well enough now. The room was a disaster. Clothes everywhere, bottles strewn about. Robert was trying to right himself, piling pillows against the brass headboard so he could sit up.

Nathaniel lifted the candleholder and passed it over the bed to see better. Robert's scars were red, his face horribly sweated.

"What did you come to my room for? To make sure I didn't escape into the night?"

"I came to ask you a question."

"It isn't that thinking or living question?"

"Is there any other kind?"

Nathaniel set the candle down on the table by the bed on a tottery stack of empty plates.

"They're out there, you know," said Robert. "Watching this hotel."

"You mean the rat and his keeper?"

Nathaniel was sitting in a chair by the wall in the shadows. Robert pointed to the mural above his bed that was just as he'd detailed it, of a chained Joseph rising up out of a prison on a dreamcloud.

"You wouldn't happen to have a dreamcloud handy?" said Robert.

Robert wiped at his face with the sheets, he wiped under his arms and his neck. He tried to breathe out the pain. "Well, actor...what's the question?"

"Why don't you really want to go home? Explain it to me." Nathaniel reached down and picked up the copy of *Frankenstein* that lay on the floor and he tossed it to Robert. "Like I was reading the first sentence of a novel, or the opening lines of a play or a newspaper article, for that matter."

"Well, I'll be damned," said Robert. "You keep turning into someone else right before my eyes."

Robert got up. He carried the book. He was naked. He was a slight person. He looked almost underfed. He wrapped the sheet around him like it was a toga. Even in that veiled light Nathaniel could see an escutcheon of discolored flesh on his back, thanks to the fire. His body glistened with the sweat of pain.

"If I wasn't feeling so bad——"

Robert set the book down on the bureau then began to rummage through the liquor bottles left there, hunting for a dreg or a pitiful swallow's worth. He leaned against that blocky piece of furnishing. "I started out believing my father was a good man," said Robert. "Strong, decent, hardworking...and honorable. And I ended up murdering my brother." He turned. "Well, actor...How was that for an opening sentence?"

Robert did not wait on an answer. He shuffled back to the bed with the sheet dragging along behind him and sat.

"My father worked for Astor for two decades. Attorney, business executive, importer. Astor originally made his fortune trading in furs. But when he was facing bankruptcy, he illegally ran opium through China. Two governments turned a blind eye. Special dispensation for the wealthy.

"That last year before the Wall Street fire I noticed a serious change in my father. He was in a constant state of tension. My suspicions grew, so I began to follow him clandestinely. His life became strange new associations, unusual business meetings with nameless people, hand delivered letters and notes arriving at all hours of the day or night. That's where I got my first look at the rat and his keeper.

"The night of the fire he received a hand delivered note. He became very agitated. Said an emergency meeting was to happen at his office. A short time after he left I suggested to my mother that my brother Tom and I go to his office. Wait for him. Cheer him up, then come home together. She thought it a high old idea as he'd been pretty morose lately. If she only knew."

Robert quieted and sat in that drafty room like someone utterly spent.

"His office was up on the third floor and when we got there the gas lamps were on, so I thought...But it was empty.

"Then my brother said, 'Look!' and pointed out the window. There was a warehouse next door. The Hart Street Warehouse. We could see my father through the windows. He was carrying a lantern. My brother was calling to him and waving his arms and when he saw us..." Robert's voice died away. "When he saw us. The look...

"A minute later I see two men running out of the place, their coats winged out behind them, disappearing into the pitch dark and a minute later there is an explosion of brick and wood sheeting, and a wall of fire blew through the glass windows."

Robert was shivering and could not quite pull himself all the way back up on the bed and it was left to Nathaniel to help. He stood over Robert who stared off into a looming past.

"It was so cold that night water froze in the pipes. The fire department was useless. The army had to dynamite a line of buildings to kill the path of the fire that had consumed Wall Street." He pointed at the black space before him. "A night watchman from the building next to the Hart Street warehouse said he saw a wagon being loaded about an hour before the explosion. The night watchmen in the neighborhood said he knew there was opium in that building.

"I believe Astor's people discovered someone was bringing opium into the city. He ordered it removed...stolen...then the building torched. But something went wrong. That's what I wrote to the editors. That beautiful building my mother lives in, that was built with opium money. And there are other developments in Manhattan that Astor is involved in. But that's not the reason I don't come home. It's not fear of Astor, though I wish it were."

There was a rapping at the door.

"The doctor," said Nathaniel.

Robert laughed. "Yeah...the doctor."

Nathaniel opened the door and there was Candy, a teenage black, alone with a sack. Robert waved him in.

"Where's the doctor?" said Nathaniel.

Candy handed the sack to Robert who held it up and shook it. There was a clanking from the sack. "The doctor's right here," said Robert. He reached in the sack and pulled out a pint sized medicine bottle. "Nathaniel, meet Doctor McMumm."

He handed the bottle to Nathaniel and took out another from the sack. Nathaniel held the bottle to the light. The label read: DOCTOR McMUMM'S ELIXER OF OPIUM.

He reached for some money on the table by the bed and stuffed it into Candy's hand, then he saluted him. "Thank you, young sir."

Robert undid the stopper and drank. He looked at Nathaniel. "Ironic, isn't it? I need opium to kill the pain. Serves me right."

CHAPTER 29

THE OPIUM PERFORMED ITS MAGIC and the pain having eased the youth fell into a sleep, bound up in the sheets like a caterpillar.

Nathaniel thought to stay and watch over him and went back to his room for his whiskey. When he returned he picked up that volume of *Frankenstein* and set the candle on the table beside the chair where he sat. He poured a drink and rolled a cigarette, and in the dim glow of midnight with a shank of moon upon the window glass, he took to reading the tale of the creature that he had once upon a time as a boy.

He had forgotten that Frankenstein's mother's maiden name, Beaufort, was the same name he had been handed all those years ago. Memories of his youth which had become with time, nothing more than nothing more.

But as he read the book this time something happened to the youth that was Nathaniel Luck. Call it God's own creative engine, or the primal urge of that all too human soul to act. So began the haunting, page after page after ever turning page.

I saw—with shut eyes but acute mental vision—I saw the pale student of unhallowed arts kneeling beside the thing he had put together.

Nathaniel looked across a room, drifting as it was in candle shadows, at this tormented youth he hardly knew yet was connected to by a reasoned fate or pure happenstance, while an idea was forming out of the chaos of those pages. Dark and shapeless at first, but alive in the blood like a nervous fever.

Robert awoke from his drugged sleep to face an inhuman shadow across the ceiling. He sat abruptly, fighting through a wave of dizziness. His lean face tried to register all that he saw about him. There was Nathaniel sitting in a chair in the corner with a guttering candle beside him. Robert's eyes shifted here and there. His mouth was dry. "What are you doing?"

Nathaniel held up that volume of fiction. "*Frankenstein.*"

"How appropriate."

"Foxworth," said Nathaniel, "or maybe it was the rat, said you were trying to write for the newspapers."

"My mother thought it a flimsy profession. But when Astor got wind of those articles he killed any chance of that coming to bear."

"One of them also said you'd tried your hand at something else…a book maybe?"

"These are strange questions."

Nathaniel seemed totally absorbed in some thought. He stopped a moment at the foot of the bed and looked at Robert.

"Why are you staring like that?"

"Because I think I got a look at the future."

• • •

Nathaniel could not sleep. The engine of his mind was going full bore as he imagined this new version of *Frankenstein*. While he shaved he rehearsed the pitch to convince Robert to come home and confront the demons that beset him.

The youth was not in his room, the bottles of opium elixir though were still on the table.

As he came downstairs, he found Candy lounging in a chair by the front desk. He was reading a newspaper and smoking and when he saw Nathaniel he stubbed out the smoke and stood. "Mister Luck, sir…Mister Harrison says for you to meet him tonight at the Walnut Street Theatre at six o'clock. And to be lookin' dapper."

Nathaniel walked the streets with his hands in his pockets. He saw nothing of the day or the shops or the people he passed. He was about putting the flesh of Robert's life on the bones of the play he meant to convince the youth to write when he was shouldered from the back into an alley where a couple of drunks sat among the trash passing a bottle. He came about to find himself ringed in against a brick wall by two unsettling faces.

"Misters Foxworth…and Katt. Good fortune reigns supreme."

Gideon ordered the drunks out of there. When they didn't move fast enough, he picked up a brick and flung it at them.

"Where's the boy?" said Foxworth.

"No idea. He was ill last night. I suppose he's out hunting up food or drink."

"He is, in fact," said Foxworth, "making arrangements of travel for Wilmington."

"I don't know where that is," said Nathaniel.

"It's south," said Foxworth. "He means to be going to Baltimore or Washington. Possibly as far as Carolina."

"But not New York," added Gideon. "Did he confide any of this to you?"

"Why would he, if he meant to go there."

"What did I tell you about this one," Gideon said to his partner.

"There is one thing I do know," said Nathaniel. "He is not the man you pretend him to be."

With one blow, Gideon knocked the youth to the ground. Nathaniel sat splay legged with his back against a brick wall bleeding from nose and mouth. Gideon then warned him, "We'll not be defamed."

CHAPTER 30

THE STREET OUT FRONT OF THE THEATRE was alive with patrons waiting on the play, listening to a black minstrel band or crowded around vendors that sold candies and soda, roasted chestnuts, imported coffees and fresh cakes and carts with oysters and ale. Nathaniel waited there in the street, all dressed up like a gent, with the sky gone lavender and the last of the sun like a fleeting match tip. The carriages kicking up clots of earth as they ushered in the well to do theatre goers. He would have tonight to make his pitch because after that, thugs would negotiate the outcome.

An arm swept over his shoulder and Nathaniel turned with his slightly blackened cheek and puffy lip. "What happened there, actor…Not the rat and his keeper?"

"Forget it for now."

Wherever the youth went there were stares, even with his collar up and top hat at a pitched angle he could not escape the disfigurement. But on this night, he seemed unfazed.

"You seem well tonight," said Nathaniel.

"I can see the future," he said, smiling. "And besides… we're going to see Edwin Forrest perform *Othello*. I thought to repay the goodwill you showed me last night."

Nathaniel took Robert aside. "I want to talk to you about an idea I had. And I want you to hear me out, no matter how crazy you think it is."

Before he could start, there was a commotion in front of the theatre. A white vendor was calling out the black man who had the oyster cart and was being assisted by a white woman who was using her charms to reel in customers. The white was ordering the black and the woman away, and there were other white vendors behind him, as he shouted, "We're not gonna let some nigger and his white whore hustle decent theatre patrons. They're just a front for prostitution and pocket picking."

Things could have gotten violent pretty quick because the black did not look intent on giving up a good turn of profit, but theatre management put the run on him and his white compatriot, threatening them with the police. And as the black labored up the street, pushing his cart through the oncoming carriages, bottles were flung.

When all the hatred and combativeness died away and the people got back to their sodas and candy, their cakes and imported coffee, Robert said, "The tongue is the only thing that gets sharper with use. I heard that from Washington Irving. *Sleepy Hollow...Rip Van Winkle...*He was having dinner at our house...a few days before the fire. Now...What is it you want to tell me?"

Nathaniel took Robert further aside so the world there would be only the two of them. "Imagine," said Nathaniel, "a new version of *Frankenstein*...As a play. This *Frankenstein* is set in America. The time is now." Nathaniel waved a hand toward the crowd. "That is the world. And our young scientist is now the scion of a wealthy Manhattan family. His home is your mother's home. His life story is your life story. The past that drives him is now the past that drives you."

Robert stepped back, but Nathaniel grabbed him by the arms. "This *Frankenstein* doesn't want to create a man out of an unadulterated ambition...but as political revenge. To exact a new kind of social justice."

"You mean for me to write——"

"You will be able to tell the story of the Wall Street fire."

"That's why all the questions you asked last——"

"You can use art to cut them to ribbons."

The youth just stood there trying to grapple with this kinetic notion——unsure, wondering, calculating. "This is your way to get me back to New York, isn't it?"

CHAPTER 31

"Art," said Nathaniel, "cannot be destroyed. What is said on stage does not ever disappear. Once written, twice spoken——it is alive forever. It is God within our grasp. How many times did I hear the Colonel preach that sermon?"

Robert leaned into this thought. "I've never written anything near a play," he said.

"So what?"

"I have no idea how."

"So what?"

"Or even if I could, if I knew."

"So what?"

"What if I fail?"

"What if you don't?"

They watched the play, this exercise of words and beauty, Nathaniel from time to time glancing at Robert. He saw that what he'd said had taken hold. That's the elemental curse of making sense to a man that thinks so much. Nathaniel leaned over and whispered, "There's a speech coming...Listen to it closely..."

Robert gave a sidelong glance and Nathaniel's expression said, "Listen now."

That is when the character of Iago began, "'Tis in ourselves that we are thus and thus." And when the character was done, Nathaniel whispered, "Sometimes it takes a villain to let us know how we control our existence."

He took hold of Robert by the lapels. "You're burning your life away. You might as well burn it away in an attempt to put out the fire. And this is something I know about. Take the chance. You can tell the audience of your suspicions about the fire. And what it did to your life. You can go after Astor, and anyone else you may feel is involved. You don't use his name. You find one that's close. You insinuate with dialogue. You hint with dialogue. Use the stage to go to war, because it's about the fairest footing you'll ever find to make the fight. And possibly find a little peace.

"As for me," whispered Nathaniel, "I'll play the monster. And I can make a very formidable monster. I know rage and I know hatred."

He had so disappeared into what he was living out that Nathaniel Luck no longer existed. That was not Nathaniel Luck who seized Robert's coat, those were not his hands trembling, or his eyes past the edge of recognition. This was some other being brought to life by the artist's dark sorcery.

"Are you dangerous, like this?" said Robert.

Nathaniel blinked. "What?"

Robert tried to pry loose of Nathaniel's grasp and Nathaniel now realized.

"I didn't know who you were there," said Robert.

Nathaniel patted his friend on the shoulder. "I'm just a poor actor, who the devil brushed by."

· · ·

There was gunfire outside the theatre. Sudden and quick and capped by a woman's scream. What followed was a violent flurry of shots from up and down the street. A wave of panic swept over the patrons in the lobby. Men in the doorway could see the white flashes of pistol fire. Someone yelled, "There's niggers outside shooting down the vendors." And then a woman, "They'll burn the theatre."

The thought of fire was as frightening as fire itself. Common sense and clear thinking, gone, when they were in conflict with the perishability of the flesh. In the rush to escape, people began to trample over each other.

The fact of what happened that night was this. The black vendor who had been run off returned with a handful of his brethren. The white vendors had been on the watch and were prepared to make a go of it. They even had the son of one of their own keep watch up on Walnut from where they thought the blacks would come. They lay in wait and began firing just as the blacks cleared the corner. The carriages out front put the whip to their animals to escape the fray before they or their animals were mistakenly shot. Women in gowns and their husbands rushed into the street and chased after them. Witnesses said it looked as ridiculous as it did violent. Women holding up their gown hems stepping around or over a handful of wounded and dead in the street.

In the theatre, people rushed the stage looking for another means out, being herded along by employees. Nathaniel and Robert had gotten separated. Nathaniel could see the youth in a mob of patrons pressed into the aisle. Robert had just made the stage when someone kicked over a proscenium light. Sparks scattered across the wooden floor and a gasp went up. People were knocked over and fell from the stage. Men took off their coats and tried to beat down the sparks before they spread.

There were still pockets of gunfire all up and down the street by the time Nathaniel made his way along the alley. Carriages sped past patrons on foot, still running away. Men held onto their top hats as they dashed off as if the hat were part of their head. Vendor carts and stalls were being ransacked and torn down. A dead black was being kicked by a white. A vision of social hatred and useless destruction to fill the pages of a lurid diary.

• • •

"Who you are often comes to you as a complete surprise, if it comes to you at all. 'Are you dangerous, when you are like this?' That question served to burn a light on me. An actor can discard a part once it's served its purpose, but a person cannot discard oneself so artfully. Acting is choices strung together, choice demands risk, risk is dangerous. The truest actors are those who thrive well on risk.

"For me it was that, and something more. From the moment I met Lucretia and her father I sensed there was a risk. I made a choice, choice brought risk, the risk was dangerous. I ended up being a hunted man. And here I am, all those choices and risks later. And I am a hunted man again.

"Is that trait in me a flaw of character? Will I emerge at the end of my life a complete stranger to myself?"

Nathaniel looked at me sincerely. "Do you have a feeling for what I'm telling you? You, of all people, must. Otherwise you wouldn't be here."

I thought about this and what he had been telling

me about the riot outside the theatre. "I could see myself fighting in the street outside that theatre, committing some act of violence," I said. "If that's what you're asking me."

"My boy," he said, putting a hand on my shoulder, "That's nowhere near what I was asking you."

CHAPTER 32

THE DOOR TO HIS ROOM WAS PARTWAY OPEN. Foxworth sat at the table drinking Nathaniel's whiskey. Gideon lay on the bed with a glass set on his chest. They both looked comfortable, and decidedly sullen.

"How was the play?" said Foxworth.

"It paled compared to the intermission."

"Go down to your friend's room."

Nathaniel walked down the hallway. The door was unlocked. The room was empty, as if Robert Harrison had never been there.

Nathaniel returned and stood in the doorway.

"What do you think of that?" said Foxworth.

Whatever Nathaniel thought, he kept to himself.

A glass flew past his head and caromed off of the door. Nathaniel acted as if the glass had not even been thrown. Foxworth had seen it all and let out a "Ha."

Then he began to verbally assail Nathaniel. And while this berating went on, Candy came thumping upstairs taking them two at a time. He saw the door open but knocked anyway. "I got a note, Mister Nathaniel... from Mister Robert."

"Give it here, boy," said Gideon, sitting up quickly.

Candy looked to Nathaniel.

"Don't be lookin' at him, nigger. Do as I say."

Nathaniel nodded. Gideon grabbed the envelope and tore it open. Reading as he got to his feet, he said, "What the hell does it mean?"

He crumpled the note and threw it at Nathaniel who flattened the paper across the palm of his hand.

The note read: *Frankenstein has escaped.*

"Who the fuck," said Gideon, "is Frankenstein?"

• • •

He took the train back to New York in despair. He had failed. He had failed Robert Harrison, failed at wresting his misery, and failed at what it would have rewarded him for not failing.

The train was crowded. It was hot. He sat across from a weathered looking chap with one leg and crutches and a cage on the seat with what looked like a fighting cock. The man had workman's clothes, and the pant leg was stitched to where the stump ended. That game bird in the cage was a pretty scarred up thing.

"Fighting bird?" said Nathaniel.

"Damn right," said the man. "Little Eli. Named him after his daddy, Elijah. Now that was one killin' bastard. Known from Phillie to Norristown."

"Little Eli any good?"

"The bird's alive, ain't he?"

"Yes, sir," said Nathaniel.

"Well that ought to be answer enough, even for an idiot."

"I see your point, sir," said Nathaniel.

• • •

Nathaniel crossed to Manhattan by ferry. Alone with his thoughts, he walked to the house on Lafayette Place. He knocked on the door——set to deliver bad news. It was Sarah who answered and before he could get out a word, the servant's arms swept over his shoulders. "God bless you," she said.

She pulled him in by his coat sleeve, taking his suitcase, calling her mistress. "He's here, ma'am…he's here."

Millicent rushed out from the parlor, her hands to her cheeks, where she was crying. Her face flush with joy. She held him and kissed him. "You brought Robert home. I had faith that you would."

He wanted to tell her that's not why he'd returned when she looked up toward the second floor landing and there was her son. "How are the bookends?" said Robert.

"They sent me home in disgrace," said a shocked and smiling Nathaniel, "while they took the train south."

"Come on up. We've work to do."

Nathaniel stood there, and all he could think of was that man on the train with one leg and a gamebird.

CHAPTER 33

AND SO BEGAN THE LONG MONTHS adapting *Frankenstein* into the play they envisioned. They worked and plotted out of the Lafayette Place home. Millicent invited Astor for dinner, so he might see for himself the positive turn in her son's behavior. Nothing was said of his blueprint to include the dark criminality he believed behind the great fire, only that Robert was adapting the novel by Shelley and Nathaniel was to play the creature himself. Even Millicent was kept in the dark. Astor was surprised to discover this sudden artistic drive within Robert, but he was glad the youth was channeling his energies in constructive endeavors. Neither youth thought Astor convinced, and in time their suspicions bore out.

• • •

On the corner of Dover and Fourth were the offices of Harper and Brothers. They were publishers, so they would know illustrators and lithographers and if there were anyone in New York yet practicing chromolithography. Nathaniel had it in mind to create a handbill for the play and he meant to bring it to theatre managers once he was prepared to help sell them on a new theatrical idea.

He dropped Astor's name and Millicent Harrison's for entrée and presented a sketch he had brought along, listening to the Harper employees' impressions while he gathered names. The rendering had come from the poster the Colonel had done all those years ago. The sketch was in color. The letters unique, robust, even fanciful. And the poster had to say Americana.

COLONEL TEARWOOD'S
AMERICAN THEATRE COMPANY

★ ★ ★ ★ ★ ★ ★ ★ ★ ★ ★

Presents

★ ★ ★ ★ ★ ★

An Adaptation of Mary Shelley's
FRANKENSTEIN

★ ★ ★ ★ ★ ★ ★ ★ ★ ★

Titled
THE MONSTER

As the play came close to completion they had to decide which theatre and theatre manager to approach. The Colonel had preached that all theatre was politics. Industrial, financial, revolutionary, conforming, sexual, burlesque was politics, satire was politics. Plays were the politics of keeping power, losing power, taking power. Even the *Dog of Montargis*, a melodrama about a beast and a mute and a murder, was built on the politics of war. "Know the theatre manager's politics," the Colonel would say, "and you will not have to hide behind facades of polite modesty or degrees of delicacy when you pitch your play, but live and die with your passion intact."

Their target became the Bowery Theatre which had been designed as competition for the Park. It seated over two thousand patrons. The Depression of '37 had hit the Bowery particularly hard, so the manager, Thomas Hamblin, decided upon a dramatic political turn to insure the Bowery's survival. Hamblin was an Englishman who was pro-American, nativist, and shrewd. He had a taste for fighting the status quo and people who criticized his tastes. He directed that all future entertainment should be marketed for the common man, the working man.

The classics gave way to spectaculars and lurid melodrama. Plays with outrageous visual effects, plays with earthquakes and circuses, huge minstrel shows with Ethiopian delineators, as white showman in blackface were called. Stories about pirates and naval battles fought in tanks on stage with miniature ships and children playing sailors to get the size right. Even using actual gunpowder. These particular shows reminded Nathaniel of the bombastic entertainment he'd worshipped in London as a boy at the Sadler Wells theatre.

Nathaniel sent an introductory note that he'd like to meet and discuss the adaption of *Frankenstein* for performance. With the note he included the handbill. The title — THE MONSTER — was done in a shade of red befitting blood, which Hamblin found particularly enticing. But that is not what had Hamblin ordering his assistant to immediately set a meeting.

Hamblin was a tall, manly creature known as a womanizer and brawler who began his theatrical life on the English stage, first in dramas and then as a part of a ballet troupe which performed at Sadler Wells.

When Nathaniel entered the office the first words out of Hamblin's mouth were, "Where'd you steal this?"

He was holding up the handbill.

"Sir?"

"Colonel Tearwood…Where'd you——"

"The Colonel! He was my mentor in London. I'm an actor. I'm staying with his——"

"You mean to tell me that impulsive, hopelessly reckless, vagabond is still alive?"

"Two pints a day and whatever he can get on the cuff," said Nathaniel.

"At Sadler Wells," said Hamblin, "he portrayed a British Naval officer with a withered arm. And the physical things he did with that arm, you'd have thought…And he did it all flat out drunk on his feet. The audience had no idea. Talk about a testament to the actor's art."

They settled down after that and discussed the play. Nathaniel brought sketches he had an artist do for the sets. They'd used the house on Lafayette Place for the Frankenstein home, and for his laboratory, they had scoured the worst and most degraded medical labs in the city. The designs were done for box sets.

"I saw the Vestrie's production in London using box sets," said Hamblin. "Here…it might be still too new."

But the three walled set, using the stage proscenium as the open fourth wall, gave the designs a kind of authenticity and claustrophobia that focused one's attention.

"How about the cast?"

"You've been known to take chances and premier American plays with unknown casts," said Nathaniel.

"And the monster?"

"I will play the monster."

"And how will you play this monster, how will he be?"

Nathaniel got up. He pointed to the window. "May I?" He walked over and lifted the sash and leaned out. There was a carriage below. He yelled to the driver who looked up. "Have Mister Harrison come and join me."

"And who is this Mister Harrison?" said Hamblin.

"He is the playwright who adapted the story to Manhattan and Wall Street and the politics of corruption. And when it comes to the monster, there is no one as qualified to discuss it as him."

CHAPTER 34

Now CAME THE WAITING while Hamblin read the play and decided. They had been honest about the politics therein, the possible corruption, a father's guilt, the fire, the opium, the changing of names. The Colonel had passed on to Nathaniel a little wisdom about the submission of plays——a blessing comes quickly, the bad news you wait for.

That first night Nathaniel had returned from Philadelphia he discovered an envelope under his pillow. He knew immediately and instinctively what it was. The note was all passion and impulse and he burned it as she requested.

She was at the address near St. John's Church, and she was much like a girl when she answered the door. Her hair was glossy, and she took him in hand. Her desire was not delicate like it had been that first night in his room. They made love in the daylight then lay on their backs with a breeze on their bodies, looking up at a ceiling white as a cloud.

"You saved my life," he said out of nowhere.

"The play you mean."

"No...not the play."

She leaned over and brushed at his hair. "What then?" she said. "Do you mind if I need to hear it?"

He thought a while, and then he answered, "Faith over sorrow." And he looked at her and smiled, all boyish and open.

"Nothing that meaningful has ever been said to me."

They kissed and remained for a little while longer, their world those four walls. She whispered to him as she rose from the bed, "If I were young and without my son, I would make you possess me...and I believe that I could."

They met when they could there. He never asked who the house belonged to within sight of the church. Sometimes he'd smoke and watch as she'd dress. One particular day she went to her purse and brought him an envelope. "From my brother," she said.

She always left first and sometime later he walked to the church. It would be there he'd open what was a letter. He wanted nothing to spoil their time at the house. The church was empty and perfectly still. The face of the Christ looking down from the cross, the same the world over, distant and unfathomable.

Inside the envelope was a note from the Colonel and a clip from the paper. The headline read:

REWARD OFFERED IN THE PICKWICK MURDERS

The law firm of Howard and Scott, who represent the estate of the late Dyer McCarthy have offered a reward of £300 for the capture of John James Beaufort.

Witnesses in Liverpool have placed the disappeared actor at a seaport inn. Scotland Yard believes he may have fled the country.

Ships' manifests are being checked and officers questioned. And traveling under an assumed name is not out of the question.

Nathaniel put the clippings aside and concentrated on the note.

Greetings Young Squire,

Millicent wrote that you're thriving in the colonies. I gather my cufflinks are working their magic. Thought of coming home myself for one last fling before I'm resurrected.

The article I sent you says it all. Except for Mister Jonah. He lost his arm up to the elbow because of the bullet. Howard and Scott have hired scrappers from Bow Street. They've been all over the theatre district with questions and threats. They believe you've gone to America using an alias. So be careful what you write.

The Colonel had left out that he had been threatened, beaten and even dragged from a pub and nearly drowned in a trough. But a good actor knows how to play the convincing coward, even when he is one, begging and pleading and swearing he had no information to give. The ignorant fool even took to weeping to seem sincere. Not genuine tears, but close enough.

And one last thing, before I close, it was good luck you never leaked to anyone the name you're living under. I'll write when I know more.

Ever, Tearwood

CHAPTER 35

AN ENVELOPE ARRIVED AT THE HOUSE on Lafayette Place which Sarah brought with dispatch to her mistress. She was in the sunroom having coffee and saw right away the embossed stamp of the Bowery Theatre. She walked it upstairs hoping to God it was good news. She knocked on the door where the two youths worked, reading through lines Robert had been rewriting. When they saw what she held, a shroud of nerves fell over the room that bordered somewhere on anguish.

"Well," said Millicent, "who will it be?"

Nathaniel told Robert, "You do the honors."

"Not me," he said, "If it's bad news, I don't want to be the one. You open it, Mother."

With all of the time, the work, and the effort, the planning and thinking, and the conniving. The youths were too shaken to read it themselves. That all too human fear of rejection, that all you've done will go unrewarded. This would be the perfect moment for a bout of indifference, or at least a healthy contempt for defeat. The note was one sentence long, that Millicent read:

> Dear Misters Luck and Harrison,
> The monster has found a home.
> Thomas Hamblin

• • •

Things happened quickly after that, with casting and set production, costuming, rehearsals. All the usual sleep stealing madness you wait your life for. Nathaniel made copies of the handbill, now with the Bowery Theatre and performance dates. The first production of COLONEL TEARWOOD'S AMERICAN THEATRE COMPANY was taking to the street. Nathaniel hired out of work actors to pass out the handbills knowing they'd make a hard pitch for seeing the show, not only to help one of their own, but to be in the good graces of someone who might one day cast them.

Robert had a friend named Arnold Fellows that he'd gone to school with and who worked as a reporter for *THE SUN*. It was through Fellows that Robert had submitted his articles on the Wall Street Fire that were summarily rejected by the editorial staff.

But they had something much more enticing this time. *THE SUN* was a frontline broadsheet, like the *NEW YORK TIMES*, but *THE SUN* was unique in that it sold on the street and not by subscription. It had advertisements. It was the first to do crime reporting, to cover murder, to write about a suicide. It sent out reporters to dig up stories. *THE SUN* had become a sensation for covering what became known as THE GREAT MOON HOAX by reporting as fact a fantastical story about life on the moon.

This paper was the common man. It fed on the lurid beauty of every-day life. And Fellows was the perfect agent for what they had in mind. He was small, lithe, and weak, picked on as a youth, bitter, nasty, out for notoriety and social revenge on real or imagined slights, and a well to do scalawag. If his own mother were drowning and saving her meant losing a story he'd rather be an orphan with a byline.

The Bowery Theatre, starting this June 19, will be showcasing a new, modern version of *Frankenstein* titled THE MONSTER. And this reporter has learned from people intimately involved with the production that during the laboratory scenes there will be actual corpses on stage.

This, of course, had the intended effect. Outraged citizen groups, religious and benevolent societies, the police, the mayor's office. All were up in arms over what they deemed an illegal travesty. Even the fire department sent their highest ranking officers to the Bowery Theatre in protest and demanding public assurances there would be no actual corpses on stage.

• • •

Nathaniel watched as some irate matron stood on the front steps of the theatre railing before a mob of similarly dressed irate women about "moral turpitude" and the "degradation of art." Robert joined him across the street from the theatre.

"I'll bet half those women will be at the show opening night," Robert said.

The two youths broke out laughing and started away. Half a block down, a pair of men fell into lockstep behind them.

Misters Foxworth and Katt had stepped from a carriage and into all that Manhattan daylight. They were talking to each other as they followed along behind the youths.

"I'm going to be at opening night," said Gideon.

"You…you bring bad luck everywhere you go," said Foxworth.

"It's one of my charms."

"Gideon, I don't think these boys have truly ever seen a dream go up in smoke."

Robert turned suddenly, near violently. "I sure have. The night of the Wall Street fire. I also saw two men running from the Hart Street Warehouse."

CHAPTER 36

OPENING NIGHT, THE THEATRE WAS PACKED. The overflow was ushered to the gallery above to take up space in the aisles or to sit on the stairs. The well to do patrons complained but were promised by Hamblin to be treated no worse than the rest. The lobby was kept clear without explanation because of the planned shock the audience had coming. And there were police stationed out front in case of disturbance, and as management had been warned——corpses onstage, was cause for arrest.

There was an unsettled atmosphere about the audience as they waited. Disquieting whispers, the slightest shuffling in their seats became this insidious sound. Women had fans they used to work off their nervous anticipation. The stage had been kept particularly dim, just a single foot-lamp lending a hint to the edge of a couch from where an arm hung. And then there was the slightest movement of fingers, the stretch of the hand, and a slight shudder from those in the front rows who saw.

The arm rose, and the figure stood in the darkness and turned up a lamp.

We are in Frankenstein's laboratory. This Doctor Frankenstein is young and handsome, with sleeves rolled up. He crossed the stage. The laboratory was a netherworld of basement brick, dark and filth, everywhere the tools of the scientist's trade and large constructs of strange unnamed machinery. He carried the lantern behind a screen of hanging gauze and shadows to an operating table, on which a body lay.

There was a ripple of sound from the audience. People in the front row stood to see better, and a voice from the gallery shouted down, "Is it a corpse?"

• • •

Nathaniel sat at the makeup table and listened. He waited alone for his entrance on stage. He looked in a mirror streamed with shadows at the monster that he had become.

He saw in that tragic and volatile creature, that the events in your life, from incident to the incidental, may not be part of the final work, but were essential to the work. They may not be discovered in the character's history or lines of dialogue, but they were essential to the character having life.

Frankenstein, the book, came into being because a group of writers and poets sat around a fire to see who could create the most frightening ghost story. In the book, the monster is born from the corpses of other lives. The play they were doing was born from the corpses of other lives. Nathaniel Luck and Robert Harrison built their creation on the corpses of other lives.

He wanted to understand, because he needed the creature to understand. He needed this to inform the creature that even though he was born from the corpses of other lives, there was more, much, much more that had caused him to be.

A voice in the doorway whispered, "It's time."

He nodded and stood and said to the tormented face in the mirror, "*Nothing* is born from *nothingness*."

The audience had settled in on this depraved tale of death now rendered through a veil of corruption and revenge. They waited for the monster, and the horror, like they were being led down narrow graveyard avenues at night, one unholy step at a time.

Then came this caterwaul from the dark and empty lobby. People in the audience turned to see, the play had stopped, the actors silenced. Men by the lobby doors scrambled from their seats to find out what the screaming was. Women by the door rose up. One screamed and fled down the aisle…men stood back.

The monster had entered.

Nathaniel had dressed like a ragged factory worker and he carried a sack over his shoulder. Nathaniel had gone to extremes to make sure he looked hideously tragic. He started by cutting his hair extremely short. And stealing from Robert's infirmity, he used a straight razor to shave patches of hair right to the scalp. These he daubed with caustics like red mercury and enamel. He let the patches blister and then he'd wipe them clean.

He stole from women's makeup tricks. An unhealthy pallor was a symbol of beauty——meaning a woman didn't work, didn't have to go out in the sun. Her job was being a vision of sensuality. To achieve this, women took small doses of the poison arsenic. Against Millicent's advice,

Nathaniel started dosing himself with the toxin, testing the limits of how pale and corpselike he could be without doing mortal harm.

And like women, he had his arms painted with white enamel and over that he had arted in blue veins. The veins went up through his grubby shirt and his neck to detailed scars along the jaw that were stitching. He had tested all this during rehearsals under the exact lighting conditions. He'd shaved his eyebrows. He had rosehead nails cut down and hammered into the soles of his boots so when he walked the iron tops would make this low but ominous scraping on the wood floor.

He did not caterwaul coming down the aisle, but rather he made his slow way toward the stage, staring at person after person, arching his shoulders to look up at the gallery as if it were some imposing heaven of judges. He had begun to cry. From this murky voice came, "What have I done…what…but be born…is that my doing…?"

He bent down and implored a patron, reaching out toward them. "You can't imagine what it's like…to have been pieced together from the dead…to know you have been rotting in the earth…" He looked up at the gallery and shouted, "You have no idea…there is no forgiveness for that…" His voice echoed, and then he was silent, just staring, all tears and anger.

A woman, just in from the aisle, saw or thought she saw something in the sack through the frayed burlap.

She stood, "There's an arm in that sack…Look…There's an arm."

CHAPTER 37

Colonel Tearwood's American Theatre Company had its first hit. Shock reviews and sold out gate. But once a work of art, or entertainment, is in the world, it is of the world and the world has many animosities and resentments to be reckoned with.

The broadsheets had a field day linking Astor with one of the corrupt characters in the play. At the Lafayette Place house, Astor demanded Nathaniel and Robert deny any such accusations. They refused.

He pleaded his case to Millicent. After all, her own late husband was a veiled character in the play, thought to be a part of the conspiracy behind the fire. Privately she had been overwhelmed. But her son's survival and happiness were more important than her late husband's reputation, especially as she'd suspected his guilt. "It's just a work of fiction," she told Astor. "Nothing more."

The next day attorneys for Astor came to the house outlining law suits against Nathaniel and Robert and the theatre company, if they didn't deny the accusations. They refused.

Nathaniel knew the play would not last. That before a pointed lawsuit would have affect there would be a more threatening form of persuasion. So every night, every performance became more cherished, more life affirming as it became more ephemeral. The dream come true through the dreamer's art, more complete and true than the world around it.

Nathaniel talked about this with Robert, who agreed. Then Robert added, "Before the play, I was a deformity, the repellent victim of a fire people avoided. Now the same people embrace me. I was pitiful then, they're pitiful now. I should hate them, but I don't. I relish the attention, I thrive on it. What does that make me?"

"It makes you what you are...a writer."

That very night, they were attacked on the way home.

• • •

After the night's performance the cast would pack into carriages and start out for the better haunts. A band of ignoble artists still in costume and ready to loosen up and go. To lock away the hard work and discipline and undry those throats. Merry pranksters straight out of the pages of Mary Shelley as adapted by one Robert Harrison, who by the end of the evening, gentleman that he was, had to be carried on the shoulders of drunken actors to his magic carpet ride home. Clip the wings of man's vexations for a good couple of hours and you can classify the evening a rollicking success——a wisdom passed down through the ages to the high priest of barrooms——one Colonel Tearwood.

The last of the revelers had been dropped off at their apartments down in Hunter's Point. Nathaniel had taken to driving the carriage. The coachman sat in the back, smoking his pipe and listening to a somnolent Robert Harrison ramble on about the ridiculous choices good fortune sometimes takes, when a carriage sped past. It pulled up in the shadow of some grimy tenements and four hooded men leapt from the vehicle carrying truncheons.

One man grabbed hold of the horses' leads so the rig could not be whipped clear of the assault. Another climbed up to the box seat and started to beat hell out of Nathaniel. The other two charged the carriage from both sides. They pulled open the doors and went at both Robert and the driver, wailing on them with their batons.

This was no robbery, but a plotted assault. Poor thugs don't make a habit of travelling in carriages. And from their clothes these weren't social dregs but professional ruffians. And along that part of the road, in that particular neighborhood, the few locals hanging about were not likely to put themselves between the victim and a violent outcome.

• • •

Millicent was shocked and outraged when they both came straggling into the house. They didn't lie to her about what had happened. They understood she would see through any flimsy story they made up. She came to Nathaniel's room that night taking the stairs barefoot in the dark, even knowing how dangerous it was with Robert in the house. They spoke in whispers, avoiding what was inevitable. Clinging to the hours until there were none left before the sun.

The play went on the next night and the night after that. Threats be damned. The next day was Sunday, the theatre was dark. In the middle of the night, Sarah came quietly knocking on Millicent's bedroom door. The two women stood in the dark of the hallway with only a candle between them. Sarah's expression was deeply strained. "There's a fire downtown," said Sarah. "It's the theatre."

The youths were awoken. The four stood on the roof and looked toward Five Points. Streams of fire pulled skyward, the block around the flames in a heated glow. At two o'clock in the morning the Bowery Theatre, with its new edifice that was barely a year old, burned to the ground. There was little the fireman and their engines could do. From what the newspapers could gather, the fire began in the carpentry shop which was just below the roof in the front of the building.

The night watchman had done his rounds barely an hour before the blaze was first sighted from the street. Some circumstances, according to the paper, led them to believe it was the work of an incendiary. The newspaper even went so far as to claim they had certain information they could not divulge that the fire had been set.

The play now was officially closed. Nathaniel approached other theatres, but no one would touch it. Colonel Tearwood's American Theatre Company had gone from its exciting premiere to an untimely demise in less than thirty days.

• • •

But Robert had come home. He had written a play. There was sanctuary in that. He was no longer a victim but a visible man who could bear his scars.

As for Millicent, she had her son back. A son in whom she could pour her affection, and her pride. She was a family now, not a lost widow. And she knew again the wonderous reality of being a woman.

Nathaniel, meanwhile, was secretly preparing to leave Manhattan. A writer can write anywhere, but an actor has to be where the theatres are. And he had no intention of waiting compliantly for the malice there to die down.

Arnold Fellows, the reporter from *THE SUN*, wanted to do a final article on the play and the burning of the Bowery Theatre, and for that, he also wanted Nathaniel's impressions.

"To destroy art," said Nathaniel, "is to destroy the conscience of man. It's meant to eradicate the beauty that comes out of the very brevity of man and so make useless his existence. But there is a twist…A work of art is like an insurance policy…it always pays off in the end."

Nathaniel decided night was best for the leaving. He waited out back of Lafayette Place. From the dark of the building he could listen to voices.

When Sarah returned from her shopping he stepped out of the shadows with his suitcase in hand. There was no need for explaining. She reached down into the good of her heart to reason him into staying. He pressed two letters into her hand and said what he'd written in the letters, "This isn't good bye…it's just intermission."

ACT III

CHAPTER 38

WHO AM I? It is a question Nathaniel the actor asked himself with every new character he was to play. It was also the question the man was to ask himself as he waited along the dock for the sun to rise and take that seven dollar ride North to Albany on the steamer *Isaac Newton*.

Unlike England, this country America was on the move. Advancing, stretching out. Everything was about now, everything was about what came next. It was not a country tied to an old history or long established ways of life. It did not have a preoccupation with tired traditions that had little relevance to the lives the people lived. This country seemed to be good at saying farewell, and then getting on with it.

Everyone seemed to be going somewhere or coming from somewhere. In this country America, everything happened fast. Centuries seemed compressed into decades. The play was the perfect example. Its rise and fall as quick as it takes to have one good meal. There, then gone in a blink. But that also meant the next rise could happen just as quick. That too was part of this country America, it seemed possessed of youthful, indefatigable attitudes.

This country America also had an unsettled, restless nature. And so, it was more like Nathaniel was than England ever was, and that fascinated him. It made him feel akin to it in some mysterious way as yet unrevealed to him.

He also came to see better that to truly evolve as an actor meant more than just finding the right part, it was knowing the part and how to enrich it. And that meant answering essential questions like…Who am I?…Why am I here?…What do I want?…What is my purpose?

To understand all that means to also understand the country you are part of, the time and the place and the people, so when you speak, you speak the language of their souls.

The light on the Hudson seemed endless, and the cool rush of the wind stirred the air. Nathaniel engaged in conversation with anyone that he could. People were travelling to places that he'd never heard of, with Indian names he could hardly pronounce. Their whole life stories pared down to minutes. There was music on board——piano and fiddle——in the salon. Mostly American songs that he didn't know. Lively tunes and heartfelt ballads.

At the dock in Poughkeepsie was a black in chains and a man toting a shotgun. Nathaniel thought that in New York all blacks were free, but a passenger explained that runaways could be brought back home for reward. It was a sobering moment, indeed. That little shadow he carried got a taste of the daylight, so he went to the salon where they were selling hard cider and whiskey and got himself exquisitely drunk.

CHAPTER 39

THE SALON WAS PRETTY WELL CROWDED with passengers reveling to the music or talking among themselves. It was mostly the upper deck crowd, all state room and gentility. There were a handful of men along the bar and the back tables whose passage was nothing more than the space they took up on the deck.

It turned out the piano player was a young woman and the fiddler a gentleman a few years older. They had the look of escapees from church service, if you asked Nathaniel. Sometimes the young lady would play a tune familiar to the patrons and call for them to sing along. Here's where that pack at the bar had to be set down by the hosteller and steward to stay abreast of good manners or they'd be booted to shore.

She seemed a shy girl, the piano player, and educated, for she spoke well. But it still surprised Nathaniel when she began a rendition of the farcical opera *The Devil to Pay*. He'd seen it performed in London, he'd even played in it himself with none other than the good Colonel——at the tail end of a lesser program, in a warehouse, by the fish market along the banks of the Thames.

And being just drunk enough and having no practical regard for making a fool of himself, and as a way of getting that shadow sitting on his heart stuffed into a pocket somewhere, he began singing to the music, musing the words was more like it, as he had when he'd performed it.

Little by little he drew the attention of the drunks around him and they began to applaud and whistle and those in the salon took notice. He stood now, giving a flick to the tip of his cap. "I'm not much of a singer," he said. "I'm an actor by trade." This brought out the usual heartfelt and spiteful hissing which he tried to quell with a smile. "I just want you to know," he said, "that an actor considers himself a rousing success if he's hissed and booed…and not drowned or shot."

The girl at the piano had done enough of these salons to invite Nathaniel forward, and her playing drifted into a soft background as Nathaniel found a spot among the tables. The actor in him had taken over, turning into the perfect cocktail of talent and drunkenness.

Nathaniel ended up performing the whole one act play, speaking out the songs. And it must have gone over well, because he pocketed quite a stash of tribute. The passengers actually thought he was part of the show, and he saw no profit in honesty.

He was stone cold sober and starving by the time he was done, and he and the piano player, and the accompanist on the fiddle, who turned out to be her husband, suggested they meet for dinner. And so the next chapter of Nathaniel's life had begun on nothing more than a lark.

CHAPTER 40

CECIL POOLE AND HIS WIFE ABIAH were Christians from Cincinnati. As members of the Swedenborgian Church, they traveled throughout the east, playing in salons, circuses, fairs, religious camp shows, raising money for Christ and spreading the Swedenborgian gospel.

They handed Nathaniel a religious pamphlet at dinner, which he took graciously, as they were paying for supper. He knew of this sect from England because they had a very different view of the black race, considering them at the very least equal, if not superior to whites, and invited them into their homes as fellow Christians.

"We've even performed in theatres," said Abiah, leaning her head toward him and looking about, as if this fact got out they'd be open to blackmail or hanging.

"You said you were an actor," said Cecil. "You've performed on stage? In theatres?"

"A few times," said Nathaniel dryly. "But I always repent afterwards."

"Abiah watched you carefully tonight," said her husband. "And she believes she could give you a few helpful pointers that would raise your performance."

He was smiling privately when someone walked up to the table and sat in the seat to his side. His eyes came up to rest upon a young woman in a simple white dress. It surprised him to say the least, and she smiled politely.

"Nathaniel," said Abiah, "this my cousin, Genevieve. Genevieve... Nathaniel."

She put out her hand to shake. Her hair was black and pulled back, with a striking widow's peak, and she wore strange looking glasses with hexagonal lenses. As he took her hand, she said, "In case you're wondering what member of the orchestra I am...I play the booking ledger and the account files. Otherwise I have no discernible talent whatsoever. Artistic or otherwise. And...I've learned to glory in my lack of talent and my lack of interest in my lack of talent."

"She went to preparatory seminary," said Abiah. "The Washington Female Seminary."

"And I have been a great cause of distress to my family ever since." As if in secret, Genevieve said, "It was a Presbyterian seminary. Turns out I am not an outstanding Christian, but just a plain old sinner."

"She's much too modest," said Cecil.

"About being a sinner?" said Nathaniel.

• • •

Later that evening, the Poole's went back to the salon to entertain the passengers. A night of Brahms and Mozart piano concertos. Soothing music to complement the darkness of the river and the densely groved shoreline. They walked the crowded deck, Nathaniel and this young woman. There were passengers asleep on chairs and benches or lying on bedrolls spread out across the bow. There was drinking and vulgarity and laughter, voices echoing out into the reaches of a stilled nightscape to fall away like thin cries.

Something had met in their eyes back there at the table. He saw it, she saw it. She no longer wore her glasses, and her eyes had a feral quality and looked as if someone had chipped off pieces of azure glass.

"When I saw you in the salon today, performing," said Genevieve, "I was envious."

"Of what?"

"Happiness. You looked extremely happy. I'm curious…What does an actor do if he despises the words and thoughts coming out of his mouth?"

"That's a strange question."

"Should I be embarrassed? I'm not easily embarrassed."

"Well," he said, "An actor does what everyone else does who despises the words and thoughts coming out of his mouth. Only the actor has to do it better, more convincingly."

"Is it that simple?"

"Simplicity is the bread and butter of good acting. Unfortunately, good bread and butter is hard to come by."

"I take care of my cousin and Cecil," she said, "because they cannot take care of themselves. So, the family enlisted me to be the mule who pulled the wagon. A well dressed mule, but a mule nonetheless."

"That's a disparaging way to speak of oneself."

"Like the good actor who despises the words coming out of his mouth…I gather I was convincing enough."

She stopped and leaned against the railing and looked out upon the Hudson. The lanterns along the deck of the steamer lit the river and there upon the blackness was the luminous reflection of the *Isaac Newton* and its peopled decks, otherworldly and alive just below the surface of the churning waters.

"We look so like a dream down there…just beneath the waves. Don't we?" she said.

He glanced over the railing, but he had been stealing a look at her.

"What a different Genevieve Wells than the one on deck," she said.

"And how is that?"

"That down there is a woman who will not stand for being a mule pulling someone else's wagon. That woman down there sees a very different world in places no one thinks to look."

The music had ceased in the salon and down the crowded deck came Abiah, searching about, finally waving to Genevieve. "I was looking for you."

Abiah had come up from behind Nathaniel, and as she passed close beside him she slid her fingers along the pockets of his coat and with such slight mastery, stole the key to his room. "Are you going to be here for a while? Cecil and I will come back and keep you company."

"I'll be here," Genevieve said. She looked at Nathaniel. "What about you? Can you bear my strange questions a little longer?"

"I believe I'm up to the challenge."

Genevieve and her cousin talked privately, and in those ensuing moments she spotted Nathaniel's reflection in the window of the hatchway door, handsome and impertinent, watching her. When Abiah walked away, Genevieve turned to him, "You've been staring at me, you know."

CHAPTER 41

ABIAH POOLE AND HER HUSBAND returned with a bottle of wine and glasses. The four drank together at the bow railing along the upper deck and they watched as towns appeared out of the darkness, sparkling pockets of light along the shore or receding back from the docks up into the hills. The river commanded one's imagination, and Nathaniel thought of Washington Irving and Fenimore Cooper. He spoke of reading *Last of the Mohicans* as a boy in England, and he looked into the reaches of the very woods Cooper had written about. As he talked of how this stirred his blood and made him feel like a boy again, Abiah deftly slipped the key to Nathaniel's room back in his pocket.

He held Genevieve's hand as he said goodnight and she leaned up and whispered to him, "I envy you."

He lay in his bunk restlessly, envisioning Genevieve as an actress onstage when there came the sounds of turmoil from somewhere out along the upper deck.

He opened his door and stole a look. People had come out of their rooms along the deck. The captain, a boatswain, and two deckhands were outside the room next door. The captain was demanding entry, and when refused, the deckhands muscled their way in.

Nathaniel shut his door. As he slipped on his trousers he could hear the muffled sounds of arguing and movement. This lasted a few minutes, and then there was a brusque knock at his own door. As he opened it a lantern was held up close to his face. He put out a hand to cut off the light. The captain said, "We need to search your room."

"What for?"

"There's been a robbery," said the boatswain.

Nathaniel barely got the word out that they could come in when the deckhands muscled past him, their lanterns swaying as they went.

"And no chicken pickings either," said one of the deckhands, as he tossed Nathaniel's clothes and suitcase onto the bunk. These the boatswain investigated while the captain commanded the doorway, his prickly fingers on the pistol in his belt.

The deckhands were looking for any place money might be hidden, any nook or cranny. Their lantern close to the wall like huge searching eyes. But it was the suitcase with the cookie tin inside it the boatswain was trying to open. The articles from the London paper about the murder caused him to panic. His hands trembling until he remembered he had done away with the damn things before he left Manhattan. He had burned them behind the house on Lafayette Place that last night, thank God. His breathing eased, but people are rarely right with their timing.

"Think I got something here, boss," said one of the deckhands.

He lay across the bed, his arm squeezed down into the space between the mattress and the wall. He sat up and the light was put upon him. He held up a wallet.

"Toss it here," said the captain.

The deckhand obliged. The captain walked outside. A man's voice, "That's my wallet...the money...there was near over two thousand dollars in that wallet."

"You're not much for hiding," said the boatswain.

"I know nothing of that."

"I suppose it just climbed into the bed with you."

The captain returned. He was slapping the wallet against the palm of a hand.

"If I stole the money, would I be stupid enough to keep that wallet and hide it here? Why not fling it into the river?"

"Maybe you're just not that clever," said the captain. "Maybe you're arrogant. Maybe this is exactly what a confidence man would do and so make an excuse for himself. It doesn't matter. The Albany court will handle you."

They chained Nathaniel to one of the stanchions outside the pilot house. He sat crosslegged in the baking sun, treated as harshly as that runaway black, with ash from the smokestacks snowing down on them.

They searched the boat for the money and questioned the passengers to see if he might have an accomplice on board. They had stopped and loaded wood at Germantown, so his accomplice might have gotten off there. Of particular interest were the Pooles and Genevieve Wells.

"We didn't know him," they said. "He was an actor who just stepped in and started performing," they said. "The passengers seemed to like him, so we let him continue," they said. "He seemed decent enough," they said.

Abiah Poole did remark, though, that she might have seen him talking to a man at the landing where the runaway slave was on the deck.

Nathaniel was brought a tin bowl of water by one of the deckhands. While he drank, the man squatted beside him. "I know the Albany jail. Done time there. Nasty place. God help you if you do time on the treadmill."

CHAPTER 42

THEY WALKED NATHANIEL from the *Isaac Newton* in chains, yet carrying his suitcase. He looked the part of the tragic joke. The Pooles and Genevieve Wells watching this rigged drama from the dock. When Nathaniel traveled, superstition kept him from wearing the gold cufflinks. These he had sewn into the belt seams of his trousers. He pressed a chained hand against them as a last vestige of hope, as foolish as it might seem.

Endless stares as Nathaniel was herded along the sunny avenues of Albany. The scales within him tipped between shame and panic. The jail was a bulky structure on Howard and Eagle. Five stories of foreboding. Dimly lit halls, stone floors, the constant echo of disappearing footsteps.

He was brought to a lonely cell in the basement that was to be his new home. That first night two guards tried to beat out of him the whereabouts of the stolen money. He lay all night in his own blood. His trial was ten days later, and he was convicted and sentenced to three years in prison before court broke for lunch.

In those first weeks he survived by living out scenes from the plays he'd learned and performed on stage, but after a time, it became its own form of persecution. His world was a long corridor of cages where men lived alone and ate alone.

"Be a good girl," he was warned, "and we won't have to introduce you to the treadmill."

Time became nothing. He began to lose sight of what day of the month it was, then what day of the week. You become like the roaches and rats that habitate your cell. Desires, longings, ambitions, you begin to view then with indifference. The heart dies first or the heart dies last, prison only accelerates the process.

What you know about the men in that dank basement is what you hear of their lives while you lie in your filthy bunk with your hands behind your head looking at a brick wall with rusty stains where water has seeped down through cracks in the foundation. You hear their hollow voices as they talk about their personal struggles and private agonies, their poverty and rage, their rotten youths, troubled minds, their lost families and bitter

loves. Some are left to scream and shiver out their need for whiskey or lau-
danum. Some are just vile malcontents, others are victims of the recession
of '37. Jobless and homeless without even a thread to hang on. Now resi-
dents of the Eagle Street Gentlemen's Club as they grimly called it. With
free room and board and maid service, only these maids come dressed with
cold grey eyes and a whip for a smile.

He spoke little about himself to the other inmates, because he believed
if he kept his private life and feelings to himself they would somehow
survive this unfair incarceration intact. He adopted a studied and silent
exterior and so was called "the actor" by inmate and guard alike.

*How is the actor feeling today?... What would the actor prefer for lunch?...
Would the actor consider putting on a show for us wretched souls?*

He often thought of writing Millicent and Robert but did not. His
shame saw to that.

You could buy tobacco and food from the guards, even whiskey, that's
how the prison worked. Nathaniel had some money in an account and he
could write up a draft and the guards would cash it, that's how the prison
worked. The violence exacted upon the inmates feared and enraged him,
but he kept mute. When the guards spit on the food or threw urine in the
inmates' faces he was enraged, but he kept mute.

He drank more than he ever had. But it did not quell the rage, it did
not lighten the despair, it did not afford him a stage to play out his hatred.
Nathaniel Luck was slowly dying of reality.

And then one night an inmate took ill and was pleading from his
cell for help. But the guards, as always, had their own vindictive protocol
about how and when they responded. The pleading got so bad that other
inmates took up the sick man's cause. Those too went unanswered. Finally,
Nathaniel stood at the cell door and screamed out, "Get off your asses, you
god damn son-of-bitches. There's a sick man down here."

What prompted him to act at that moment would be the cause of
endless questions. The torment of endless questions. Maybe the torment
of his own existence had finally broken him. Maybe crying out on that
sick man's behalf, he was crying out for himself. Maybe he thought this
intercession would free him somehow. Maybe it was a plain and simple act
of defiance. It did create utter silence along that dim corridor of cells, and
it did inspire the respect of his fellow inmates. It also earned him a date
with the treadmill.

. . .

There was an open sided shed out back of the prison that was enclosed by a twenty-foot wall. Under the shed roof was a paddlewheel about forty feet long that pumped water. Along the length of the wheel, a series of rails had been constructed that ran to the backwall roof, sectioning off the wheel into ten numbered slots. In each slot was a man walking the wheel while his hands gripped yet another railing that ran the length of the wheel so that he would be kept upright and not fall from exhaustion between the slats.

The paddlewheel turned by human effort, human effort was the engine. Nathaniel was booted forward and ordered up into slot 9.

This was no violent, all consuming, momentary punishment. This was not created in a moment of vengeance or wrath. This was the slow and steady exercise of cold blooded will. A man got onto that paddlewheel and walked. He walked all morning and he walked all afternoon. He walked for ten hours if so ordered. He walked on half rations and he walked on bread and water. He walked in the scorching heat and the hellish cold or when the rains leaked through that shoddy tin roof. If he collapsed, he was rallied back by the guards and set to the wheel. He was made to walk until his body was broken, until they'd subjugated his spirit, his soul left in ruin.

Embittered and exhausted, he took it in silence. He was now a warning for the inmates to heed about what could happen. The canary in the mine, so to speak. Nathaniel Luck was a death waiting to happen——and then came the letter.

CHAPTER 43

HE COULD ONLY STARE AT THE LETTER the guard held through the bars of his cell.

"No one knows I'm here," said Nathaniel.

"Bein' you're such a famous actor and all," said the guard, "maybe one of your fans located ya." He flicked the letter toward the slop bucket.

Nathaniel grabbed for it, missed. He picked up the letter, an edge wet with urine. On one side of the folded paper it read:

Nathaniel Luck
Albany Prison
Albany, New York

It was beautiful handwriting, with delicate flourishes. He turned the letter over and just above the wax seal it read:

Genevieve Wells

He went and sat on the cot. He looked at the name and remembered and thought, "Why in the world would——"

He broke the seal and opened the folded up double leaf of folio paper. It was a short letter in that same beautiful handwriting with the delicate flourishes:

Dear Nathaniel,

I don't know if you remember me, as it has been two years since we met on the Isaac Newton. You performed in the salon with my cousin and her husband.

I just wanted to tell you how that night changed my life. Do you recall answering my questions about what an actor does if he despises the words and thoughts coming out of his mouth? And that simplicity is the bread and butter of good acting.

Your mind was so agile, and you, so beautifully alive and free with your experience.

I no longer work with my cousin and her husband. Do you recall how I defined myself as a mule pulling someone else's wagon? Soon after that night, this mule escaped the wagon. Like so many people in life I have done things for which I hope someday to be forgiven. But that is a subject for another time.

I am sorry for what happened to you. I know in my heart you are innocent. Have faith, Nathaniel. I believe one day I will see you perform on stage, because that is your God given calling.

I send you my tenderest sincerities.

Genevieve Wells

After he read the letter, he cried because it had sparked in him a surge of hope from this most unlikely source. One of the inmates heard muffled sobbing from Nathaniel's cell and said, "Hey, actor…someone die?"

"No," said Nathaniel. He wiped at his burning eyes. "Someone lived."

He saw the world ever so differently after that. Even the suffering he experienced on that "endless staircase" as the inmates had christened the treadmill. Nathaniel could admit to himself that he had killed a man in London, rightly or wrongly, that he had beaten him to death and escaped that crime and so in some respects, he could say he was paying for it here.

The hours of punishment on the wheel were no longer painful lost hours, but the time where he could think out a life after prison…and the rebirth of Nathaniel Luck.

He wrote to Millicent and Robert. First to apologize, and then explain. And in Robert's letter he added: *Come to Albany if you can. Have an idea for a play. Need you to meet the characters in person, as they are in the cells around me, and readily available.*

• • •

Millicent arrived first. She had decided this with Robert. She waited in a dusty room just down from the warden's office. There were bars on the window and they cast their presence across a table and two chairs. Nathaniel was led in silently by a uniformed guard. She watched as the chains were unlocked from his wrists. They made such a weighted sound, she thought, in that little room.

He was no longer a youth, she could see that, but a man. He was unshaven and filthy, and his face had hardened lines and his eyes had deepened and grown stormy, and maybe even more attractive because of it.

When the guard left, they came together hesitantly and kissed and held each other. He was so pitifully thin, she could almost cry, and she went on about why hadn't he contacted her right away? That she would have come to Albany and hired him the finest defense and that she was going to work now to see how she might get the rest of his sentence commuted and that she would bring him better food and a doctor if he needed one. He took hold of her hand and had her sit. He just watched her as she went on and when he kissed her hand she stopped talking. His head came to rest on her hand and she reached out and ran her fingers through such unkempt and bug ridden hair.

"Just seeing you is enough," he said. "And your being here more than I deserve."

She pressed the side of her face against his and whispered, "I would never say this to anyone for fear it would get back to Robert. But you are the love of my life."

• • •

When Robert was in that dusty box of a room alone with Nathaniel, he quickly got to the point. He took out a flask of fine whiskey from his coat pocket and set it before his beaten down friend. "Is it worse than you look?" said Robert.

"How I look is makeup and wardrobe," said Nathaniel. "It's inside they kill you."

They went to work after that, sipping whiskey and talking up theatre. No one had done a realistic play about life in prison. Nathaniel handed Robert a sheaf of paper he'd brought along. For the last two years he had been writing down the inmate's stories he heard along that hallway of cells.

Here was the premise———a youth is convicted to a term for a crime he claims he did not commit. It is there the youth confronts this machine of realities. Souls can't hide in prison. Indifference reigns supreme. Men walk about with the heart ripped out of their voices. Guilt or innocence means nothing. Their life stories are the stories of this country. And they all end up on the wheel sooner or later. The youth has had his will expended, his pockets emptied of hope and faith. He is in the presence of a blackness that will feed him to the grave until——

"He receives a letter," said Nathaniel. And he hands Robert the letter from Genevieve Wells. Nathaniel had written Robert the whole story about that night on board the *Isaac Newton*.

"Whether it was the girl, the letter itself, the mention of faith and God, or that one day I would perform again…my life was changed."

Robert rented a room near the prison where he came and went, interviewing inmates and writing the play. He went up to the roof of a nearby building where he could look down into the enclosure with binoculars and bear witness to the treadmill——the everlasting wheel.

The first time he saw it was an afternoon of striking heat. The shed roof, tin white hot from the sun. On the ground the men's long shadows climbing. Robert was reminded of Sisyphus from mythology class in school. Pushing that forever stone up a hill never to be scaled. Robert hired an out of work theatre artist and brought him to the roof and handed him binoculars. He was to draw a wheel in detail as a working prop for the play.

When they next met, Robert brought with him a thought, more than a thought really. And he didn't know how it would be taken. "Our play is missing something," he said.

Nathaniel looked up from the detailed sketches of the wheel. "It looks so benign…that's the beauty of it."

"Did you hear me?"

"You said our play is missing something. What is it?"

"A woman."

CHAPTER 44

THE IDEA HAD STARTED ACCIDENTLY. Robert had read the letter and passed it to his mother, thinking it not only a godsend in how it affected his friend, but also as a perfect catalyst for the third act, keeping the youth in the play from an act of self destruction.

"You realize," Millicent had said to her son, "this Genevieve Wells committed the robbery. Along with the Pooles, of course."

They were in a well appointed Albany restaurant having a quiet lunch. His mother had said this so offhandedly that Robert had no idea how to take the comment. He just sat there staring amidst the slightest clatter of silverware and conversation. Then Millicent gave her son a dressing down with her eyes, and he knew.

"Men are so naive when it comes to women," said Millicent. "Women have a secret language all their own. And let me share with you one of those secrets. We are anything but the fairer sex. Women have poisoned many a man...both literally and figuratively.

"Read the letter, Robert. Not the words. She talks of innocence...She talks of forgiveness...Of breaking with her cousin...Meaning her past. It's as close to a confession as a coward can get."

Millicent saw that her son could not or would not allow himself to accept this. "Scares you to know what a woman might do, doesn't it?"

"You could be wrong."

Millicent drank her coffee in righteous silence.

And it wasn't long before she was proven right. Millicent had hired a man to investigate similar robberies on the paddlewheelers that coursed the Hudson. Three weeks after the crime on board the *Isaac Newton* there was a similar robbery on a boat called *Eden*. When checking passenger lists it was discovered a Genevieve Wells and a couple named Poole were on board.

Robert wanted it to not be true for the most human of reasons. But as a writer, he was thrilled. This was perfect for the woman's character he had conceived to be part of the play.

"He shouldn't have gone to prison," he said to his mother.

They were in her hotel room at the time. It looked out upon the dark waterway of the Erie Canal. It was a night of hard rain and lightning and she just stared and stared out the window. Finally, she spoke, "I could imagine killing her." She turned to her son, "Surprised to hear your mother say such a thing?"

What so affected him was the sense that his mother's fondness for Nathaniel ran so much deeper than he'd realized and of a decidedly more intimate nature. It came as a shock and made him feel that what she'd said before——men are so naïve——went to the heart of that moment. He was not sure if he liked what he was feeling, and suddenly thinking.

• • •

"Imagine this beautiful young woman in the prison setting," Robert said to Nathaniel, "that only our central character can see and talk to. Is she a ghost, a dangerous spirit, an angel, a person he created to keep from losing his mind?

"She knows everything about each prisoner. Their secrets, their past lives. She tells him things that seem to presage violent events. Our central character wants to know why she is there, why only he can see or talk to her. She refuses his entreaties. She only offers that someday he will know. And then he receives a letter."

Robert and Nathaniel sat in that musty paint chipped room doors from the warden's office. Robert held up the Genevieve Wells letter.

"And this spirit, ghost, angel," said Robert, "tells him that Genevieve Wells committed the crime. That the letter was a stumbling attempt at a confession, an attempt to elicit forgiveness. Our character doesn't believe it. But our spirit, ghost, angel tells him that three weeks after the crime a similar robbery was committed on a boat and who should be passengers... but Genevieve Wells and the Pooles."

At first Nathaniel had no idea and said, "Is that the reveal in the play? Cause it's great. Is this apparition telling the truth, or is it a lie? Does she mean in the reveal to destroy him or save him?"

"It's the truth, Nathaniel. That's the reveal."

Nathaniel blinked. His body began to stiffen and sit back. This was more than a state of unease overtaking him.

"My mother hired a man to investigate. There was a robbery on another paddlewheeler three weeks later. Wells and the Pooles were passengers. What are the odds? She is going through everything with the warden right now to see if she can affect some shortening of your sentence."

When he truly realized what Robert was saying he came up out of his chair and flung it aside. It hit against the wall and cracked apart. A sound came out of him as if a knife had been plunged into his throat.

• • •

"I was destroyed, Jeremiah. Destroyed. Hours passed where I was devoured by rage at being used like that, only to be replaced by hours of despondence over the years of my youth I had lost in prison.

"I thought I would kill someone. I came close. I thought I would kill myself. I came very close. I wanted to commit acts upon that woman that are too vile to even think, let alone say.

"I was leaking poison everywhere and wanted to escape my own being. And because I could not I began to hate myself. The walls of my cell shrank down until the brick pressed against my body from all sides. I could not breathe. I could not sleep. I could not eat. I could not close down my mind. And those exhausting hours on the treadmill only made it worse. And then I could not speak.

"I lost my voice. I lost it completely. I could not even swallow. I was mute. For days...mute. For weeks...mute. I believed I would never speak again. I lay in my cell moving my mouth, but nothing happened. That was my introduction to hell.

"And then providence saw fit to raise the actor in me. Agony is nothing more than agony until it is turned into art. And the actor saw how to play the part of the inmate on stage in the last act...without a voice. Having to connect with the audience, to have them experience and understand through my silence. First to see my fall...and then maybe, just maybe...for a moment...my rise."

I listened to Nathaniel and the more I listened I came to think...that was me. I leaked poison. I wanted to escape my own being. And because I could not, I harbored hate against myself. I had not lost my voice, though. I had no voice. That was until providence came into my life, in the guise of this hunted murderer.

CHAPTER 45

Nathaniel was released in the Albany rain three months early. He walked to a carriage with Millicent and Robert and stopped in the street and put his head back and let the drops teem down on his face. It was his first moment of freedom in almost three years and he had shaved for the occasion and had his hair cut and was wearing the cufflinks hidden in the seam of his trousers since his arrest.

They had not come to this moment unprepared, but had decided this would be the place where the play would premiere, and they'd find out what they had. There were no theatres in town at the time. The Green Street had been turned into a church, and the Albany bought by Saint Paul's was being refitted for Christ. But there was a warehouse on the south side of town the owner was desperate to rent, in a neighborhood flooded with immigrant workmen on the Erie Canal.

Nathaniel wanted to go straight to the theatre to burn off the bad years as soon as he could. It was a dreary old building, drafty and leaking, and their voices fell heavy in that vacant brick shell. Robert had had built a proscenium and flanked it with tarps to create a backstage of sorts.

Waiting in the half dark there was the treadmill, and the bars of one large community cell. They watched as Nathaniel got up on the wheel and it made this strange clicking sound as he walked it that rose up to the roofbeams and just hung there.

· · ·

It was still raining that night when he went to her room. She took him by the hand and they sat in the darkness. A single candle through a doorway shined and left its slightest trace on their faces.

"I would have died in prison, if it wasn't for you."

"I'm sorry I had to bring you bad news to save you."

She rested her head on his shoulder, and they watched the rain stream down on the window. They were calm and quiet together, and you'd never guess they just walked out of the Albany prison.

146

"Robert has a sense," she said, "of what goes on between us."

"What do I say if he confronts me?"

"There'll be nothing to say, because after opening night, I'm going home." He was surprised, and disappointed besides.

"Sometimes," she said, "life exceeds all your expectations. And I'd like to leave it like that."

• • •

They had flyers made up and saturated the South End where the working stiffs lived.

COLONEL TEARWOOD'S
AMERICAN THEATRE COMPANY

✮ ✮ ✮ ✮ ✮ ✮ ✮ ✮ ✮ ✮ ✮

That Created the Hit New York Play
THE MONSTER

✮ ✮ ✮ ✮ ✮ ✮ ✮ ✮ ✮ ✮ ✮

Premieres Its New Play on June 19th
THE TREADMILL
The story of Seven Inmates
and
The Women Who Knew Them All

They had junkmen cart seats from the two gutted out theatres, and carpenters hammer benches of scrapwood. Enough to fill out the front of the warehouse. After that, patrons were left to their own devices to stand and take up spots by the walls. The discount seats, as they say, where patrons can drink and smoke and get rowdy.

The actors were locals or ne'er do wells passing through. Wardrobe would be their own filthy clothes. For makeup, they were told not to shave or cut their hair and the worse that they looked all the better. The woman they cast was ideal for the part, but no one could say that her talent was sterling.

It wasn't a packed house the night of the opening, but it was a lively one. The setting and the seating had seen to that. There were those of the better set who'd arrived in carriages with their private invitations. There were members of the press from the *Gazette* and the *Journal* thanks to Millicent's persuasive luncheons. Even Horace Greeley, editor of *The Log Cabin,* was there. Already famous for his progressive political stands, Greeley had become the voice of a whole generation when he coined the phrase——"Go West, young man"——enticing a nation of young men the future lived somewhere out there on the road beyond the conformities of the era.

But most of those in attendance had come on foot from their homes or the local bars and pool halls, and they brought their own liquor. They were canal men, foundry men, men of factories, men of labor, who lived paycheck to paycheck. A lot of them knew each other and shouted hellos across the warehouse or flung epithets and lewd remarks. And their women, sitting there, stubborn and resourceful creatures, for whom a night out was as much a relief as it was a blessing.

When it was time for the play to begin a makeshift curtain strung from cables stiffly parted and there was the wheel, a bleak and ominous device towering above the proscenium. And from the audience came this collective exhalation.

Most of them knew what it was and what it meant. Brothers of their class had done time on the wheel and lived to sing of its pitiless joys. But no one had ever seen it in a play.

Someone yelled from the back of the warehouse. "Burn that damn thing!"

There was a round of applause.

Robert was backstage. Nathaniel glanced at him. They knew without fault now, no matter what, this would be a bucking night. Nathaniel managed a few moments with the girl playing the only woman in the drama, who they had appropriately named Genevieve. She was tense. "Brace yourself...we got a lively audience tonight. Forget a line...take a deep breath and improvise."

Nathaniel was, in fact, talking to himself, through her. It had been three years since he last performed on stage. There was a lot of emotional dust underfoot, besides all the usual caged up actor insecurities. It was one thing to fail as a man, as a loner, as an inmate, but as a performer——

That was the ultimate door slamming in your face. The cold, ruthless aspect of existence that terrorized him. He could only liken it to the smothering of a baby.

CHAPTER 46

IT WAS AN UNTAMED AND UNTETHERED NIGHT. When the actress playing Genevieve made her entrance on stage there was rowdy applause and lurid whistling.

She stumbled through her first lines and someone out there in that mob of standing patrons shouted, "Speak up honey, we can't hear you over all the heavy breathing." There was a swell of applause and other patrons yelling to "Ssshhh…"

When Nathaniel came on stage, he was shocked to hear his own voice echoing high in the roofbeams. It was as if he were out of his own body and staring down at this former convict who was trembling inside. "Keep a brave face," the colonel would say, "and the audience will never realize they are witness to a sniveling coward."

Nathaniel's performance at first was unsteady. Storm tossed would be a more accurate description. He was not the character, he was a rusty actor playing a character. And then, strangely enough, when he was set on the wheel for punishment, he steadied up. It was as if some compelling pulse of the earth had taken hold of his performance.

He was that tortured man on the wheel. And when he spoke he was that tormented man on the wheel. And when he cried out in anguish, it was genuine anguish and the audience felt that anguish, and not just because of his performance, but because it was their anguish coming through him. It was their lives he was crying out. Their existence in a world that ignored them, that denied them, defaced them, devalued them. That turned a blind eye to their misery and death. That saw them put to the road with nothing if they could not climb the wheel day after day to no avail.

As the guards abused Nathaniel on stage, there were shoutdowns from the audience and a flurry of bottles were flung from beyond the seats. Whiskey bottles, medicine bottles, elixir bottles, and pieces of fruit, a tobacco tin, bits of scrapwood that had been left piled along the warehouse wall. Even an old shoe that clunked one of the guards in the head, cutting it open. As he escaped off stage, there was a mighty round of applause.

The actor playing the part refused to go back onstage. He could not be ordered, coerced, or even bribed into returning. He had lines of dialogue and there was no one backstage to take his place, so it fell to Robert. They got the guard stripped down there in the wings, and Robert was booed and hissed, and he thought he'd need help from the Almighty to just keep from throwing up right then and there.

One of the actors playing an inmate who was also on the wheel had the resources to improvise. He began to sing the campaign song from the last political presidential election——Tippecanoe and Tyler Too. *"Who has heard the great commotion, all the country through..."*

There was a sea change in the audience. They stopped harassing the guards and began to chant along. The brotherhood of an American moment. The wind in their voices and spilling with urgency. Then the actor and Nathaniel went back into their lines, and the scene continued like clockwork.

The dialogue was the common language of the street, and it grew more tensile as the play proceeded. There were a handful of vulgarities spoken that stopped the audience cold. And the defining moment came at the very end with Nathaniel's character's final lines.

Whether it was an accident or his intent, no one ever knew. He would never tell. The final lines after he came to grips with the reveal that the woman had intentionally marked him for the crime was to give the audience the absolute sense that he had risen above circumstances and suffering.

But when he came to say the lines——it had been such a warm night and his voice was so dry and he hadn't performed for three years——they were barely audible. So, as the curtain closed, those in attendance didn't know, and this left the play open to interpretation. Was it a tale of redemption, or a man's destruction, was it some tenuous station in between?

The reviews were harsh. The *Gazette* and *Journal* particularly so... *"A plate of vulgarities the audience was made to feed on...shameful misuse of a woman...Trash of the lowest denominator...Violence personified...The curtain should have gone down before the play started."* Horace Greely saw something else. *"The destruction of theatrical decorum...Stark reality disguised as a fiendish sentiment...As violent as the country itself."*

The actors were neither praised nor panned but rather taken to task. One reviewer said, *"The performers did not respect the audience. They were more like a ratpack in an alley or a bar. Or a prison, I guess. I have heard the lead actor Nathaniel Luck was a convict himself. And it shows."*

At first, Robert and Nathaniel were discouraged by the negativity, until they came to realize they had stumbled upon something. What they had stumbled upon was the future.

CHAPTER 47

THEY SAID GOODBYE TO MILLICENT AT THE DOCK. She and Nathaniel had not spoken since that last night in her room. He watched Robert and his mother as dusk fell. The last of the sunlight across her face. So like a painting of a woman in the graces of life. She was looking longfully over her son's shoulder. She mouthed the words, "I will miss you." Something was slipping from his life. He thought of Lucretia at that moment, and the vexing temporariness of it all.

When he and Robert walked from the dock in the dark, Robert said, "It's good she's going home. For both our sakes. Otherwise you and I might have had a falling out."

• • •

The reviews, harsh as they were, had not had a toxic effect on the nightly attendance, which grew slowly and steadily. Maybe the play was just blessed being uncivil enough that civility could not thrash it. In fact, it was quite possible the reviews generated what one *Gazette* editorial called a *"...vulgar curiosity in the salacious art of jail cell denizens being showcased in Albany."*

But the people who saw the play seemed to recognize their lives in the characters' lives that were in doubt, day in and day out, and whose futures were just as uncertain as the muffled final lines of the lead actor after the third act that he had played mute.

Sitting in the hotel bar getting drunk Robert read aloud the latest barbs, adding a dramatic flash here and there.

"At least," said Nathaniel, "they're not trying to burn down the theatre."

The comment touched upon an undercurrent of trouble that had caused them to be drinking. Having a financially successful play on stage they began to contact the better houses in Philadelphia and Boston to see if they could engineer dates for a theatrical run, after they were done in Albany.

But they were getting locked out. And the letters had an eerie similarity to them. The fire, the threat of lawsuits. And the subtle intimations that any manager who would do business with COLONEL TEARWOOD'S AMERICAN THEATRE COMPANY might essentially alienate the more renowned companies and their financial backers.

"The people we have to deal with now," said Robert, "are provincial when it comes to their profit and loss. I don't see a way past this."

Nathaniel did not either.

"What if we tried something like…changing the name of the company?" said Robert.

"I wouldn't be here if it weren't for the Colonel. And besides…keeping the name is spitting in their faces."

"Well, we better get shrewder then."

Nathaniel stood and used the moment to be humorously dramatic. "We shall not yield to the moral bankruptcy of others." He'd said it loud enough and was pompous enough to turn a few heads.

"Unless, of course," added Robert, "it pays."

• • •

Nathaniel walked until his body was too tired to carry him. Instead of the hotel, he went to the warehouse. When he was restless, confused, uncertain or troubled, a theatre was his church of escape.

He stood in the lofty silence on the makeshift stage. He could breathe there, be himself there, be true there——he was home there. Nothing else anchored him to this world. For all the rest, he was just a gypsy thief wandering a landscape of rooms, hotels, and apartments.

He confided to those empty seats and benches his private rage at the reception the play was getting from those theatre managers. That his talent and force of will was not enough to overcome a group of monied elites and the professional sycophants who grazed in their shadows aroused a driving hatred that seemed to have existed within him since time itself.

He had a pint of whiskey he'd bought after leaving the hotel. He drank in the stage shadows. "Hey boy," he called out mimicking Tearwood, "blood always flows downhill, so remember to keep on the upside."

He was startled by a faint trace of footsteps. He looked across the backstage, past the treadmill and the prison cell. A limping outline, its weight shifting in awkward steps, slowly made its way.

"Is that you, Luther?"

"It me, Mister Nathaniel."

"I thought you did your rounds by this time."

"Did, sir, but——"

He looked out toward the seats. He bent his shoulders left and then right, squinting. "Did you see her?"

"See her?"

"Yes, sir."

"Who?"

"Da woman."

"What?"

Luther came up alongside Nathaniel. He was a hunched and worked down old chap. He pointed a bony arm out into the warehouse. "Da woman."

Nathaniel looked about as if he was missing something he did not quite understand. "What woman?"

"Da woman sittin' out dere in da seats."

Nathaniel looked again to where the old man pointed.

"Not a half hour ago."

"No woman out there, Luther."

"Dat's why I come back. Cause of da woman."

"What was she doing here?"

"Here to see you, Mister Nathaniel. Dat why I surprised she gone."

"Me...?"

"Yes, sir. Here ta see ya. Strange lady, Mister Nathaniel."

"I don't get it," said Nathaniel.

"Say she was da lady in da play. Sat out there like one a God's own righteous angels and says it...'I da lady in da play. Da real lady.'"

CHAPTER 48

LUTHER WENT THROUGH THOSE FEW MINUTES with the woman. Nathaniel stood listening and rolling a cigarette, he thought to himself...*It's a crazy person or...he couldn't imagine she'd have the audacity.*

"I come back with my dinner," said Luther. "Sat at dat table."

He'd meant the staff table just offstage. There was a lantern on it Luther lit that he might eat by. That is when he heard some movement out there among the seats. He stood and took the lantern and walked around the stage curtain. He wasn't sure what it was. Some creature might have slunk its way in. He shuffled out to the edge of the proscenium. There was something all right. Seats don't make that creaking sound all on their own. He'd felt a little nervous and told Nathaniel so. He held the lantern out. He couldn't see much. Then he heard a voice, a woman's voice. "Yes," she said, "there's someone out here."

That old man leaned down, his shoulders curled, and he held the lantern out as far as he could from the edge of the stage. There she was. A young woman in a simple light blue smock sitting alone. The light falling upon her a little smoky and golden, her hands folded, her face still and somewhat unreal in that setting.

"Ma'am?"

"Yes."

"Why you sittin' dere?"

"I saw the play."

"Da theatre been closed for hours."

"It certainly has."

"If you do'n mind, ma'am...you do'n wanna be sittin' in dis filthy old warehouse so late."

"Don't I?"

"A fine young lady like yourself."

She laughed slightly. Her voice carried in a soft flutter up into the rafters. "In some quarters, people might not think I'm so."

"Ma'am?"

"If you don't mind my asking...What's your name?"

155

"My name? Luther, ma'am."

"Luther…would you be so kind as to do me a favor?"

"A favor, ma'am? Sure, a favor."

"Would you give Mister Luck a message?"

"Mister Nathaniel…Yes, ma'am."

"Tell him the lady *in the play* was here."

"I do'n understand."

"It's all right, Luther. Mister Luck will."

She stood and started through the passageway of seats toward the warehouse doors.

Luther called to her, "Ma'am?"

"Yes."

"Do'n you wanna leave your name?"

"I just did."

When Luther was done explaining, he just stood there shaking his head and said to Nathaniel, "Just walked outta here silent as a ghost."

"Young, my age? Dark hair? Slender, tall?"

"Yeah…Beautiful girl. But let me tell you, Mister Nathaniel…and dis comes from an old man who been burned. She do'n look da kind dat sits at home."

• • •

The actor in him said this kind of drama meant she would appear again at the time and place of her choosing. Yet he watched from the wings when he was offstage and searched out faces as he performed. He stayed in the warehouse night after night, becoming obsessed. Existing on one unanswered question.

"Don't let a moment of grief become a tradition," Robert warned, when the two of them stood on the stage alone on a wind riven night. "After all," he said, "if it wasn't for her, we wouldn't have a hit play."

Nathaniel eyed him in anger.

"That's mighty selfish I know," said Robert. "And easy for me to say. But I speak from experience and have the burn scars to prove it."

Robert took up his coat. "Let's go hunt up a couple of demigoddesses," he said. "And see if we can't overwhelm them with our charm."

Better than sitting there empty handed, thought Nathaniel, and rose up to join his friend. It wasn't but a moment later that Robert began snapping his fingers to get Nathaniel's attention. A figure stood in the moonlit doorway.

"Can we help you?" said Robert.

It was a boy. "I'm lookin' for a Mister Nathaniel Luck."

He was carrying a note, or possibly a letter. Robert pointed to Nathaniel. "This is your man," he said.

The boy handed him what was a note. Nathaniel dropped some pocket change into the boy's hand. Nathaniel struck a match and held it close to the paper. He squinted over a tiny yawing tip of match flame. "She wants to meet," he said, "and you'll never guess where?"

"Inspire me," said Robert.

"At church."

CHAPTER 49

Nᴀᴛʜᴀɴɪᴇʟ ʀᴇɴᴛᴇᴅ ᴀ ʜᴏʀsᴇ and rode out Broadway to Troy Road. From there it was about another two miles or so. Both sides of Troy were lined with orchards, apple orchards for hard cider mostly, at least that is what a farmer explained to him as he rode past. The day kept shifting between brilliant warm sunshine and spikey grey storm weather.

He had not slept. He did not know what to make of himself. He was as contradictory as the weather. An actor searches for a character's motivation to know how to play him on stage. But Nathaniel could not understand this character that was himself. At times he felt he was riding into the teeth of a terrible judgment. And the last time he'd felt that, he'd killed a man. He should turn back and let her desire to meet die a natural death. But he could not. He was compelled by irrational needs, as if she had some power over him that he could only exorcise by meting out a measure of his rage. But he detested himself for these feelings, because they made him seem weak to himself just like he detested the fact that he'd shaved that morning in anticipation of seeing her. That he'd wanted to look his best seemed to him a slap in the face of his own manhood.

He could hear singing from a choir long before he sighted the buildings. It wasn't a church so much as a meeting house where they were to come face to face. It was well off the road in an open plat between orchards. There was a barn and a mill and set about the place were saddled horses and wagons, enough for maybe one hundred people.

She had written she would be at service, and they could talk afterwards. He assumed the setting was to keep his darker impulses in check.

The sky had blackened considerably, and a wind had blown up as he entered the service. The long pews were filled with parishioners and to his surprise there were black people sitting among the whites there. The person administrating the service turned out to be a woman who sat in one of those three wheeled chairs for people who can't stand or walk.

She was a reedy thing with plain unorthodox features, and as Nathaniel scanned the other faces, she talked of a new world order where the races would share God's bounty together. And women like herself would not be forbidden to speak in churches or from offering their insights on the world. That the "new Christian" religions such as the Swedenborgian Church were at the front of the human revolution that saw equality in all things as the foundation for everlasting peace. But look as he tried, there was no Genevieve Wells.

There was a small loft that had been transformed into a gallery where the choir of about a dozen or so stood and sang. She was not there either. And with the grey sky upon the windows, he did not understand.

The people there were country poor and a study in frayed collars and patched shoes. There for some restful piece of the good that God has promised. And he thought…why have I been brought to this place if she is not here?

A woman began to sing. *Just as I am, though tossed about…With many a conflict, many a doubt…Fighting and fears within and without.*

He knew that voice, as only an actor knows the lines of a play years after it has been performed. And even though he'd only heard her voice that once, it still resided inside him with all its plaintive urgency.

He looked up, and there she was standing in the gallery with the hymn book in her hands, come forward a step from the others and graced in a pale blue smock. She must have been sitting in the back row, that's why he hadn't seen her. That was his guess anyway.

Just as I am and waiting not…to rid my soul of one dark blot…To thee whose blood can cleanse each spot.

There she was, in all her touching simplicity and clear throated direct-ness, her airish voice bearing sorrow only to rise like some pure instrument of God with transcendent ease and unwavering grace, the very thief and cheat whose actions led to his imprisonment and suffering.

So tell me, he thought, why am I so moved, so touched, so captured, so caught between breaths by this singular vision of a choir singer? Am I more a fool than the fool himself, because I am even considering forgive-ness? Is a seduction being performed on me with a surgeon's skill? There was a terrible arsenal of actions racing through his mind, so he just walked out. But he did not leave.

He stood outside the church and smoked and watched the sky change shades and it was not long before the parishioners began to file out. The chil-dren scattering wildly, the parents talking in small groups. When Genevieve stepped into the light, she was with the woman in the wheelchair.

Genevieve confronted an unpleasant stare, then said, "Nathaniel...I'd like you to meet Sister Evangeline."

The woman offered Nathaniel her hand to shake, and he took it hesitantly. "Genevieve brought me to see your play. I was quite taken. And I had a thought...As the world changes, I can envision a time when all the inmates in your play will be women and that ghostly character a man."

He put on the actor's smile, the stealth smile, and glanced at Genevieve. "That time may be closer than you think."

"If you don't mind," Genevieve said, "Nathaniel and I have to talk."

CHAPTER 50

SHE WALKED FROM THE MEETING HOUSE toward the orchards. He followed a half-dozen paces behind her, not a word spoken by either. He wished lightning would strike those soft blue eyes dead. They walked as the clouds broke apart and the air through the trees speckled with dust.

"I've no intention to chase you across creation."

"You're not chasing me…and I'm not running away, Nathaniel."

He did not want her calling him by his first name and told her so.

She walked him so far, he could no longer see the meeting house or the mill, and she stopped. The sky was turning gun metal grey as she turned. He looked about the countryside, nothing there save the trees and chirp of birds, a perfect place for lovers…or murderers.

"Why are we here?"

"I'm giving you a chance to exact your will upon me," she said.

This was not what he expected.

She took a step forward. "Go on," she said. "Take your due."

He did nothing. He just watched this. He did not even know what to call what he was witnessing.

"I could stand here and cry innocence. I could tell you honestly that I was the unwitting fool of my own family. Naïve, exploited, debased. In so many ways. And that I did not find out how it was until so much later. I could tell you how I have lived shame, humiliation, and disgust. That I walk or walked away from my life, my family, my past with a single suitcase…and penniless. I could make you believe what is true, and probably even what is not true. There is not much difference between them. A few words here and there. Remember what you told me on the *Isaac Newton* that night when I asked you…What does an actor do when he hates the words and thoughts that come out of his mouth."

He remembered.

"I've had a long time to think about everything we talked of that night. Memory has a will of its own. I never realized what a deadly weapon that was. I could lie my way into your good graces…I'm talented enough to do that. I saw your performance. On the boat, in that play. I can be that good.

161

I could make you forgive me."

She took another step closer.

"Show me how you hate what I did. Get it off your soul. Get it off the books, as they say. And I'll show you how much you affected my life."

He was staring at her, looking for the answer to his pain and fury. She had pressed into his boundaries, gotten so close they could touch.

"You're staring," she said, with the same gentle sincerity that she had said the very same words that night on the *Isaac Newton*, and without even realizing he cracked her across the face. His open hand sounded like a leather strap when it hit. From both of her nostrils blood spurted. Stunned, she grabbed at the air with her arms, but ended up down on her knees in the bending grass. She cupped the blood in her hand and looked up. "Is that all I get for ruining your life?"

• • •

When Robert finally found him, Nathaniel was abysmally drunk at a bar in the hotel's shadow. A mindless starer at the wall in palpable defeat, he confessed what happened to his bitter shame about beating the girl down. Frightened to no end at the violence inside him. "As a man, I'm a failure," said he, with the sweep of a hand knocking over his whiskey. The glass spinning like a top on the floor.

He was helped to his room draped to Robert's shoulder. He lay him on the bed and undid his boots. Nathaniel covered his eyes and cried in confusion. "It was she who did wrong, so why am I crying?"

"My answer to that is, be careful. Because she's coming back." Robert turned down the lamp till the room was pitch dark.

"How do you know that?"

"By waiting for her in the theatre…you opened the door."

• • •

It might not have been a faint knock at the door, but something woke him. The moon was motionless there in the sky, but it wasn't the moon and it wasn't the sky, but a hallway lantern there for a moment as the door opened then closed.

Had he said 'Come in'?

He raised himself up in the bed, or tried to. "Robert, is that you?"

"It's not Robert."

His splayed fingers reached around the bedside table for a match. He found one and struck it. A ripple of light across the hotel room and there she was in the shadows in the same blue smock with a cape over her shoulders and a suitcase in hand.

"Why in God's name are you here?"

The match had burned down, and he shook it. A column of smoke rose in the dark. He was feeling for another, when she told him, "Don't put up a light."

He could hear her crossing the room.

"I wanted to know if you were all right, or nearly all right. If you've had your fill of retribution."

The bed creaked in the dark as he sat up, or tried to. "That's not why you're here and both of us know it."

"It's why I should be here. May I sit?"

"Are you a cool one," he said.

He wanted to roll a cigarette, but he'd downed so much liquor his hands were unsteady. "For today...I am sorry."

"Don't worry, because I'm not."

There was a bottle on the table with a few last dregs which he downed to clear out his dried throat. "I'm a troubled man. A flawed man. I think I'm also a desperate man. Who almost did something terrible today."

"What stopped you?"

"Having done terrible things in the past."

She took a moment and slipped back the curtain and looked out the window. "You saved my life, you should know that."

"What...by going to prison?"

"Everything I said in the letter was true. Except for the facts. Facts never do."

"What do you want?"

"We're very much alike. You must see that. Everything is temporary with us. Intense, of the moment. We burn with passion. Like you on stage. You're another person. It's as if there's a hole to fill in your soul and that's what those moments on stage are meant for. When I sing in the choir, it's like that. You found your calling. I want that in my own way."

"Don't you get that from being a thief?"

She made a funny little laugh. How cynically he'd said that actually appeared to charm her.

"If I were a thief…yes," she said. "But I want to better myself. I want to be on stage. Simply put…I want to be you. And I mean to. And then I'll pay you back for that night on the boat."

He wanted a drink but there wasn't one there to be had. At least his hands had steadied enough to roll himself a smoke. He took his time about it too, staring, as he was down into the deep side of an emotional canyon. "I don't know who's more mad," he said.

He struck up a match and pointed the flame at her, and then himself. "You for believing what you suggest…or me for being even a bit susceptible to what you're suggesting." He lit the cigarette.

There she was, sitting in the chair by the curtained window. A veiled image, like a painting in ancient shadow. She had taken off the cape, her hands were folded, the suitcase at her side, still wearing the blue smock that had her bloodstains on it.

"We have been with each other since that night on the *Isaac Newton*," she said. "You know it, I know it. And you live with me every night on stage. I am that woman. I will always be that woman."

He blew out the match.

"What is it you want?" he said.

"I want the same things you want. I want to be on stage. I want greatness…success. And all that comes with it."

He had never heard such blunt hearted directness come out of a woman's mouth. And he told her so.

"That's because men see the world as only for themselves," she said, "and leaving nothing for women."

He smoked and wrestled with the moment.

"Why the suitcase?" he said.

"I could tell you I've nowhere to sleep. Or I have no money for a room. I could say I'm lonely. I will say I need to leave it somewhere safe for a few days while I do a favor for Sister Evangeline."

• • •

Nathaniel was always late and had to be driven from between the sheets, whether drinking or not. This had become such a sorry routine for Robert, who had a watchman's personality, so he didn't bother to knock. He just martinetted his way into the room, kicked the bedpost, and pulled back the curtains to throw a wall of sunlight across the bed, then he'd stride right out without so much as a word. Only this morning when he turned from the window there was no Nathaniel in bed to curse him out, but a woman. She lay there alone, staring at him and composed as a silver dollar.

When he got that moment of shock in check, he said, "Jesus Christ."

"No," she answered. "Not Jesus Christ…Genevieve Wells."

CHAPTER 51

"I THINK YOU'RE MAD. You know that. And it scares me."

Robert had taken over the upstairs parlor of a brothel. Robert was play-ing the piano, and he was a deplorable musician. He sat stark naked at the keys but for a shiny black top hat and was tanked on Doctor McMumm's Elixir.

"Can you hear me down there?" said Robert.

Nathaniel was lying on the floor on his back, naked himself. A pros-titute was asleep, or unconscious, her head resting on his stomach and her legs pulled up like a baby.

"Hey…do I need to write you a letter?"

"Maybe," said Nathaniel, "we need a touch of madness to do what we do. Maybe what's bad for you is the fuel to get you to what's good. When I think of all the destructive things I've done, without them I might have ended up a drummer of kitchenware or a clerk in some gloomy office counting the hours. Maybe we need what's destructive to keep us a step ahead of our doom. Maybe it's our scars that people will know us by."

Robert started this dirgy melody straight out of bad melodrama as background for what Nathaniel was saying. Rotten playing, but funny. Then Robert got up and urinated out the window.

"And so ends the scene," said Nathaniel.

• • •

Night after night people came to the warehouse as much to curse the guards, throw bottles, and shout obscenities as to see the play. They had become a sort of local treat. Along the way, letters of interest soliciting the theatre company began to arrive from small theatres as far west as Buffalo. They weren't exactly on the heels of fame, but they weren't broke either.

Genevieve still had not returned for her suitcase. It remained just where she'd left it by the window. Damn reality set in, he began to worry for her safety. He decided to open the suitcase as if an answer might be packed away there.

It didn't tell much of a story: A few unassuming pieces of clothing, plain undergarments. A pair of beat up walking shoes and heavy wool socks. Not exactly the legacy of a successful thief. When Nathaniel got to the last of it, he found a sealed letter. He turned it over to see what was written there:

LAST WILL AND TESTAMENT
Genevieve Wells
A notarized copy is with
William Fuller, Attorney — Cleveland, Ohio

The next day he rented a horse and rode out to the meeting house on Troy Road only to discover its walls were charred and the roof caved in. There were a handful of men about the ruin with rifles that converged on Nathaniel as he came down that rutted causeway. He was ordered at gunpoint to put up his hands and he obliged immediately.

He was pulled from his horse and roughed up some as he was explaining. "I'm here looking for Sister Evangeline. I'm trying to find out about a woman named Genevieve Wells." It wasn't until a woman shouted from the mill that the men quit their harassment. It was Sister Evangeline herself. She was in her three wheel chair there in the doorway.

"I know this man," she said. "Let him come."

She had taken up residence in the mill. She had a desk and a cot. Her possessions were on shelving made of brick and plankboard. The mill was for the production of hard cider, and Nathaniel was offered a drink.

While a man with a rifle stood guard in the doorway, Evangeline explained that the meeting house was a stop on the Underground Railroad helping runaways escape to Canada. And that the burning had been an act of revenge by slave catchers for the loss of a bounty on a couple of blacks they'd been hunting.

As for Genevieve, she was thirty miles away in Schenectady where she was to wait for a family of runaways, then deliver them to a secret rendezvous point on the Hudson River. There they would then be escorted north to Canada.

The man at the door with the rifle broke in on the conversation. "You should never have sent that one."

"I send who I have faith in."

Evangeline asked the man to leave her and Nathaniel. He slammed the mill door closed behind him. Once alone, Evangeline said, "She should have been back by now. And I can't send someone there. There's slave catchers about, and I don't want them to learn of our other stations on the route."

When she'd finished, Evangeline pointed to a mug on her desk and asked Nathaniel to fill it with hard cider. This was no gentile lady. She was an armed militant. About thirty years old, who had been crippled when shot as a teenager. Her parents had been first generation abolitionists who'd lost their lives in a violent clash with slavers just outside Cairo, Illinois. She'd watched as the men dragged her mother into the Mississippi and drowned her. Looking as if Evangeline were to die herself, the slavers didn't bother with her. Her spare white body lay in the river sun for most of a day. Her prayers were answered when a hunter's dog came upon her at dusk.

She drank the mug empty and set it down. "Genevieve told me all about herself," said Evangeline. "And all about you."

He should have been surprised, but he wasn't. He'd seen already that Genevieve Wells had a trait, like certain actors, of being and doing the unexpected.

"Someone needs to go to Schenectady," said Evangeline.

He was being studied by this woman and he knew it. The expressive power of a simple stare never ceased to amaze him.

"I'm not the kind of woman who is in the grips of character and motive when I make decisions. I deal in courage, friend. If you get my meaning."

CHAPTER 52

NATHANIEL BOARDED THE DEWITT CLINTON TRAIN FROM ALBANY. The three cars were nothing more than rickety stagecoaches hooked together and riding on iron wheels. They travelled through wild country the likes of which Nathaniel had never seen before. The gent beside him explained that this was a desolate and dangerous place known as the Pine Barrens. He pointed out how the higher ground was all sand dunes spotted with spiny looking pine trees in desperate need of green. The lower traces were wetlands, densely thicketed and deeply grottoed, and tricked out with swamps and quicksand. A living cemetery of the foolish and the daring.

Robert had been against Nathaniel going but said nothing about it because he knew, even at his young age, you cannot stop the inevitable. As for the actors in the cast, they couldn't see him off soon enough as it meant some of them would get a chance to play his part, or the part of the actor who was to play his part. That is what is so wonderful about actors—— they are always ready and willing to climb over your grave for a good cause.

• • •

Schenectady was on the Mohawk River. The Erie Canal had turned it into a manufacturing town where mills and factories processed raw products sent up from the South. The locks of the canal followed the river then turned west to the Great Lakes which was why Schenectady was being called "The Gateway to the West." Patches of sky were already greasy with smoke, like the manufacturing hubs he remembered from England.

His destination was Union College. He bought a ride with a wagoneer who was heading out to the lumber mills east of town. Union College was a hot bed for abolitionists and home of the Anti-Slavery Movement. The wagoneer asked Nathaniel his trade, and he admitted to being an actor. With a dismissive stare, the wagoneer said, "Prove it."

So there Nathaniel was, swallowing dust from the ass end of four mules and reeling off scenes from Marlowe and *Paradise Lost*. The wagoneer was not duly impressed and asked, "Is it true that actors talk so much they chew down their jawbones?"

Nathaniel said it was a tragedy that did not affect enough actors. The wagoneer nodded solemnly.

When they were within sight of the college, the wagoneer told him how the school had been carved out of swamp and sand hills, and was the first in America of its kind——built from the ground up at one time, from one grand design.

"Sort of like creation," said the wagoneer.

Nathaniel had stepped into the road and had not really heard the man and asked what he'd said.

"The college," he said, "sort of like creation itself... built from the ground up...by one grand design...God's own creation...it's all God's work, ain't it?"

• • •

She was sitting alone on a bench in an arcade that ran in a half moon around the north end of the campus. She was in a plain working dress of brown check, wearing her glasses, a straw hat on the bench beside her. He watched for a long time how she maintained a quiet and faceless presence, as someone in a church pew. And even as he approached her, and she saw him, her reaction barely changed.

"You cannot stop here," she said. "Keep walking."

She waited there until the light died away and the campus fell under the spell of long shadows and the stream of students moving in and out of the lecture halls trickled down to a handful of silhouettes. He kept her under watch all the while from the window of an empty lecture hall when a boy, he could not have been more than ten, came past sprinting across the campus.

What caught Nathaniel's eyes, the boy looked back over his shoulder more than once, and then he veered suddenly toward the arcade. Nathaniel lost sight of the youth against the dark brick of the lecture halls then caught sight of him again as he sprinted up into the arcade and then down the arched passageway.

He went right by Genevieve who had stood suddenly. If something was said or passed between them, he would never have known from her manner. She was coolly distant but immediately came down the arcade steps and started away.

She walked out Union Street where the wagoneer had dropped off Nathaniel. She crossed the timber bridge over the canal, her walk measured, unconcerned, never looking back. Nathaniel sprinted across campus after her to the Union Street bridge to find that she was gone. He stood in the quiet, turning like a slow weathervane, when she came sweeping up alongside him. "Come with me," she said. "And hurry."

She led him down Maiden Lane keeping back from the road, and when she thought it safe, she stopped and looked back struggling to catch her breath.

"Evangeline?" she said.

"She hadn't heard from you in days and———"

"They hadn't shown up until a little while ago," She held up a scrap of paper. "You were watching."

"How else?"

"She didn't come to you," she said, "did she?"

"No. I'd opened your luggage———"

"You went to———"

"I did."

"I knew it on the boat…I knew it for the year I was thinking about writing you the letter…By the time I wrote the letter, I knew it was too late."

CHAPTER 53

AT THE FAR END OF MAIDEN LANE stood a crooked house on a sandy incline just above Grootes Creek. A sorry clapboard you could hardly see back in the trees with a porch that was all but collapsed. The house was dark, but someone must have been watching because as soon as Genevieve was at the front door it cricked open.

An old man greeted them from the pitch dark hallway with a shotgun. He kept the barrel on Nathaniel."

"It's all right," said Genevieve. "He's from Evangeline."

• • •

They lit neither lantern nor candle, and just waited.

Genevieve whispered, "They'll signal us with a light when they're here. And we'll signal back it's safe to come on."

The old man took up a post at the rear of the house. Genevieve stayed up front, peeking out from a burlap curtain.

"I gather they'll shoot you down if they must," said Nathaniel.

"I know what you think," she said.

"Do you now?"

"Don't even say it...the word. I know. And I don't want to hear it. I am not here to amend my life. Understand. Or to be saved from my sins and errors. Some of the most valiant people I know are scoundrels and thieves. Some are even murderers. Am I wrong?"

"I know some people who are blacker than this room...that I would trust with my life."

"Be careful, Nathaniel. You don't want your sins showing."

"There's more truth to that than you realize."

She kept watching the road. But it was dark and quiet, and not a sign of anything stepping forth.

"Nathaniel."

"Yes."

"The next time you look for an actress for your play...I would like the

172

chance to prove myself."

"Just like that."

"My father used to say… 'Would you rather be the lowest branch on the grandest tree, or the highest branch on a sapling? He, of course, personally is scum."

· · ·

She was always on the game, no matter how the world was burning down around her. A living, breathing plot, if ever there was one. Her eyes wide open, filling in the blanks to get what she wanted. She was a revolution on the natural order of things. Those two, they were a creation together, as they both swam in the deep waters of life. And don't think it didn't give me many a sleepless night asking that same question about myself.

As for her daddy, he was scum of the first order. He would prove that when his cunning racist self came crawling up out of those human tarpits we're preached about. There weren't enough hymnals in the world to get that man righted, that would be the business of a pistolshot.

· · ·

"They're here."

The old man's voice carried through the quiet house. He was gathering up a lantern when they joined him in the kitchen. He pointed to the window. Back in the loomwork of the trees a small bore of light mechanically going up, then down.

He answered with a lantern, passing it across the window. The reflection of Nathaniel and the girl flanking his shoulders, watching. The light in the woods went out and it wasn't long before figures were coming on single file, up through the matted undergrowth with the boy Nathaniel had seen earlier leading them.

They entered the darkened kitchen. The boy first, followed by a black man and another black man carrying a small child and then a black woman with a boy in tow. In the crowded kitchen, the old man pointed to a doorway. "In there," he said. "Food and drink. But you have to be quick, as tired as you might be. We have to get you to the river by dawn."

They were an exhausted and malnourished lot saying, "Thank you" and "God bless you," and this was as close as Nathaniel had ever gotten to the plights of these people.

Genevieve filled plates in the dark and passed them to Nathaniel to hand them out to the runaways crowded in around the table. The boy was leaving, and he said, "Good luck to you all." He no sooner stepped onto the porch when the crack from a big bore rifle cut through the evening stillness and blew him back into the house.

He lay on the floor convulsing with a gaping black hole in his chest and Nathaniel and the old man dragged him back inside and got the door shut as a volley of shots blew out windows and shanks of woodwork.

Nathaniel knelt over the boy who was choking on fleshy bits of lung that had vomited up into his throat. His pupils in a sea of white, petrified. The only way he could plead for help was beating his feet wildly on the floor as if trying to escape his horrid end. *I have seen this before*, thought Nathaniel, *I have seen it and lived.*

A voice from the trees demanded, "Send those niggers out here, or we'll burn the house down."

The old man stormed over to the entry and wielded up a smoothbore that had been leaning against the wall. He shoved the barrel out through the broken glass and fired. "Answer enough," he shouted.

There was more gunfire. Bits of wall and door were ripped apart. The runaways huddled together at the edge of the kitchen. The old man looked to Genevieve. "Take them outta here like I showed you. Can you do that?"

"I can do that," she said.

"Bundle up that child's head in sackcloth," said the old man, "so they can't hear her outside if she's cryin'."

Genevieve told the runaways to come along and be quick. There was a door to the root cellar. She ushered them forward one at a time, telling them to be careful going down the stairs.

The old man asked Nathaniel if he knew how to use a gun.

"Some," said Nathaniel.

"Gotta get educated fast." The old man searched a bureau drawer blind as he kept his sights on the window for movement outside. Came up with a Colt. Slapped it into Nathaniel's hand. "Got no trigger till you pull the hammer back."

"You in there. We got Greek fire out here. Now send those niggers out or we'll cook the lot of you."

Before she started down to the root cellar, Genevieve looked back over her shoulder. Her arms folded across her chest. She could not make him out in that pitch dark room any better than he could her. The old man stormed over and shoved her down the stairs. "Get out."

She was gone before Nathaniel could see she was gone. Her shadow now the shadow that was there before her.

Bottles were being thrown at the house. They could hear them shattering against the walls. One crashed through a porch window. They could see it on the floor in a small patch of moonlight. There was clear liquid spilling out of it.

"There's naphtha and kerosene in those bottles," the man outside shouted.

Nathaniel looked toward the root cellar door. "How they gonna get out?"

"Same as us…after we bloody up those boys out there a little."

CHAPTER 54

By the following morning the building was a skeleton of charred ruins. The ground around it scorched, the trees boned black hands rising up through dried and crusty sand.

Neighbors walked the property. A body was discovered in a shallow ravine near the house. How he died, there was no way to know, his clothes and flesh had melted together. The fire had spread down to Grootes Creek. There was discovered the entry to a tunnel just up from the riverbank. Carrying lanterns, a search party made their way through a hundred feet of carved out earth. It led them to the root cellar. A wreckage now of collapsed timbers. Not one of the old man's friends had ever known about the tunnel.

● ● ●

Robert had taken rooms on the upper floor of a whorehouse down by the Canal Basin and just off Montgomery Street. It was on a row of shoddy rooming houses and apartments with empty lots where the unemployed and their families had set up camp among the weeds and the refuse. He claimed it had the right creative atmosphere for his writing, but it was where a disfigured man could most easily hide the loneliness that haunted him.

He awoke in the middle of the afternoon to a faint stream of mottled light seeping through the shutters. And there in half shadows, sitting in a scored up leather club chair that Robert had bought with the spoils of their success, was Nathaniel.

He had his shirt off and was slouched there, drinking from a bottle of Doctor McMumm's elixir. In the slatted light, Robert could see one arm had a nasty wound. Robert got up and wrapped the bedsheet around himself and shuffled over to his friend. He leaned down and looked at the arm. Long and deep slash marks there.

"You need a doctor, brother."

Nathaniel put his head back and took a throat full of painkiller.

"I saw a boy shot dead yesterday night," Nathaniel said. "He couldn't have been but ten, maybe twelve. Assassinated right before my eyes. With cold intent. He was helping runaways." Nathaniel tried to move, but he was too damn exhausted.

"What about her?" said Robert.

Nathaniel put his head back and drained the bottle. "This country is on fire. And I had no idea how on fire."

He closed his eyes and put his head back and swallowed hard. "I need to rest a while and then see a doctor."

"That girl…What happened to her?"

Nathaniel's voice was falling into a drugged sleep. "No idea. We were in a house that slave catchers set on fire."

• • •

The play was near the end of its run. For a number of scenes, Nathaniel went on stage bare chested and without bandages. He meant to exploit the wounds——authenticity for authenticity's sake. Keeping ever closer to the burning footlights so the sutured, violent slashes had a theatrical luminescence.

Robert could see better now that Nathaniel savored these moments. That the play, in some way, was a manifestation of Nathaniel's personal scars. Realized, externalized, turned to art. He began to wonder, do men like this search out conflicts, danger, risk, even self destruction to feed creative hunger? A hunger that in and of itself is unexplainable, unfathomable.

Had Nathaniel Luck become a manifestation of my own personal scars? This was the question that Robert now confronted in himself.

On the night of the last performance Sister Evangeline appeared at the theatre with men armed to protect her, as there were threats against her life for her underground activities. She and Nathaniel conferred in the alley alone. She held his hand in both of hers. She had not come just to thank him for the risks he'd taken in Schenectady, but to give him a letter.

"She's in Canada," said Evangeline.

She kissed him and was then lifted from her three wheel chair onto a rattletrap wagon and tramped off into the business of her life.

In the light of the stage door, he tore open the wax seal. The letter was brief, to the point of being spartan.

Dearest Nathaniel,

Envy is the least of my feelings when it comes to you. I do not know when I will be back. But I hope the time will prove worth it.

Yours,
Genevieve W

ACT IV

CHAPTER 55

THE PLAY WAS SHUT DOWN FOR THE WINTER. The actors and stage hands, wardrobe and props, had one last night together in that drafty old warehouse. They reveled and reminisced, relived their finest moments, their botched readings, the night the treadmill didn't work and the audience cursed them out, or when the curtain collapsed on the performers and they had to wade through a sea of cloth to carry on. They went from one drunken memory to another, holding on as best they could to what was already gone. They were grasping for the beauty that had already escaped their being. The joy, the passion, the connection with the audience, already gone. Like the wisps of smoke from a stage lamp, the clang of glasses in toast, a bit of laughter, a tear simply brushed away...gone. Those nights on stage belonged to time now. They belong to a world of shadow memories with faces and names you can't remember, but who forever have your heart. It is so cruelly beautiful, that for a brief time you are one in perfection, and then it is no more. And you are left holding out an open hand to the darkness.

After all the goodbyes, actor and writer sat alone at a table on the stage. The candles half melted down and smoky as in a church setting. Used up bottles of liquor and plates of food scrap all that remained. Nathaniel was a portrait of brooding silence as he smoked.

Robert got up and moved about. Lifting bottles, shaking them, looking for dregs to pour into his glass. "I'm going home, Nathaniel. To Lafayette Place. For the holidays."

Nathaniel's mind was elsewhere. He nodded blankly.

"Thanksgiving...Christmas...New Year's. My mother knows how to put on a holiday. Why don't you come along? It would make her happy to see you, I'm certain."

Nathaniel's eyebrows tensed as he looked out into the warehouse of empty seats. A deathly stillness and the shadow of that treadmill over it all.

"I think I'll travel," he said. "See some of this country of ours. I'll catch up with you in the spring."

"After hunting through all those bottles," Robert said, "you won't find her."

"I'm lost, Robert."

"Did you hear me?"

"That's not why I'm lost."

• • •

He wanted to see more of America and its entertainments. To feel, then understand, the nature and sweep of its peopled tapestry and so become a more true actor in its drama. It was also a way of keeping the desolation at bay.

He followed the train stations and the stagecoach lines west. He took in the small town circuses and dog acts and musicals in dreary smoke wracked halls. It didn't matter if it was a naughty second hand burlesque or child ballerina in their fireside costumes. He went to tent shows and revivals with their powerful sense of music and hard tone sermons. Street orators, road house entertainers, itinerant balladeers who sang in local libraries——they were all American art to be absorbed.

In Buffalo, he watched the Seneca Indian National Band play on the steps of city hall. Not exactly the murderous aboriginal "red" man that Nathaniel had read about as a boy in England. But proud, even a bit haughty in their stiff but decorous outfits. At the Eagle Theatre, he took in a well mounted performance of *Othello* one night, and the next the house put on a degrading blackface parody——*Othello... The Noblest Nigger of Dem All.*

There was a righteous free for all feeling in the rurals. Everywhere wagons and itinerant foreigners headed out to places that didn't have names yet. Carting along their dreams with threadbare defiance. Crude and dispossessed as they might be, but driven. With stumbling English, but all bustle and go.

There was a sense of wonder to all of this that did not exist in England. England was too tied to its ruins and mythic knights, its fashionable landmarks and the castles of kings. England was the staid old gent lecturing you on manners and morals and Shakespeare, while America was the hot tempered youth who said the hell with all that. But there was one thing that was the exact same——actors.

It was bitter cold in Cleveland as Nathaniel made his way up along Superior Avenue. His head hatcheted down against the ungodly wind coming off the lake from the frozen reaches of Canada. Only a madman would be out in this kind of weather. A madman…or an actor.

He was tracking through the snow to Watson Hall. It was the only theatre in that faceless construct that dared call itself a city. They were having auditions for a new theatre troupe, and he just wanted to be there.

Not to read, himself. But to be among actors. To be where they live and breathe. To feel their anxiety and anticipation, to watch them nervously prepare a scene, then endure the silent wait for their moment. To see how they reacted to the subtle promptings of the theatre manager, then how they responded to having their psyches dragged around stage before an audience of their peers.

He needed to be part of all that, because without it, he was nothing. He was just an empty vessel without a voice. His success in Albany made it all the more apparent.

This, he came to see, was one of the trappings of success. It afforded you the quiet time alone you no longer had to spend struggling and suffering to attain success. You can lie to a stagelit face, but not the face behind it. And there he was trying to steel himself against the swirling frost when he had this sudden image of a tombstone. His own. In some as yet unnamed cemetery, and at some unmarked date. And what it read:

NATHANIEL LUCK
His life was the lines of a play —

CHAPTER 56

THE THEATRE WAS ON THE SECOND FLOOR, and was he surprised when he entered the building to find the lobby and stairwell up to the theatre mobbed with children. The youngest looked to be about ten, the oldest fifteen or so. They were in some noisy packs, and they had sheaves of paper, and damn, he could hear they were rehearsing scenes from plays.

He grabbed hold of a sprightly kid shuttling past him. "What goes on here?"

The boy looked him over. "The winter pageant, of course. The schools and dramatic societies, even the foundlings. We get to perform scenes upstairs, and the chosen ones will be part of pageant night."

"And what play are you and your mates rehearsing?"

The boy held up his pages. "*Harlequin and Mother Goose.*"

"That's a challenge."

The boy gave him a pantomime thank you... and good-bye. And it had more than a touch of good riddance implied in it.

It took some maneuvering to get upstairs through that loud and scrappy mob. All that buoyant urgency, that's the domain of children who still have their liberated souls. At the entry doors to Watson Hall, he stopped and looked back. He'd known a boy like those down there. Could still see and remember him from those far off corners of by gone days with all their hardships and unhappiness. He wouldn't part with it, none of it, the suffering especially, for a lifetime of sunshine and summer rain. After all, the actor was the progeny of that boy.

• • •

Inside the theatre, it was an altogether different story. There was a deep, nervous hush akin to funeral homes. One group of actors performed on stage under the taxing demands of the theatre manager. Those listed to perform next were hovering about the wings like hunted birds. The rest of the actors were scattered about the theatre alone with their ambitions and anxious stomachs.

Every time you enter a theatre there is something new to learn——this is what the Colonel had taught him. Nathaniel took up a quiet back corner, his legs up over the back of the seat before him and rolled a cigarette. He watched the actors come and go for hours——dancing, burlesque, pantomime, drama, comedy upon comedy——and what did he learn?

Nothing…that's what he learned, and it was a valuable lesson. Everything he was witnessing he had witnessed before. It was quite unsettling. All those actors. The way they dressed, the way they comported themselves, the way they performed, the material they chose to perform. It was as if Nathaniel had walked through the doors of Watson Hall to find himself in London a decade ago. The actors dressed like middle class merchants, or decorous personages of worth. They were gentlemanly and womanly and appropriately mannered and tailored and subdued. They were living copies of earlier copies, riding clichés into the sunset. Same everything, just different faces.

This was America, for christ's sake. Nathaniel had been here only a handful of years, but it was enough to birth a thought. America had its own music. He'd heard it in the churches and revivals, on the streets, around the bars and taverns and music halls. America had its own writers: Hawthorne, Irving, Fenimore Cooper.

Where were the plays that looked and felt and talked and smelled American?

And what about the actors? Where were the actors that looked and felt and talked and smelled American? They were still suffering from that English volume and pitch, intonation, kingly diction, formal enunciation, heads and eyes aimed at the heavens, voices booming like baby cannon, alone on the stage even in a crowd.

His legs came down from the seat and he leaned forward, intent…This was why *The Treadmill* was a success. It was American. It did not feel like a play, but rather, an eavesdropping on a violent aspect of life.

• • •

As the exhausted and browbeat actors were filing out after the auditions, the theatre manager intercepted Nathaniel and took him aside. "I noticed you when you came in. Albany, right? *The Treadmill.* I saw the play."

"Did you?"

"Yes. And I thought it…" He was very tight faced, and he moved his head from side to side. "Different," he said.

"Different." That review was usually reserved for those who didn't want to tell you how little they liked it, or how much they hated it. At least that was Nathaniel's experience. He smiled politely at the theatre manager and privately hoped he was thrown down a flight of stairs.

Once the theatre doors opened, the children came swarming in. Anyone or anything in their path…trampled. They charged up the aisles, leapt over seats like they were stepping stones. You'd have thought a riot was in progress.

The theatre manager asked Nathaniel, "Every year I try to have a working actor make a few introductory remarks to the children. Give them a sense of hope and promise. What do you say? Just a few minutes. They'll be a rapt audience."

While Nathaniel looked over that collection of laughing, shouting, nose blowing, cross talking, fighting, misbehaving, incorrigible cast of future performers, the theatre manager noticed a black youth standing by the door.

"You're not with any of the groups here," he said.

"No, sir," said the boy.

"Go on now."

The boy pointed at Nathaniel.

"Get out!"

The youth obeyed silently.

It took Nathaniel a moment to realize——there was not one black child in the audience.

He said to the manager. "Don't they have——?"

"No. Not even the foundlings will send one of them here. No point."

While the theatre manager quieted the children down and started the introductions, Nathaniel was staring at the theatre doors. One was slightly ajar, and he knew——

Nathaniel was standing at the entry when his name was called out, and there was this wave of enthusiastic applause and whistling as he shoved the doors open. The youth jerked back from where he'd been peeking, and Nathaniel grabbed him by the collar. The theatre got quiet mighty quick as Nathaniel led the young black along, holding him by the collar of his coat like he was a sack of laundry.

"Let's talk acting," said Nathaniel. "Here's a question. How many of you young ladies and gentlemen would perform on stage with this rascal here?"

Well, if that didn't dim the lights, so to speak, and there was no confusing the put upon stare the theatre manager was wearing. Out of a few hundred, maybe five, six, seven hands went up. And they rose as if admitting to a transgression.

"And now," said Nathaniel, "all of you who would *not* perform on stage with this rascal here, raise your hands."

A wave of hands rose and held there.

"All of you with hands raised. I want any one or more of you to get up and give me a reason why you *should* perform on stage with this rascal here."

The poor black stood there in the grip of what he knew not.

The hands slowly went down, but no one among their number stood. A nervous hush came over the children. They began to look among themselves for an answer. There was slight tittering.

"First lesson in acting," said Nathaniel. "Being an actor is being able to portray a character you have nothing in common with, who you do not agree with, and possibly don't like, and maybe even hate. And, from where I stand, I don't see an actor among you."

The lesson over, the youth followed Nathaniel downstairs. "Why did you do that?"

"I'm an actor. That's why."

"Oh," he answered, as if that explained it.

"What's your name?"

"Jeremiah Fields."

"What you doin' 'round here? Don't tell me you want to go on stage. I couldn't bear it."

"I'm here to give you a message."

"What are you talking about? Message? From whom?"

"My cousin."

"Your cousin? Who's your cousin? Who are you for that matter?"

"My cousin is Genevieve Wells."

• • •

And so, I met Nathaniel Luck and through a trail of accident and tragedy and choice, I ended up being the one relating some of this to you.

I had seen Nathaniel once before. I was at the theatre that night in Albany when my cousin Genevieve went to see the play. I was outside at the shipping doors by the actors' dressing rooms, which were nothing more than squares of sheeting hung from wires. Most of the stage hands were black, so they let me come in and watch with them.

You get to see a play from the other side of the world back there, where it's all a confusion of props and flats, pacing actors, agitated costumers——the faceless people the world of the theatre is built on. How many of them were black? I hadn't ever known. They all were pressed into the dark around the edges of the stage, lit as it was like some place steeped in mystery.

Strange...backstage was more like the real world, and yet more unreal than that unreal world on stage.

I didn't know then that I was home. That mysterious darkness rimmed by light where a nether life was playing out possessed me. How or why, I don't know. I had never given it a thought, but some invisible force executed its will over me. This world, this place, I wanted to be part of *that*...whatever *that* was. Nathaniel told me once...Life is the art of trying to find your way, even after you find your way.

CHAPTER 57

THEY WALKED OUT OF THE THEATRE TOGETHER and into a raking wind off the lake. The snow had turned to ice.

"Where is she?" said Nathaniel.

"Not here yet. But she will be. Tomorrow, the latest."

"You eaten? You have a place to stay?"

"No, sir...and no, sir."

"Well, come on."

They trudged along shoulders bowed against the wind. The powdered snow packed and cracking under their boots.

"That's a pretty raggedy coat you're wearing, son, for this kind of weather."

"Raggedy...yes, sir. It was raggedy even before I got it. You might say it's second generation raggedy."

Nathaniel gave an arched look. "That sounds like a sense of humor. You got a sense of humor, son?"

Jeremiah dipped his head. "Which answer makes sure I get my lunch?"

Nathaniel smiled into a bitter cold. "She's your cousin?"

"Yes, sir. Our mamas are sisters. Both black. Jennie's daddy, white as an angel except for his soul. That's how she can pass."

Nathaniel's mind churned. Every fractious conflict, every traumatic and consequential state of being in the country at that time just dropped into his lap.

He walked along now with the youth shadowing him.

"Every day brings a new role," said Nathaniel.

"Mister Luck?"

"How old are you?"

"Eighteen...almost."

"Read and write?"

"Hobart Christian School for Coloreds. Had a scholarship for the seminary. But that's not me!"

"There's a term...a phrase...*la piece bien faite.*"

"I have no idea what that means, sir."

189

"You will. Because we're living it right now."

The youth followed Nathaniel down Central Avenue, past shop windows highlighted with frost and done up in holiday splendor. Everything that a teenager in a raggedy coat could imagine except respect.

Nathaniel turned into the entry of the Danville Hotel. Jeremiah knew what Nathaniel obviously did not——a black entering this hotel was getting an armed stare and then shot in the ass. Now, Cleveland was a liberal town with strong abolitionist leanings. Schools there were integrated, blacks and whites lived among each other in the Haymarket district. But there were quarters in the city where it didn't take a flash of lightning to educate you on reality. Jeremiah followed Nathaniel, whispering, trying to get his ear, but too late——

The lobby was small and quiet with a marble floor and check-in desk with brass motifs. A few men sat by a huge fireplace reading their newspapers or playing cards who suddenly became aware of this ratty looking black in their midst.

The day clerk also noticed and rose up from his seat. He was tall with a schoolish manner and pale eyes, and as Nathaniel said, "I'd like to get a room for this young gent——"

The clerk cut him off with, "Not on your life."

It took a few seconds to register what he'd done. Nathaniel became angry for compromising himself, but even more so for opening the youth to humiliation.

He told Jeremiah, "Wait here a minute. I'm going up to my room."

"He can wait outside," said the clerk.

The men by the fire, with their newspapers set down, and that poker game on sudden hold, were a backdrop of pure umbrage.

"I'll wait outside, Mister Luck."

Jeremiah went out front. He walked over to the hotel window and wiped the frost from the glass with his frayed coat sleeve. He cupped his hands around his eyes and peered in.

When Nathaniel came back down to the lobby he was carrying two small suitcases. He went to the desk and paid his bill. As he started to leave, he turned back and said something to the clerk that put the man into a state of enraged panic. Next thing, the clerk was sprinting up the stairs, taking the steps in bunches.

When Nathaniel walked out into that freezing noon, he was smiling maliciously. "Well," he said, "know a hotel around here?"

"What did you say to make that man jackrabbit like that?"

"I told him I set my room on fire."

Jeremiah led the way down to Haymarket. Along the Cayuga, farmers brought their goods to sell, including hay. Nathaniel had enough of watching the kid shivering and pulled him into a riverfront clothier and outfitted him with a pea coat and scarf and seaman's cap. Jeremiah was a lanky youth, the image of someone taken advantage of, with sensitive eyes and refined features. He stepped out into the cold all bundled up, hands fisted in his pockets, "How do I look?"

"Formidable," said Nathaniel.

• • •

The Wylie Hotel was two stories of brick, and there was a brick building behind it that had been a horse barn turned into a workman's eatery and a bar. There was a walkway through the snow between buildings covered by galvanized sheeting where ice hung in long tears.

They sat and ate after Nathaniel got rooms for himself and the youth. It was a drab, windless place, but thank God for the three wood burning stoves spread about the place with their grimy stacks piped up through the roof that was black with tar. There was a heavy smell of men and stale beer, and Nathaniel wondered aloud how many fights had this bar recorded in its time? An evergreen tipped the pitched ceiling and was decorated for the holidays with whimsies, and beside it a piano player was tinkling out Christmas tunes. On top of the upright, a bowl for donations and a sign that read: **I PLAY EVEN BETTER WHEN I'M DRUNK.**

Over in the corner, tables had been moved and a homespun manger set up with straw on the floor and a crib made of crate strippings. They'd even brought a lamb and a goat and tied their leads to the floor. The lamb kept hopelessly bleating, and a couple of drunks took to amusing themselves by letting the goat nurse from a soup bowl of ale.

"She's crazy, you know," said Jeremiah.

Nathaniel had been taking in the place, the people. Every loud drinker or poker faced eater. They were all the soul and bones of a character in some future play. Bits of human documentation to be stolen, like you lift someone's wallet, memorized for the future. Nothing was ever inconsequential.

"What...Who's crazy?"

"My cousin."

Jeremiah had Nathaniel's attention now.

"Well...there's all kinds of crazy. Good crazy, bad crazy, and just plain crazy."

"I believe she's got traces of all of them." Jeremiah snapped his fingers real fast a couple of times. "She can do good, then do bad. Just like that. She shot her daddy when she was a girl. Maybe twelve. She ran away after that and married a man old enough to be her grandfather. He's passed on now. She came back home with the Pooles. Who are not cousins. I know their name is poison to you. Her father is alive... somewhere. Sharpening the blade for her is my bet."

"Why'd she shoot him?"

"Don't know. Jen had a sister. Died right before the shooting. The women know why, but they are shut up tight about it."

"Why are you telling me all this?"

"I love my cousin. We share black blood. That's as deep as religion can go. But you're a decent soul who bought me a coat and a room. She'll break your heart, Nathaniel. Before you even realize it."

He thought of telling the youth that's how it always was when it came to having your heart broken. That your ruination had begun with the first kiss, because love was hopelessly impractical and more suited to witchcraft than wisdom.

But he had something else on his mind. He pushed aside his finished dinner plate and leaned forward resting his arms on the table. "What's it like," he said quietly, "being black?"

"What?" said Jeremiah.

"In this world. Enslaved...hated...defamed. Watching white people in black face mock you, exploit you, stealing your human treasure."

No one had ever asked him such a thing. His people talked of it when they could safely hide behind whispers. They spoke in their music and their hymns, and in places without names.

While he thought away, Nathaniel watched his face, that was at least as important as the words. An expression captured. Hatred painted by masters.

"Imagine," Jeremiah said, "being made to lie in the road. And every-one who passes stops to piss on you. Even the few that don't, you are unsure. You lay there and lay there just like your father and his father before him. You lay in a grave rutted out by all the urine that flowed over your ancestors. And the ground never dries 'cause you can't figure a way to stand while keepin' alive so the sun light can get at it."

CHAPTER 58

IT SNOWED ALL CHRISTMAS WEEK. It came down over Manhattan in stark white flakes that made the earth silent, but for the sleigh bells on the carriage horses that coursed up through Lafayette Place. The sky was hard grey stone, the wind blowing up icy swirls against the windows of the homes, when there came a knock at the front door of the Harrison house.

Sarah answered to find a man she did not know or even recognize. He wore a long black cape and a top hat he kept in place by a scarf wound over the top of the hat and under his chin. The man was also missing part of his left arm from the elbow down.

"I'm looking for Millicent Harrison," he said.

Sarah eyed him cautiously from head to foot. The wind blew a bitter chill through the doorway.

"I was given her name and address from her brother," he said. "Colonel John Tearwood. I'm from London."

"May I have your name, please?"

"Certainly. It's Mister Thaddeus Jonah."

"Mister Thaddeus Jonah," she said, repeating him. "Wait here, please."

Sarah made her way down the hall to the sewing room. Millicent had been standing inside the doorway and could only pick up bits of the conversation. As Sarah entered, Millicent whispered, "Shut the door.

"Very strange," said Millicent. "Showing up like this the day after Christmas."

"Said he giv'n your name by your brother."

Millicent ran a fingernail along the edge of her lower lip.

"He look like a severe fellow to me," said Sarah. "And he missing part of an arm." She made a sawing motion with a hand at her elbow.

Millicent felt a gasp but suppressed it. Sarah noticed.

"You all right, ma'am?"

She turned away and paced.

"Ma'am?

"Have Sam come over…if he can." Millicent pointed. "And bring that one in here."

Millicent sat in a chair by the fire and took up her sewing. She hoped this wasn't what she believed it was. Sarah ushered the gentleman into the room. His top hat and cape left hung in the entry. He wore a rumply black suit and he bowed with a clumsy heft to his back.

"Merry Christmas, ma'am. And greetings from your brother."

"Good holiday to you, too. And how is my dear brother?"

"Hale and hearty when I last saw him."

He was lying, of course. The last he knew, the Colonel was in the hospital ward for the poor with liquor poisoning, which afforded Mister Jonah the luxury of going through Tearwood's possessions. Tearwood, he'd learned over the years, had been religious in destroying correspondence. Mister Jonah believed the old drunk knew where John James Beaufort had gone and was still in contact.

For a few shillings a week, Mister Jonah had in his secret employ a stagehand at the theatre where Tearwood lived. That a letter had come by chance when the sot was in a filthy ward gave him a promising lead.

The letter had been from Tearwood's dear sister...

As luck will have it...Your protégé is doing admirably well, acting up a storm...And your nephew is now a writer of plays...Bravo to us all...And I must say that Colonel Tearwood's American Theatre Company has a hit...albeit in Albany. You should come home, you darling man. I'm sure the boys could find a part that would fit your immeasurable personality.

"So...Mister Jonah...What brings you to New York? In the dead of winter."

"An errand of mercy, ma'am."

"Dear me," she said, looking up from her sewing. "That sounds so very serious."

He was warming his hands near the fire. He was about to undertake a risk. "I am trying to locate an actor," he said. "By the name of John James Beaufort. Though he might have changed his name. I believe he has come to this city."

"And of what importance is he?"

"Importance...he committed the brutal murder of a stage manager and his daughter. A daughter to whom this John James had been secretly married."

Millicent set her sewing down in her lap. "Please, continue."

"Not only was Beaufort married to this fair lady, but he had a child with this woman. Lawyers for the girl's estate…Her grandfather was quite well off…Hired me to see justice be done."

He stood now by the fire. He was uncomfortable trying to evaluate how the woman was taking all this. She seemed immune to what he was saying.

"This Beaufort has to be about thirty now," he said. "Dark hair. Sure voiced. An actor's speaking voice."

"Well," she said, "I don't envy you your task."

"Would you know such a fellow? I only ask since your son writes plays and has that troupe…Colonel Tearwood's——"

Millicent finished the thought. "American Theatre Company."

"Does he sound like anyone you might have seen?"

"It sounds like most every actor in creation."

She rose from her seat, making a polite excuse, and with her sewing in hand cordially walked Mister Jonah to the door. Being an acquaintance of her brother, Millicent asked Mister Jonah where he was residing, so that she might invite him to the house for a holiday get together…if he were still in town.

He stood in the windswept street, the snow like ice against his face. The instincts that made him treacherous said the woman was too dismissive, too unmoved.

She fingered an open eyelet of drapery and looked past the colonnade and there he was, this blackened cutout staring at the house in tracks of filthy snow where the carriages and sleighs had sewn a path up through the square.

She threw her knitting aside. An anxious fury consumed her. Had he secretly been married? Did he have a daughter? She felt like a woman betrayed, but she was wise enough to know better. She could match him sin for sin anytime.

She went to the kitchen. Sarah stood by the stove. Sam sat at the table having coffee. "The man that just left here," said Millicent. "I will pay you to follow him and tell me all you learn."

"I'll see it done," he said. He stood. Put on his coat that was draped over a chair. He kissed Sarah, then was gone.

Millicent sat, and Sarah got out a cup and set it before Millicent and filled it with coffee. Millicent motioned for Sarah to join her. The two women sat drinking in silence.

"You're worried over this man."

"I'm worried over this man," said Millicent. She stared into her coffee cup. "As women get older," she said, "they get smarter…Men just get old."

Millicent noticed a chip in the rim of the porcelain cup she drank from. She picked at it. "Throw this cup away when we're done here."

"Yes, ma'am. That man means trouble for Mister Luck, doesn't he?"

"He means trouble." She set the cup down. She set her elbows on the table, raised her forearms, folded her hands and rested her chin on them. "But we know how to handle trouble, don't we?" said Millicent.

CHAPTER 59

You could hear Christmas carols coming from the eatery well off into the chilly Cleveland night. The warehouses all around the hotel stood dark and lonely beneath a moonless sky and lent an air of sadness to those without.

Nathaniel and Jeremiah joined the celebration. Whites and blacks alike took part. The piano player was joined by a fiddler and a small handful of carolers. The people packed in there sang along to *Deck the Halls* and *Joy to the World*. Faces in the grey haze of smoke and candles consumed with the hopes Christmas brings.

At midnight the piano player stood up on his bench so he towered above the patrons, and he stilled the crowd with the wave of his hands and told them it was time for the Christmas Nativity. He sat back down and began a slow and poignant rendition of *Oh Come All Ye Faithful* accompanied by his fiddler and flock of carolers.

Through the swinging kitchen doors, with steam from the ovens and boiling pots clouding the entry, came a man and woman dressed as Joseph and Mary, and she, carrying a small child, and followed by three gruff looking wise men bearing gifts.

What they wore could hardly be called costumes. It was little more than headdresses cut from the roughest cotton over their everyday clothes. The child in a bit of gold swaddling shorn from a section of drape.

A clumsy path was cleared among the patrons for this immigrant Joseph and Mary with child and three riverfront magi weaving their way to a scrapwood manger, everyone singing now. You could feel the choral singers pressed together and all around them the lost, the lonely, the needy, the unwanted, the fearful, those in the grip of some insurmountable grief. Everything else about them swept away, except this moment with its invisible grace that makes them all one. And Nathaniel, he leaned over and whispered to Jeremiah, "I have to go outside for a few minutes," and as he turned back into the crowd, Jeremiah could see Nathaniel was crying.

Nathaniel trudged along the pathway between buildings then veered off into a vacant lot where he could cry in his aloneness. The scene in the bar brought back the thousand heartbreaks of his childhood, the private defilements, merciless and unrelentingly exacted upon body and being, that he had never spoken of to a living soul. These were just insidious details, but they were not the story.

The tale was that empty hole within you that the wind blows through and your only escape from was the theatrical stage. The one place where you are free of your own worst enemy…your agonized self. It was and is a special form of suffering that only the artcraft of performing can vanquish. The magic of a few hours in constant battle with the misery of a lifetime. "All rewards are momentary, it is only suffering that lives forever"———a little quote he remembered from some forgotten, nameless actor.

He listened to the singing through the wind, making it seem the voices were reaching out from some heavenly darkness. He stared into a snow so white against the blackness of the sky, wiping at his eyes, thinking, the days are a long time coming at moments like this, when somewhere behind him a voice in a sing songy whisper———"*Oh come, All ye faithful, joyful and triumphant.*"

He turned to find this ghostly figure in a hooded cape, with a cold grey mist coming from her mouth as she sang. He wiped at his eyes, there was anticipation in his voice. "I have been endlessly thinking about you."

"I suffer the same fate."

He came to her and she slipped her hands out of her cape. "Why were you crying?" she said. She wiped at his cheeks with a gloved hand.

He swept one arm across the scene as if to take in all that was about him.

"Christmas," she said. "There's been nothing like it since the beginning of time, is there? It frightens me, Nathaniel. I don't know why, but it does."

They were close together, and he took her by the front of her cape and kissed her. Their flesh was bitter cold but the warmth coming from their mouths———

"I thought about never seeing you again," she said. "I argued with myself over this, but I am stubborn. I am also too selfish and driven to do anything that decent. I must also warn you, I am notorious for making bad decisions."

CHAPTER 60

JEREMIAH PUT A CHAIR BESIDE THE WALL OF HIS ROOM where he sat and cupped a glass against the paltry slats, his ear pressed to the bottom of the glass as if it were a stethoscope, so he could eavesdrop on some good old fashioned fucking. He caught drags on his cigarette between the lurid moanings and pleas that begat wild pictures, grinning with near evil pleasure. Once they'd finished, when the cries and creakings of the bed had subsided and there was nothing but that boring rustle of whispers, he got up and finished off a beer. He toasted toward the wall before he drank.

• • •

"We're a play," said Genevieve.

"We?"

"You and I. Our life."

"And what kind of play is that?"

"A comedy, of course."

"I see," said Nathaniel. "How could I have missed all the jokes piling up around my existence?"

They had been lying in the bed together, but she got up now. She was animated, openly intense. "At least we start out as a comedy. Until we become a tragedy. Tragedy is always better, isn't it?"

"Always better," he said with a little edge in his voice.

"I meant in the theatre."

"I had the notion that's what you meant."

"My cousin," she said.

"Yes?"

"He told you about me...us?"

"He told me."

She stood there naked in the candlelight. She did not seem to know the meaning of shyness or reserve. "No one would ever guess about me, would they?"

"I have no idea about such things."

"Did you have any idea?"

"I did not."

She moved about. Drifting into the shadows, clasping her hands together. "I'll be discovered one day."

"Maybe not."

"I'll be discovered…and destroyed."

"Don't think like that."

"Once you are discovered…you are destroyed. That is how it is in the America of right now. That is the tragedy. The one I'm carrying around inside me."

"Funny," he said.

"It's not funny. Not funny at all."

"I didn't mean that. I meant…Every actor has that same kind of thought at one time or another. *I'll be discovered…and then destroyed.*"

"I don't understand."

"They will be discovered to have no talent…and their career will be destroyed. It is the irrational fear."

"I have no such feelings. From what I've seen of actors on stage, I can do at least as good. After all, I've been doing it all my life…and successfully."

"Just because you're a good liar, confidence artist, charlatan, does not make you an actor on stage."

She sauntered toward the bed all confidence and brass. "You're going to put the play back on in the spring. Yes? I can play the woman. Just give me——"

He laughed out loud.

"Don't you dare laugh at me. Do you understand?" She completely turned on him. There in the half-life of the light, her face had hardened. "I have lived and suffered and died. I've had to survive on other people's leavings." She began to cry. "Is it so much to ask? A pitiful request. Haven't you ever…I can swallow my pride with the best of them if I have to…I can beg with the best of them. Do you want me to pour out all my grief? Do you?"

He did not know what to say. This was a suddenly sad woman child crying, her eyes hidden behind her fingers. Sobbing. He sat up.

"They'll hear you out in the hall," he said.

A moment later she peered out from between opening fingers. Her tormented features softened in a slickster's smile. "How was that as a performance?"

CHAPTER 61

As the spring approached, the theatre season had to be plotted out. Troupes began the yearly hustle to interest theatre managers and financiers in their respective entertainments. It had all the decorative trappings of respectability and art, but at its core it was about the deft religion of money——and on very, very rare occasions, other things altogether.

When Genevieve announced to Nathaniel that she had arranged a meeting with financiers, he became suspicious.

"Are we sailing into illegal waters?"

"You are at least partly right," she answered.

They arrived by carriage at midnight to a dock along the Erie Canal. They were to board a packet boat and that is where his suspicions were rewarded. When Nathaniel stepped down through the door and into the low ceilinged and lantern lit cabin that ran the length of the packet, he understood this was no ordinary meeting.

Sister Evangeline was sitting at a table in her three wheel chair at the far end of the light. With her at the table were two men that Nathaniel recognized on sight. Misters Dean and Davids——theatrical entrepreneurs to be sure, but men with an unflinching political agenda.

The cabin had a low ceiling. As Nathaniel came forward, Sister Evangeline said, "Nathaniel Luck...I'd like you to meet..."

"I know these gentlemen," he said. He put a hand out to shake Mr. Davids' who then asked that he sit. Mister Dean brought out a bottle of fine bonded whiskey and set it on the table. Nathaniel glanced back over his shoulder. Genevieve had taken a seat by the door, where she could watch and listen and be ready.

"We saw your play in New York," said Mister Davids. "*The Monster.*"

"Mine and Robert Harrison's," said Nathaniel.

"You took on Astor," said Mister Dean pouring out a glass of whiskey.

"Robert Harrison took on Astor. I took on the character."

Mister Dean slid the glass of liquor Nathaniel's way. "You were not afraid of making a political statement."

"And for our efforts, we managed to get a theatre burned down and then were politely run out of Manhattan. I don't see how that would make us attractive to theatrical entrepreneurs."

Mister Davids glanced at Mister Dean. "He's probing, Mr. Dean."

"That he is," said Mister Davids. "He's a clever lad."

Nathaniel sipped at his whiskey silently.

"Are you familiar with the Lakefront Consortium?" said Mister Davids.

"Theatres in Buffalo, Cleveland, Detroit," said Nathaniel. "And one down in Columbus, I believe, along the Erie Canal. You gentlemen control what shows perform the circuit."

"Yes. Mister Dean and I are here to discuss giving your show a run for the Spring and all through the Summer."

"It'll make your career," said a quiet Genevieve.

Nathaniel looked back to where she sat by the entry, her hands folded in her lap, the moon through the open door above her shoulder. Ever the demure hustler.

"The offer comes with a caveat," said Sister Evangeline.

"Yes," said Nathaniel. "I assume that's why you're here. *You* are the caveat."

"I never thought of myself as such, but...yes."

"Your theatre crew," said Mister Davids, "is mostly black. We want to use your troupe as a———"

"Front," said Mister Dean, "to help us smuggle runaways into Canada."

"They will be brought to you," said Mister Davids. "You will have them work as members. We will have them transported on to determined locations."

"You're to be a moving station on the underground railroad," said Sister Evangeline.

"Of course, there's the obvious risks," said Mister Davids.

"And," said Mister Dean, "the obvious reward. Your troupe will have bookings, it will thrive."

"It's not enough," said Genevieve.

This brought about a concentration of stares. And none too happy with the young lady.

"You can't just book the play," said Genevieve. "You have to insure its success. Promotion...advertising. And that means money."

"Who are you suddenly?" said Mister Davids.

"Suddenly...nothing," said Mister Dean. "She was always a conniver and she's a conniver still."

"I'm heartbroken at your assertion, gentlemen. But hear me out. If the play is only passably popular, if it has a thin gate, people will wonder why you keep giving it a run. You don't need suspicions for any reason. But by promoting the play, and the players..." she pointed to Nathaniel. "The more popular the actor, the more likely the play will be a success. People come to see their stars, their idols. The greater the audience, the longer the tour. The longer the tour, the more runaways find their way to freedom."

"I suppose," said Mister Davids, "you have a plan for this."

"You can bet," said Mister Dean, "the little conniver has had a plan, since she approached us with this notion of hers."

Genevieve smiled. She had a plan all right. As selfish as it was selfless.

There was to be no answer anyway. Nathaniel told them this as he stood up to leave. Robert Harrison had as much to say about any of it as he did himself, and Robert was about a week away from joining up with him in Cleveland. There'd be no decision until then.

• • •

It was left to me to stay on watch along the canal with a rank old pistol tucked up under my shirt. Anywhere Sister Evangeline travelled there was the threat of spies and bountymen working for the slavers to bring back runaways. Sister knew it too...she was surprised she had not been shot down already.

I was standing guard when Nathaniel joined me in the dark and rolled himself a smoke. It was pretty quiet out there all around us, but inside that packboat cabin there was still some pretty high tensions over Genevieve's sudden demands for more money.

I could see Nathaniel was conflicted. You tally up opportunity in the light of a good cause and its attenuated threat, this was a man who was gonna sweat out the harvest.

"I told you," I said. "About my cousin."

He looked at me through the dark with the fullness of a hard stare.

"And you know what else? She's not done yet. She got plans. And her plans got plans."

Smoke came out of his nostrils on one long breath.

"That woman," I said, meaning my cousin, "she could talk Jesus down off the cross. And that's gospel."

CHAPTER 62

ROBERT'S SUITCASES WERE PACKED AND IN THE HALLWAY, and when there came a knock at the front door, he was sure it was the carriage meant to carry him to the river for his journey to Cleveland.

But the man at the door was no carriage driver.

"My name is Lord Halsey," he said, having removed his hat. "And I'm here to speak with Millicent Harrison if I might."

This was a hard looking gent with an imposing size and thick rasher of sideburns. His hair was sparse and black and slicked down in long strands across his huge white skull.

"And what matter of business might you have with my mother," said Robert.

"A man came to this house last Christmas by the name of Jonah to speak with your mother about a murderer. He went missing shortly after. I am investigating his disappearance."

Robert watched his mother be politely questioned about this Mister Jonah who was searching for a murderer from England and appeared at their home in Lafayette Place thanks to a conversation that he'd had with a Colonel Tearwood, who was her brother.

Millicent was the epitome of unwavering calm, even for her. And when it was explained that this Mister Jonah had disappeared less than two days after their meeting at the house, she did little more than shake her head and say, "How misfortunate. How utterly misfortunate."

She apologized again that she could not offer Lord Halsey anything more by the way of information. Even when he read to her a description of the murderer from a London newspaper, she gave little more than an unindulging shrug.

He then turned his attention to Robert. "I hear you're a man of the theatre. Might you know an actor who fits that description? Remembering it was a number of years ago."

"I know endless actors who fit that description," said Robert. "And most of them are murderers." He stood then, and smiled, "Of the English language."

It was Robert who walked Lord Halsey to the door. "I'm sorry we couldn't be more helpful in your quest."

"You'd be surprised," said Halsey, "how helpful you have been."

He left Robert with a business card and told him if he cared to contact him at any time, to leave word at the British Embassy in Manhattan. Halsey glanced at the luggage. "I hear you have your own theatre company."

"With a partner."

It must be an exciting life adventure…the theatre."

"In between the hardships, disappointments, and failures, it's fantastic."

"I will have to make it my business to see your next show."

When Robert returned to his mother, she was in private conversation with Sarah that ceased immediately when he entered the sunroom. Sarah left without a word, without even so much as glancing at Robert, which was entirely unlike her.

"You know, Mother," said Robert, "over the last few years I've come to realize I don't know you as well as I thought I did."

She had been in quiet thoughtfulness, letting the sun touch upon her face. She turned to Robert then and said, "And that, my dear son, is a blessing for both of us."

CHAPTER 63

NATHANIEL WOKE TO SUNLIGHT ACROSS THE WINDOW and the sight of Genevieve stretched across the lower part of the bed holding, of all things, a bank draft.

"Well, Colonel," she said. "Do you see what I have here?"

The way she stared at that check she looked astonishingly fresh and young.

"So," he said, "Jesus did come down from the cross."

"What?"

"Never mind...Just something a wise man told me."

She began to rub her bare foot across his chest then ran her toes down the length of him.

"Colonel...we are striking out for parts unknown."

"Where I hope to find they can hit their mark and know their lines."

She crawled up on top of him like some slithery witch and she set the check down on the table by bending it, so it stood up on its edge and was easily visible, and for the next hour between them, it was all about saliva and sweat.

· · ·

She had a surprise for him and he was not told where she was taking him. She actually blindfolded him for the last half block, leading him along by the front of his vest, his arms reaching out, testing the space before him, a picture of humorous curiosity to everyone passing. She ushered him into a shop whose windows were blacked out with drapes.

"You can take off the blindfold now," she said.

There was a dusty light about this small shell of storefront that looked to have been turned into a photographer's studio of sorts.

She pointed over his shoulder where he should turn and look. The light through the open doorway fell upon a draped section of wall where there was a life size wood cutout of the COLONEL TEARWOOD'S AMERICAN THEATRE COMPANY flier that Nathaniel had made up and passed out on the New York streets. The words attached to the draped wall with bolts. It was an exact replica of the original painting that Tearwood had conceived all those years ago, but with the empty chair framed by the words, which Genevieve pointed to and said, "The chair is waiting for this era's Colonel Tearwood."

The photographer was a little man, a slight man, who stood with folded hands by the chair. Politely silent, smiling. The artist in residence, ready to serve another artist's dream.

"The lady brought clothes," he said. "Costumes. A makeup kit. Create the image you want to present."

The photographer pointed to a table where everything he had described awaited.

The scene as it was, silent, but for intermittent street noise and shadows passing across the open light of the doorway. The empty chair, waiting, the image all but complete.

He noticed now, there was Jeremiah, casually sitting on a crate with his back to the wall, legs stretched out and crossed, smoking. He made a fanning wave with a hand to say hello. He was grinning like a young devil.

"You're a star now," said Genevieve, quietly leaning over his left shoulder. "You're the one they will come to see. You…carry the American Theatre Company on your shoulders. That's what stars do. And everyone should know."

There was that cool, sensuality in her voice that stirred the dark in him. He kept looking at the chair. The idea was pure intoxication.

"I would give everything for that one moment of fame. Do you know that?" The Colonel had been lying in bed, stricken with pneumonia and coughing up poisonous phlegm when he told Nathaniel this. *"I'd give up everything…everything for one moment…"* He leaned over and spit an evil looking clot of infection onto the floor. *"Fortunately,"* he said, *"I did not have everything to give up."*

Nathaniel sat at the table with the makeup kit open. He looked into a mirror and conjured up an image. He tinted his hair a smoky white and detailed his face with a trim moustache. He turned himself into the vision of a timeless, ageless actor from any era, a persona inured to the ways of life on the stage.

But it was not him. He turned and looked at the set, the final details being prepped by the photographer. Lastly, at that elegant empty armchair.

He wanted it for himself. That moment, that everlasting image. He wanted it in all its selfish glory.

He peeled away the moustache and washed the smoky coloring from his hair and then he combed it neatly. He put on his waistcoat and a tie, which he seldom if ever wore. He went and placed himself in the chair, draping an arm over the sidewings and crossing his legs. He was the portrait of cocky and cool assurance. And the moment the picture was taken, he regretted it.

CHAPTER 64

MILLICENT ACCOMPANIED HER SON TO THE DOCK. She spoke as if that morning had never happened. She was only concerned about her son's health and wellbeing. As she kissed Robert goodbye she held his hand for a moment afterward. "If you write about me someday," she said, "be fearless. The more truth you tell, the greater the telling. By the way…when I married your father, I knew exactly the kind of man he was. And he was the man you wrote about in your play. There is very little innocence in the world, Robert, even among the innocent."

• • •

At the hotel, Robert had been told Nathaniel had taken over a suite on the top floor. He knocked on the door, and when it swung open, who should it be greeting him?

"Robert," said Genevieve. "Come in, dear. Come in." She threw her arms around him and hugged him as if they were long lost intimates.

The first thing he noticed, her clothes were everywhere. And Nathaniel was nowhere to be found.

"He's not here. Come on. We'll go see him. He's been talking about you incessantly." She grabbed him by the arm as one would a child.

"You've got a lot of decisions to make," she said. "But I'll let Nathaniel tell you. Auditions have already started."

"What are you doing here?" he said.

"Among other things, I'm reading for the lead of the play, of course."

"No kidding…"

"Robert, at least sound enthused. Passably enthused. Pretend enthused. Are you hungry? Do you want to get something to eat first? Coffee, maybe? A drink?"

"No, I——"

"I read a book, by the way. An English author. Ellis Bell…It's called Wuthering Heights. It would be perfect for our next play. It's up to you, of course. You're the artist," she said. "You look well and rested. How's your mother? Nathaniel talks of her so much, I feel as if I know her. Have you been writing? I want to hear all about it. You should hear some of the wonderful things people say about your play. I get a thrill just telling strangers I know you."

She led Robert through a barren lot across from the hotel and down along foundry row on a rutted causeway where she had to hold up her dress to keep the muck off it, then weave her way through a loose flock of goats being herded along by a couple of kids shaking cans on a string, and her talking theatre all the while, highlighting their plans like she was the Queen of Things to Come.

She pointed to a small abandoned warehouse where workmen between shifts peered into the grimy and broken windows. It didn't take a genius to realize there were probably a slew of pretty young actresses in there trying to stake their claim to destiny.

It wasn't quite a madhouse, but it was the next best thing. There was a black youth sitting at a table Robert didn't recognize and he was taking the names of actors and actresses waiting in line and setting up a day and a time in a ledger for them to come back and audition, while Nathaniel talked to each privately.

Robert knew the speech by heart now. They had their own brand of auditioning. "I don't care if you can breathe fire while you dance like a ballerina. Don't care if you can sing while you perform on the trapeze or juggle while you recite the classics." He would then hand the actor a few pages of script. And just as he was about to set off on his last few lines, Robert cut in and said, "You're not gonna give them that tired old line that 'We do straight drama here, so come back and show us something.'"

Nathaniel looked up. Saw his comrade in arms had arrived. "I believe I was…Of course, I stole those lines."

"Doesn't surprise me. Though they could use a polish."

"I stole them from the playwright."

"Yeah…but not as written."

• • •

When they were done for the day with their theatre business and the actors had left, clinging to a few pages of dialogue they imagined would change their lives, the two men went off together to talk, as each was carrying around a little private truth to unveil upon the other.

"I've got something important to talk to you about," said Nathaniel.

"How timely," said Robert. "I've got something of some urgency to relate to you."

"Well," said Nathaniel, "why don't we flip a coin and see who goes first?"

As Nathaniel reached into his pocket for a piece of silver, Robert said, "You call it…Mister Beaufort."

To hear the name was like waking up in a grave. Nathaniel didn't bother with the coin now. Instead he listened to the whole damn story, sickening at each turn, and filling in bare facts where he could.

"We were never married. I had no daughter with her. From the day Lucretia and I met to the moment she was murdered was just short of a year."

"This Lord Halsey…he will show up, eventually."

"I don't know how he can prove it was me. Mister Jonah… That is quite another story."

"Mister Jonah, it seems, has inexplicably disappeared, and without leaving much heartbreak in his wake. A question…Could the girl have had a daughter that you did not know about? That she kept secret from you? Her father…The way you describe him, seems capable of——"

"Don't say such a thing. Because it feels like it could be true."

"What do you want to do?"

"Nothing. We go about our lives. If it should come to be, I know how to make an exit." He needed a smoke, he needed much more than a smoke. "You might have the premise here for another play, my friend. First love, craven murder, lives tragically destroyed. It reeks of success, don't you think?"

"Sometimes there's nothing more painful than sarcasm."

Nathaniel pointed his lit match at Robert and nodded over how right he really was.

"You had something you wanted to talk to me about," said Robert. "Is it the right time, or——?"

"The hell with the right time. The right time isn't all it's cracked up to be anyway."

They walked into in a small glassed in office in the middle of the warehouse floor. Some of the glass was broken, some of the panes badly spidered. There was one chair in the room and Robert sat in it. Nathaniel was thinking on where and how to begin. Robert glanced across that vacant building.

Jeremiah was at the table as before, writing in the ledger. Genevieve was with him, but she was not stealing glances their way, she was flat out staring.

"Is it about that crazy woman?"

"Her…and the young man out there. We've been offered financial backing for a full season. It's called the 'lake circuit.' A theatre here, Buffalo, Detroit, and Cincinnati. They'll even put up advertising."

"But it comes with a price," said Robert. "Yes?"

"I guess you've seen that play."

CHAPTER 65

G<small>ENEVIEVE KNEW IT WAS BAD</small> as soon as she saw Robert come out of the office, his chin crammed down into his chest. "He's got on a judge's expression," she said to Jeremiah.

"If anyone ought to recognize a judge's expression, it's you."

She glared at her cousin.

Robert came right toward her. Nathaniel followed along behind him.

"I'll say this much for you," said Robert. "You're a world class conniver."

"My father used to say I was a second rate conniver. I must be coming up in the world."

"Or the world is sinking down to your level…Now, I'm not against taking a political risk. And I'm not adverse to putting myself in harm's way, when I have a compelling reason."

"It's me you're against…I've tried to make up for my sins…Which are many and ongoing."

"You're here because you're trying to hustle up a career. And you'll use us to try and get it." Robert turned to the youth. "I'm not against you being here. God only knows, the theatre is always looking for people it can work to death for a pitifully low wage and little hope of reward."

"Well, Mister Harrison," said Jeremiah, "being born black prepares one perfectly for such a position."

While they talked Genevieve went over to the table and opened a box. She took from it a salted paper print of the daguerreotype she had done of the American Theatre Company with Nathaniel and she walked over and slapped it into Robert's hand.

He looked at the print long and hard. What he saw there he did not like for a number of reasons. He turned his stare to Nathaniel. "Whose idea was this?"

"Mine," said Genevieve. "I've already got someone in Buffalo passing them out for important theatre people there. I want you to succeed. I'm doing everything I can to help you succeed. I want Nathaniel to succeed. I want you——"

"The fate of our dreams are sealed by our mistakes," Robert shook his head. "At least be honest. This is all about your own selfish self-interest and that makes you dangerous."

She took a breath and reared her head back dramatically. "My fate was sealed at birth…And I don't walk in the grip of a handful of truths. I'm a conniver and a con artist. My cousin here can tell you. There is no good I would not do, there is no shortcut I would not take, there is no ploy I would fail to use, to achieve my selfish self-interest. Which makes me like most every person in the world. Judge me harshly, fine. But don't condemn me yet. After all, it was my scheming that got you a season's worth of prestige bookings."

With that, she walked out.

• • •

Nathaniel asked Jeremiah to go along with his cousin, to take the books and ledgers with him, leaving the two men there alone with the sun setting through the windows. It was a harsh light that bled across the rooftops and the windows were so grimy that the glass looked to be almost scorched.

Once alone, Robert held up the print and said, "The only thing missing from the photo is your crown."

Nathaniel walked about. Bits of broken glass on the floor crackled under his boots.

"Since when," said Robert, "were you voted to replace my uncle in that photograph?"

"I fell party to pure vanity. I saw the chair there…" He pointed to some imaginary chair… "And I wanted it. I knew I shouldn't do this without talking to you and Millicent. But I was…It represented success and achievement, I…I could not control myself." He forced his hands down into his pockets. He was uncomfortable, ashamed, and yet… "We live in the present, don't we? We sell the present, don't we? We need an image that says———"

"She had the chair right there waiting for you."

"She did."

"And that's not the worst of it." Robert approached Nathaniel, holding up the print. "Halsey will show up someday. You can deny who you are all you want, but if he sends one of these photos back to England there are going to be people who will swear that is John James Beaufort…the murderer. Legal affidavits can be sworn out." Robert took the photo and stuck it down inside Nathaniel's vest, right where his heart should be. "Not exactly the apple from the tree of knowledge. But as a prop, it will do very nicely."

Robert turned and started to leave, bits of glass now cracking under his shoes. "She's dangerous even when she doesn't realize it."

CHAPTER 66

WE WERE WALKING BACK TO THE HOTEL and what was the first thing Genevieve said to me. Take a moment and wonder. She had not been brought down by Robert's berating of her. She seemed immune. Genevieve Wells was somewhere out there on the horizon where the sun was going down in a burning flame.

"I need you to teach me how to roll a cigarette," she said. "Got to do that right away. Starting tonight... Roll one and smoke one."

That is what she said.

"What are you talking about, Jen?"

"I'm going to be the first woman on stage to roll her own cigarette. And I'm going to be the first woman to smoke on stage. No one has, you know."

"How can you be sure?"

"I've talked to everyone who knows the theatre. I've talked to every actor I've met. In every play I read. Never happened."

I doubted she'd read ten plays in her whole life. And she could have talked to what, a couple of dozen actors. Slightly less than the whole world, for sure. But I never interrupt someone in good conscience even if they are out of their mind.

"I'm going to be famous for it," she said. "They're going to write about me for doing it. Don't say a word to Nathaniel or Robert. I'll never work on it during rehearsal. I just got to figure out where in the play."

She actually stopped and with her long slender fingers rolled an imaginary cigarette and lit it. She stood there in the fading light smoking away. "I can see the moment," she said.

"Yeah?" I said. "But you must have stolen God's eyes without his knowing…because I don't see shit."

• • •

The two young men walked the Cleveland streets together. A different slant of life to follow them wherever they went.

"Is she crazy and dangerous…or just crazy?"

"She's a steady dose of drama and risk," said Nathaniel. "Like the theatre business."

Nathaniel noted Robert didn't look particularly well. The flesh around his scars now paler. "How you feelin'?"

Robert slipped a pint of Doctor McMumm's from his pocket as an answer.

"Do you want to go someplace quiet and eat?" said Nathaniel, "or somewhere and get completely debauched?"

"Both at the same time."

Nathaniel nodded at the efficiency of the plan.

"I wonder," Robert said, "what they'll write about a playwright who lived half the time with his wealthy mother and the rest in a brothel?"

• • •

Genevieve was sitting at a table near the window and reading a book by lantern light, when Nathaniel entered. He was, as they say, exquisitely drunk. She looked up from her reading, the light sparkled upon her eyeglasses. He stood there staring at her and swung the suite door shut behind him. Not a word or a nod or a gesture passed between them.

"You're like a painting there," he said. "One of those cherished English portraits. The modern woman. Not only beautiful and demure, but enlightened." He undid the buttons on his waistcoat, removed it while wobbling a bit, then flung it across the bed. "You probably picked up the book like you were reading just before I came in. How long did it take you to think up that phony pose?"

Her nostrils flared. She slammed the book down on the table and peeled off her glasses. "I won't be insulted like that."

"You don't want to be insulted…Improve your melodramatics. That pose went out with Moses."

The bones in her cheeks pressed against the flesh as she was biting down on her teeth so hard. She leaned her head back and then broke out laughing.

"You son of a bitch," she said. "How do you know me so well, and so soon?"

He grinned back at her. "I've logged more sins than you have, dearest. So, I have more experience with these…expressive sideshows."

He dropped down on the bed. They looked at each other with a kind of wicked pleasure at the sparring they played at.

"Why don't you come over here and kiss me?" she said.

"Why don't you come over here and kiss me?"

"Well…I have my pride, you know. You come over here."

He reached into his pocket and took out a silver dollar. "I'll toss you to see who gets to have pride."

She grabbed the book and flung it at him. He wouldn't even have gotten slightly clipped on the side of the head if he wasn't so drunk."

"You didn't defend me tonight at all," she said. "You didn't come to my aid once. Not one word's worth with Robert."

The book had gashed the flesh along his temple and he wiped at the blood trickling down into his eye with the tip of his fingers, then licked them.

"Robert and I came up this road together. He fought through pain to write a play. He took on Astor. He gave me a chance. While I was in prison in Albany he was there writing that play to help me survive. Especially after your letter."

"I knew that would surface. It was so predictable."

"The plays are him," said Nathaniel. "I wouldn't put in a good word for you. You want it…You earn it."

"You could have at least said, 'Give her a chance.'"

"You should have been smart enough to just ask him. You should have been wily enough to throw yourself at the feet of his goodness and decency. But you're too damn proud."

She was up and pacing now. Her eyes bearing down on him, her pupils, four white sided. And all those dark pent up emotions. "This is your chance to get back at me, isn't it?"

"I've had plenty of chances. I'll have plenty more."

She stormed over to the table and swept her hands about, knocking books and papers to the floor until she found an AMERICAN THEATRE COMPANY print which she promptly flung at Nathaniel. "No shortage of vanity there."

"Matched only by my stupidity and bad timing."

"All of that belongs to me," she said. She screamed out, "Me! I created this opportunity."

"But you have to go further back. La piece bien faite. Something people of the theatre know. This story begins before the beginning. We're here because a thief had a bout of remorse, and Robert used that act as the central plot in a play which you saw as an opportunity…for yourself."

"God damn you. You are throwing it in my face."

"I'm giving you perspective. Something real actors know is central to their craft."

"You are going to find every way you can to put the knife in." She walked over to the wall between the rooms and started to slam her fist against it. "I know you're in there listening, Jeremiah."

Nathaniel had no idea, until she turned on him, and wagging a finger, said, "He listens you know." She kicked the wall. "I know you're there." She kept kicking the wall.

CHAPTER 67

"Wake up, honey boy."

Robert rolled over and splayed himself across the womanly flesh beside him. "Come on now, honey boy," she kept saying. "Wake yourself."

She shook him hard, but he was in an addled, drunken stupor.

"What, what?" he finally said. Speaking to…who? He didn't remember her name.

"There's a lady wants to see you," she said.

He spooned up alongside her and burrowed down into that warm woman body. "I should hope so," he said.

"Not me," said the woman.

"She means me," said Genevieve.

One groggy burst and he was sitting up in the dark looking about him.

"Dear God," he said. "Where the hell are you?"

She turned up the lantern. There she was, Genevieve Wells, resting in a god damn armchair and staring at his naked self.

Robert tried to cover himself with a sheet. He pulled it so hard the woman beside him got swept up and toppled to the floor. He looked like a god damn school boy suddenly, caught in the act. He'd thought himself ridiculous to feel that, but that was the way of it, that's how he felt.

"What the hell are you doing here?"

"I came here to plead my case."

"Well, I certainly question the time and place of your choosing," he said. He sat drunk and huddled up in a sheet, the sodden potentate.

"From a man's point of view," she said, "I could see you questioning it. But women have a different sense of such things."

Her eyes grew narrow and glisteny. He had a terrible thought——was she smiling?

"What's going on here?" said the other woman. She was gathering up her clothes, her shoes, her purse. "You two married or something?"

Genevieve held out a silver dollar. "Be gone now."

The woman gave Genevieve a whored up stare. "I was to be paid more than that."

"You can come back and earn it later. Now get out. Or I'll throw you out as you are."

"Well...you don't have to be such a bitch about it."

"But I'm afraid I do," said Genevieve.

When it was just the two of them cloistered in that room, Genevieve said, "I'm going to be destroyed one day. Of that I'm sure."

Robert reached an arm out from under the sheet and pointed to a bottle on the floor. Genevieve rose and picked up the bottle. She held it to the light. "Doctor McMumm's...This will settle out the scars," she said, "when there's nothing else."

As she handed it to him, he said, "Explain yourself."

"I'm black. I pass. Nathaniel told you. I say nothing. Hardly anyone knows. Sister Evangeline...my cousin. I always wanted to be on stage. How much time does someone like me have? I'll be exposed one day. Then what? I'll never get a chance to be on the white stage after that. And there is no other stage."

Robert was a dark shadow in a white sheet staring up at this picture of sincerity.

"I'm asking you...I am humbling myself...Just give me the opportunity. I know I am a bundle of selfishness and conniving. That I'm a walking contradiction. That you could look at me and call me liar and I'd not argue." She turned away, started for the door. She stopped. Her voice tender, light as smoke. "When I was a little girl, I was an angel in a church play. A black church. I had white wings made of wood strips and old sheets. I sang and read from the Bible. And it was the closest I ever got to who I wanted to truly be."

$\bullet \ \bullet \ \bullet$

There's an old saying——*There's limits even to wisdom.*

They let her read with the other actors in Cleveland trying out for the part. There was no doubt about it——she stank. She took this fact as any aspiring actor would——badly.

Nathaniel and Robert had decided rather than have one cast they would do something different. Actors from each city would perform in that city, the only constant would be Nathaniel. This, they felt, would keep the play fresh and alive. So, they let her read with the actors in Buffalo. She was right there at the bottom of the talent pool. In Detroit she proved to be only marginally lousy. There were some things about her performances that were in her favor. She had an outstanding memory. She knew every actors' lines. And she had an impeccable sense of timing.

She caught Nathaniel and Robert talking privately, and as she approached them, they took on that nervous silence. She knew then she had been the subject of their whispering. "I do have one thing in my favor," she said out of nowhere, "I seem to have both of you feeling bad for me."

Later, as she lay beside Nathaniel in the dark silence of their suite, she said, "Is there anything you know to help me?"

"I am helping you," he said.

"How? I don't understand."

"I'm letting you fail," he said quietly.

She sat up. She needed to see his face there, even in the shadows, to know and understand. She saw that he was serious. His stare bluntly on point. She was suddenly furious, not at him, but at herself, but she slapped his face anyway.

CHAPTER 68

WITH EVERY CASTING TRIP THEY UNDERTOOK, they brought an entourage of runaways posing as personal servants and wardrobe for the actors, working under the supervision of Jeremiah, who was now defacto stage manager for the company. Nathaniel and Genevieve played the part of self-centered and demanding actors ordering their black employees about.

A private one man steamer had been conscripted through Sister Evangeline that would carry the runaways across Lake Erie to the Canadian shore just south of Chatham—Kent. A place runaways had heard of, a place that said freedom. The trip across the lake could be treacherous. Hard rains and high winds, violent waves and choking fogs. Many a ship had been lost, and then there were the abolitionist haters and slave catchers who patrolled the lake. More than once in their crossing they heard distant gunfire upon the night waters. The reports steady and horrifying then falling away like a fading dream.

In those frightened faces of that stark crossing of the night sea, Robert saw where the future of the theatre lay. He whispered this to Nathaniel beneath the chugging boiler of that lowly steamer. Nathaniel understood. "Undivided reality," whispered Robert.

It was terrible and wonderful and endlessly true.

"Your uncle," whispered Nathaniel back, "used to tell me to be ahead of the times was dangerous. That if you wanted to survive…you should be one step behind the times. Which puts you just far enough out front not to be shot dead."

Courage in the face of adversity will not enhance your skill as an actor. It should, but the stage does not embrace any of the spiritual laws. Its roots are soiled in mystery. After all, some of the finest actors in the world are blazing cowards or selfish and self-possessed losers. It was not unusual to find popular stars to be nothing more than whining miscreants of the first order who disbelieve the Copernicus rule that the earth travels around the sun and not around themselves.

Sadly, Genevieve was kept on as understudy out of pity, and because she risked her life on these midnight missions. She understood this, though it was never said outright. Robert had been the final vote behind this, to his own surprise, and she told him, "You can't hide behind your kindness. Even though you are." The other actors in the casts of the different theatres were quietly resentful of her. It was that mean spirited and jealous indifference that actors do so well with just a smiling turn of phrase. Of course, they had no idea what was going on right before their eyes with black stagehands appearing and disappearing.

Alone with Nathaniel in the theatre Jeremiah looked up from the company ledgers and his nightly count of the box office and asked, "Is there any chance she'll get better?"

"Chance…chance is a blight on talent."

"She's such a practiced conniver and liar, you'd think she'd be perfect for the stage."

"Who said she isn't?"

• • •

The way he said that left me little room to wonder. There was a God given plot afoot in the cunning mind of that gent. "Jeremiah," he said, "let me ask you… Do you think you could handle a bit of kidnapping?"

He had already rolled a cigarette and was lighting it when he asked the question and waited upon my answer.

"Is that part of the stage manager's duties?" I said.

Which if it wasn't the most foolish answer I've ever given to a question, it was near about the top of the list.

CHAPTER 69

It wasn't exactly a kidnapping, not in the truest sense. Nathaniel sat with makeup kit and mirror, and Jeremiah watched as the actor conjured himself into a hard-bitten thug with a pugilist's nose and scraggly beard. Nathaniel then walked the waterfront searching until he finally came upon two denizens of its trashiest quarters he felt worthy of solicitation for his plan.

It was an hour before the night's performance and the actress playing the lead had yet to arrive, which was totally unlike her. To claim a sense of trepidation was settling in over the cast that Genevieve would have to go on in her place was an understatement. Within half an hour of the curtain's rise she had still not arrived, and patrons were already filing to their seats. There was now unqualified, unquestioned panic backstage. The actors stared at Genevieve as if she had typhus.

From out of nowhere, Jeremiah came rushing into the theatre with a concocted ransom note. He had been in the alley when a man handed him a note, told him to give it to the theatre manager, and then proceeded to run away. Nathaniel read the note aloud to the cast. The actress had, in fact, been spirited away outside her rooming house and if the troupe ever expected to see her alive and well again, a ransom of one hundred dollars had better be delivered to the appointed place, at the determined hour. Jeremiah had watched Nathaniel write and rewrite the note in a barely legible script———to make it seem more realistic.

Robert, who had not been brought into this scheme, had pulled out a bankroll and was peeling off bills. Nathaniel decided it would be best for Jeremiah to deliver the ransom as he had been given the note and could recognize the man who'd fled.

As for Genevieve, with opportunity thrust upon her, she took these few minutes before the curtain rose to go over to an empty bucket backstage and puke into it. She wretched again and again pitifully. Nathaniel stood beside her, and as she rose up, pale and sweating, he told her quietly, "Your performance so far is brilliant."

Her head swam, her skin was clammy and waxen. Her entrance was about ten minutes into the play, giving her enough time to be plunged into every station of panic. Nathaniel would be on stage alone when she would appear in his cell, an apparition dramatic and silent at the edge of the footlights.

Would she have even made it from the wings had it not been for Robert standing behind her and spearing her in the back with a steady hand? "Please," he whispered, "get the fuck out there."

She found her mark, and as she waited for Nathaniel to get through his monologue and notice her, she could feel the audience staring at her like some immense and shadowed jury of every person she had ever hustled and connived and lied to or robbed, ready to indict and convict her with their tacit disapproval for the fraud she truly was.

"Who are you?" said Nathaniel.

That was her cue to say, "Who I am is not important…But why I'm here is…you see…I've come to destroy your life." But it was as if her throat had been melted shut.

He came toward her, slowly, stretching the moment, letting the drama heighten, and covering for her at the same time.

"Who are you?" he said again.

He, like Genevieve, could feel a rising sense of uncertainty in the audience at her silence. Her not answering seemed to be going on forever.

The night's play was hanging in the balance of the next few moments. There is something beautiful and terrifying in that. To have moments fraught with such dire urgency is the essence of a living theatre. Nathaniel existed for such moments, they flooded his being with something almost holy. He was of the moment as he came toward her. "Who are you?" he said, but this time there was a fearful ferocity as he spoke, and he brought an arm back and slapped her so hard across the face he knocked her from her feet.

There was a collective gasp from the audience. A woman in the front row stood and pressed her tiny fists against her cheeks.

Genevieve looked up at Nathaniel. She was bleeding from her nose and mouth.

There were shouts of outrage from the audience, disgust, they seemed untethered from the comfortable entertainment of a play and brought to some other level of experience. They were involved, they seemed at one with this wounded creature of a woman on hands and knees just beyond the footlights.

As Genevieve wiped the blood from her face, a voice from the balcony came booming down, "Get up darlin' and have at the bastard." And then there was a run of applause, and whistles, and women calling to her, and something in her head clicked.

It happened so quickly, so empathetically, it was as if a toggle switch flipped on, and it felt so loud inside her head it almost hurt. Her voice, stuttering at first, came out with, "Who I am is not important..." then rising, "But why I am here is...You see...I've come to destroy your life..." Her speech was animated and alive and she began to improvise as she stood. "And I will bleed with pleasure at your undoing..."

That night the play had a violent energy impossible to duplicate, the emotions a fevered pitch beyond technique and training. Her performance was such the cast fully embraced her. She was conceived and born that night. It was like seeing some far flung star for the first time, and she kept asking Nathaniel, "What happened out there? What was that?" Nathaniel didn't know what it was, only that it was. That his actions had been driven by some actor's dark instinct.

Their sex that night put all that wild and unholy energy to good use. Afterward a sweating and naked Genevieve leaned out the hotel suite window and shouted down into a street of blue moonlight, "I'm an actress... do you hear?"

Her voice carried across the rooftops. Either a gaudy embarrassment or the rush of honest childlike expression, what difference?

She sat on the floor by the window with her back against the wall and cried into her cupped hands. "God," she said, her voice choked with joy, "was looking down on me tonight."

"Darlin'," Nathaniel said, "if anything, God was looking the other way."

CHAPTER 70

THE ACTRESS WHO HAD BEEN KIDNAPPED returned with Jeremiah after he'd paid "the ransom." She didn't go immediately to the authorities like any sane person would but rather set her sights on the newspapers instead. Her sense of self-promotion was second to none, and by the time her story hit the streets it was an incredulous concoction of lies and self aggrandizement.

The kidnappers were now part of the notorious Banditti of Illinois and Ohio. Cutthroats known for their heinous acts of violence. Once kidnapped, she had managed with her feminine wiles to escape into the woods where she was ultimately chased down. In a rage her kidnappers decided to murder her, and it was only through her calmness under pressure and talents at manipulation did she keep herself alive long enough for the ransom to arrive.

"All that's missing from the story," Nathaniel said looking up from the newspaper, "are the hunting dogs snipping at her heels."

Jeremiah was curious. "Is everyone in show business a blatant liar?"

Nathaniel tossed aside the paper. "That's one of the primary requirements."

The actress was quickly pursued by a number of theatre company directors who saw in her story an exploitable play——the modern American maiden, a pure working girl, contemporary villains, drama, suspense, violence——which she herself could star in. One theatre director even had a promotional flier made up—**THE KIDNAPPED ACTRESS.**

Backstage she met with Nathaniel and Robert to hand in her notice. She was quitting the play that very day for a "grand opportunity." Did she give them a chance to match her other offers? Certainly not. She was being promised Boston and New York, not Detroit and Cincinnati.

She shed a few polite tears, there were the cursory hugs, the holding of hands, the wishing someone well. The scene was just dripping with faux sentimentality.

For quitting them that way Robert would have liked to chop her head off. But at least they had Genevieve in the wings. Hopefully, she wasn't just a one nighter. Robert could not understand why Nathaniel took this all so glibly.

What could he tell Robert? That what actually happened was a lot more play worthy than that phony melodrama in the newspapers.

As the actress left the theatre, she had to walk past Genevieve who was conversing with some of the other performers. The two women took a moment for what was to be their good-bye. There had never been bad blood between them, just quiet disdain. The actress was glad to have Genevieve as her understudy as she considered her an untalented whore who slept with the leading man.

"I hear," said the actress, "you gave a reasonable performance last night."

"Judging from the applause you usually got," said Genevieve, "I would say my performance far exceeded reasonable."

"I also hear," said the actress, "that your finest moment came when you were retching into a fire bucket. That's when your talents really shone through."

The other performers found all this deliciously nasty and they tittered accordingly, egging the ladies on. Nathaniel and Robert, on the other hand, from their work table far across the stage, saw all this quite differently.

"There's going to be trouble," said Robert.

"One can hope," said Nathaniel.

Well, while the actress went back to her extended goodbye to the cast, Genevieve walked over to one of the fire buckets, picked it up, lugged it across stage then called to the actress. As she turned, Genevieve gave her a damn good dousing. There was a throatful gasp from the actress. Her body stiffened, her arms spread out, her hands fisted. She looked down at herself. She was dripping wet, her new dress a sloppy wad of ruffles.

It would be an insult to call it a fistfight. The women preferred to kick and claw and tear at each other's clothes. They dragged each other around by the hair like wild Indians. Genevieve beat the actress over the head with the heel of one of her shoes, while the actress bit into Genevieve's arm, gnawing at the flesh like some maniacal ghoul.

• • •

The *Kidnapped Actress* never made it to Boston or New York. But, it did play in Baltimore, Charleston and Charlotte. Only by then it had been reenvisioned and

rewritten any number of times and was now called *The Southern Belle.*

In this version of the play, the maiden was the daughter of a well to do Southern planter who was kidnapped by abolitionists and their "nigger henchman." It was a driving hit across the South that aroused violent reactions in its audience. It was, to the Southerner, the antidote to such works as *Uncle Tom's Cabin* and other anti-slavery plays.

I saw *The Southern Belle* once with Nathaniel and Robert. We sat in the farthest reaches of the balcony. My people were the "nigger henchman," but we weren't even allowed to portray the violent subhuman dregs they cast us as. That was left to whites in black face. Emotions cut so close to the marrow that people in the audience flung bottles at the whites in black face. I wondered, did that speak more to the power of the theatre, or the profound hatred within man that he cannot understand or control.

"They're throwing bottles at themselves," said Robert. "And they don't even know it."

• • •

Genevieve looked like serenity herself resting up after her sideshow with the actress. Her performance that night was more assured than the first, and the following night more refined than the previous, and the following night more refined than the last. Wherever she went, she was a work in progress, throwing her lines at perfect strangers, at children walking with their mothers, at sidewalk vendors, shop clerks in doorways, drunks, reprobates, policemen. Even an emaciated dog sleeping on a sunny patch of sidewalk got her full dramatic performance.

Around a week in and during a long monologue, she pulled out paper and tobacco and rolled herself a cigarette to the shock of her audience. It had been improvised and secret, just as she'd told Jeremiah, who watched from the wings. She lit up. Her fellow actors knew they were being upstaged, and women in the audience looked on with stunned interest, some stood to see better. A gent from the cheap seats shouted, "Smoke away, honey. Give them lips some exercise." A round of applause followed, and not to be outdone, Genevieve threw her head back and blew out a small storm cloud of grey smoke.

Her vanity was at least a match for her talents, and her vanity was boundless. She was in the grasp of her dream and gaining on it every day. She had a paper carte de visite made up with her photograph and name, to be given out to well to do fans and admirers. This was done before it became the rage.

Secretly, the company actors wished she was still backstage puking into a fire bucket. Knowing that, Genevieve made light of her fellow thespians. She had a fire bucket with her name plated on it, which she kept outside her small draped off dressing room.

Colonel Tearwood's American Theatre Company was beginning to feed on its notoriety, while behind the scenes they still quietly delivered runaways to the shores of a free Canada. On those nights the actors gave way to the raw material of humanity, moving in darkness and on bleak tides for the betterment of man. And where even their shallowness was a thing to admire.

As for Robert, he was deep into an adaptation of the book Genevieve had given him, *Wuthering Heights*. He had changed the moody and impassioned love story from the moorlands of Yorkshire to the mansions of Fifth Avenue, with their neighborhood carriage houses and stables.

In Robert's mind this play was to be the American Theatre Company's triumphant return to New York. This was to be where they artistically spit in the face of the powerful who had run them out. He would, with the same sleight of hand as in *The Monster*, transform this dark and brooding piece into political and social theatre.

Robert was quietly in love with Genevieve, and this would be his attempt to turn her into a classic tragedienne. The play was for her. He wrote as he always did, isolated in his room, feeding off his loneliness and sobriety. In these late still hours, trying to weather his emotions, he came to realize he and his mother both suffered the same fate——unrequited love.

Nathaniel knew this, but would never hurt or demean his friend by even mentioning it. He made sure Genevieve never did either, knowing she would take advantage of Robert's sensitivity, warning her in no uncertain terms as they lay in bed. "Don't let the beautiful crystal goblet prove to have a flaw in the glass."

She pulled the sheets up, covering her face, except for those depthless pooling eyes staring up at him like something from *The Arabian Nights*. "Why Mister Luck, I believe you're jealous."

"I save my jealousy for the stage," he answered.

"Can I tell you something, Mister Luck? If I lost you…I believe I'd die."

He kissed her. "No one lies as wonderfully as you…even when you're telling the truth."

They both broke out in gaudy laughter and Genevieve slammed her hand on the wall. "Can you hear us in there, cousin?"

CHAPTER 71

"Who would have thought the stage the perfect hiding place for an actor who'd committed murder?" came a man's voice.

They were in the empty theatre running through scenes of *Wuthering Heights* that Robert had been drafting. There was he, there was Nathaniel and Genevieve, and there was Jeremiah, who by now was the endlessly overworked stage manager who answered to no one but his two employers.

The four looked out into the darkened theatre. The man who had spoken was coming through the shadows and Robert recognized him right away. What he'd feared most had materialized. The man was coming down the aisle just as the monster had all those years ago in another theatre, carrying an arm in a sack.

"Colonel Tearwood's American Theatre Company," said the man.

Nathaniel knew from Robert's description this was the English gentleman known as Lord Halsey.

"Did you know he's a murderer?" said Halsey, directing his comment to Genevieve. "He killed his young wife and her father. She was an actress… just like you. And…he left a daughter behind." Halsey held up the flier with Nathaniel's image. "I sent a number of these back to England. People will be able to identify you. And we'll see you taken back." He stood at the edge of the stage, looking up.

Lord Halsey said no more. He did not try to press an advantage, if indeed he had one. He turned and started back into the darkness, just like that. If Nathaniel knew nothing more, he knew the constellation of his career, as it had been, was no more. It shocked him to realize it was his career being ruined, and not his life, that so affected him.

"Is it true?" said a stunned Genevieve.

Halsey could hear her, and she knew that.

"I did not kill the girl," said Nathaniel. "She was not my wife. We did not have a daughter together."

"And the father?" said Halsey.

Silence fell about the stage that as an actress and woman she understood. "God damn you," she said. "You've allowed me to feel hatred for myself over my failings while you hide behind your secrets——"

Her cousin told her to "hush her mouth," and she turned on him with a vengeance. "You keep your place, or I'll have you sent packin'. You understand me, boy?"

"The way she'd said "boy," they all knew she meant "nigger.""

Jeremiah looked worse than defamed, this coming from his own blood. "It's all just chance, woman," he said. "Just chance."

"And no one," said Robert, "sends anyone packing from this company but Nathaniel and me."

"Yeah...well, don't confuse the past with the future," said Genevieve.

"What does that mean?" said Nathaniel.

She pointed to their treadmill prop, cast by shades of the moon slipping down through the skylight. "Someday a woman will play the convict and the man will play the ghost. And that day is coming."

• • •

There was a knock at the hotel room door just as he expected. He reached over from the chair where he sat for the revolver he had placed close at hand on the table. "You can come in," he said.

As light from the hall fell flat across the widening doorway, there stood Robert Harrison. He looked into the dimly lit suite that smelled stale with smoke and musty old furniture.

"How is it they chose you?" said Halsey.

"Natural selection," said Robert. He closed the door behind him. He had noted the heavy calibre weapon in the Englishman's lap.

"I expected it to be that loud mouthed bitch."

"No...we thought at least to give you a fighting chance."

"I'm not Mister Jonah...who disappears after talking with a worn out middle aged matron and a pair of nigger servants."

Robert went and sat on the edge of the bed. He could look Halsey eye to eye now. "My mother would take umbrage at being called a middle aged matron. She rather thinks of herself as splendid."

Robert went to reach into his coat. Halsey sat forward, everything about him on guard, the revolver hoisted. Robert carefully removed from a pocket a pint bottle of the good doctor.

"Addict, hey," said Halsey.

Robert wiped at the sweat accumulating on his face. "Being an addict…
makes you aware that everyone is addicted to something…Everyone."

As Robert drank away, Halsey said, "How did you and your mother
get involved with such dregs?"

"As you should have discovered, my mother's brother is the original
Colonel Tearwood, which suggests it's in the blood." He pointed the bottle
at Halsey. "My mother learned about you from friends at the embassy.
You're a remittance man. Reviled at home. No more a lord than you are the
Queen of Egypt. There's a whisper that your predilections have damned
you of all deliverance. Too bad you could not find something akin to the
theatre for expression. It's a lot more forgiving than the world in general."

"I don't need to be preached to, and I won't be persuaded."

"How might you be proffered?"

"If I can better my station by taking a man down…I shall better my
station."

Robert stoppered the bottle. He stood and started for the door. "John
James Beaufort is dead."

"To say it and prove it are two different matters."

"Like a good play…one must prepare for the last act right from the
beginning."

As Robert walked out, the suite closing behind him, he heard Halsey
remark, "Tell that to the reporters."

Whatever that meant left Robert cold.

CHAPTER 72

NATHANIEL SAT FROZEN AGAINST A MOONLIGHT WINDOW. The nightmare returns in all its justice and injustice. Is it God's hand making him wake every day to uncertainty? He thought of the wonderous beauty that had been lost to him. He had barely been old enough to play *Romeo and Juliet* let alone live it. He will always see her in that broken down auditorium on the pulpit, unloosing her hair during the balcony scene as he auditioned for her father. It was the future she was unloosing at that moment, with all its dreams and hopes and dark recourse.

From somewhere in the darkness, Genevieve said, "I would give anything to have been loved like that. I never was at that age. There was only desire and desperation."

"You're loved now," he said.

"But not like that."

She was right, he thought, but didn't say it.

"I will remember this," she said, "someday onstage. I will need this. I will need to know what it's like." She felt foolish and shallow for having said it. She felt selfish because she knew she was selfish. And that is what she had to give...her selfishness.

• • •

The story broke the next morning and very quickly Robert knew what Halsey had meant when last they'd talked. As he came out of his hotel room, the playwright was ambushed by a reporter with the draft of a story he was working on. He wanted Harrison to confirm or deny the facts, as given to him by Lord Halsey. The lead was as follows:

IS ACCLAIMED ACTOR
WANTED PICKWICK PAPERS MURDERER?

Robert showed the story to Nathaniel. Genevieve hovered over his shoulder, reading along with him. "Well," said she, "divine intervention is out of the question…so what do we do?"

She was shocked the men were not as panic stricken as herself. Jeremiah was sent out to organize a press conference for that afternoon at the theatre. A black being put in a position of such authority, and over a matter as cutting, aroused partisan political emotions. Even in a city as liberal as Cleveland. This was treacherous ground and it could have a negative effect, as there were no black stage managers of theatrical companies, except for the few black troupes in existence, and they didn't count.

The theatre that afternoon didn't just swarm with reporters and other men of the press, but with vipers of every shape and stripe, claiming a story to sell or a promise of secret information. On stage stood the members of Colonel Tearwood's American Theatre Company. Nathaniel stepped forward as spokesman.

"The man you are looking for known as John James Beaufort is dead. Both Robert Harrison and I knew the youth. He was an actor we befriended. He was also a friend of Robert's uncle in England…the original Colonel Tearwood. That is how we met."

As Nathaniel spoke, he was relentlessly shouted down by Halsey calling him "murderer" and "liar." From all quarters, questions by reporters were hurled at him to test his veracity. Nathaniel remained calm and collected, as being the accomplished actor that he was, could play the part of the calm and collected actor.

"Next week," Nathaniel said, "we will be in Buffalo performing our hit play *The Treadmill*. We ask you to come there, as John James Beaufort is buried in a public cemetery in that city. And if you care to…we will have the body exhumed, and you can see for yourself…"

What followed was a whirlwind of bizarre actions and a treatise on the unconditional defects of human character. The actors were approached and offered money from reporters for anything about Nathaniel that would prove newsworthy or lead to his guilt.

The blacks who worked backstage were approached in a more iron-handed manner. They were intimidated and threatened. They were beneath being bought off, you see. As for Jeremiah, he returned a beating he got for his ignorance with reserved silence.

When Nathaniel wasn't being insulted or accosted, called out or condemned like a dangerous criminal, he was being asked for his autograph. His suite was broken into, it was ransacked, he was robbed. A hat was stolen right off his head by a youth who outran him. His belongings were being sold as souvenirs.

If Halsey believed going to the press would lead to the downfall of Luck's stage life and hasten his reckoning, he was a triumphant failure.

Nathaniel Luck was becoming that most problematic of human characters——a celebrity. The last days of the play were sellouts. People will gladly pay to see a possible murderer who has escaped the law. They will watch him perform and imagine him strangling his beautiful young wife and then beating his father in-law to death. It's all that pent up violence behind the pleasant, handsome face that had women sending him notes of introduction and proposals of marriage.

Each one of these notes enraged Genevieve all the more. She tore them up, she set them on fire, threw them out the hotel window, ground them into the sand with a shoe heel, and when she could no longer bear it, forced them back into the bustiers of the women who asked she pass them on to Nathaniel.

As for Nathaniel, he had committed a murder, and the terrible memory of it, and the tragedy that led to it, that he'd hid in the hushed blackness of his soul was being relived now in the real world. There was no escaping its sorrow. Drink did not help, sex did not help, affection and love did not help. His only freedom from its menace was the stage. That's when Nathaniel Luck no longer existed, when John James Beaufort was dead and gone. When life was a beautiful five acts and a few minutes of applause.

And yet, there were flashes when a fear struck him. What happens if I lose this? What happens if the world invades my stage?

CHAPTER 73

THERE WAS A BURIAL GROUND IN BUFFALO run by the Charity Foundation of the Episcopal Church. In its office records was paperwork that said a John James Beaufort was buried in a common grave: Grave 19———Casket 6. He had been interred for over a year. His age was listed as twenty-seven, his cause of death being alcoholism.

The Foundation agreed to exhume the body. Rumor had it a number of newspapers had banded together and offered the foundation a sizable stipend.

There were well over fifty people there. Two dozen reporters, at least, from Cleveland, Buffalo, Albany, one from even as far as New York. The rest were the devotionally curious.

The unearthing of the grave would take hours. The people set out blankets, they brought basket lunches and drink. It was an unkempt burial ground, uncommonly sad with some of the trees being dead, their bark scored and black, the ground uneven and deeply weeded.

Halsey stood among the reporters with his arms crossed claiming all this a sham. A conspiracy to disguise the truth.

Nathaniel waited and watched from a small patch of shade away from the grave. He was stared down at, remarked at, questioned. Tensions rose with the heat and the slow cadenced gutting of the earth. Robert and Genevieve, with her parasol, even Jeremiah, bore their stations beside Nathaniel. They too suffered remarks that stiffened with insult and injury.

"All they'll dig up is more lies," said Halsey. "Because that's all there is to dig up…lies."

That huge block of a man was trying to stoke up a little anger, create some rage. You could feel the bad will in the steamy air.

Genevieve certainly could. Maybe it was being a woman and black she could feel tense militancy before it surfaced in the words. Then something happened to cut into the moment. She handed her cousin her parasol. "Don't run off with it," she said.

She walked out into the sunlight to the grave where she picked up an unused shovel. The gravediggers took to staring when she asked to be helped down into the two feet of dug earth and began to work alongside them. She shoveled until she knew she had aroused absolute curiosity, then she looked to Nathaniel and slipped right into the gravediggers scene from *Hamlet*.

"Did you, sir," she said, "just ask me… 'Whose grave is this?'"

With that, he was in the moment, as only an actor could, "Why, yes," he said… "and I'll ask again… 'Whose grave is this?'"

"Mine, sir," she said. She began to sing and shovel and sing and shovel… "O pit of clay for to be made…for such a guest is meet…"

• • •

Had it been a spontaneous revelation, or a well planned ploy? No matter. In that blazing sunlight, they were beautiful to watch. They didn't need sets, or props or wardrobe, they just were. Put all their personal vanities and ego aside, these were righteous performers, and the reporters were all caught up in the scene. They had out their notebooks and scraps of writing paper…Playing the gravediggers scene from *Hamlet* **during the actual exhumation of a body… buoyant, joyous, maybe even a touch jaded. Wonderful press. Wonderful. And the fact there was a photographer there…though he never said how he had been informed of the exhumation.**

Halsey stood among the reporters and the ridiculous, towering over this sycophantic mob, shouting, "You're not actually listening to them like they're human beings. They're actors—Deluding you is their stock and trade."

I had to laugh privately. This was coming from a man who put the word 'Lord' in front of his surnamed. Of course, he wasn't incorrect in all that he was shouting.

I'm sure most of you have seen the photographs of the scene, as they have been printed and reprinted everywhere. Nathaniel and Genevieve posing at

the gravesite; with the gravediggers, them alone, Nathaniel holding a stone as if it were the skull of Yorick taken from the grave. And the casket when it was first brought up from the earth, with Nathaniel and Genevieve flanking it. Who knew then that those photographs of both of them with the casket would come to have so many meanings.

• • •

While the gravediggers pried open the casket boards, the reporters crowded in around them. A slat of dusty light fell upon part of the face of what was a boy around the right age. His beard had grown after all that time, as it will. His face was like a dried out footprint and streaked with the muddy grime where the groundwater had seeped through what was little more than a crate. He lay in a plain and rumpled suit that had been eaten away with rot.

Halsey had muscled his way to the head of the casket. "This proves nothing..."

"Take a look there," said Robert. He was pointing to the withered folded hands of the dead youth. The shirt sleeves peeking out from the coat. The gold cufflinks done to look like dice. Too expensive and beautiful by far for the corpse they adorned.

"This is all just an ingenuous fraud," said Halsey, and he kicked at the casket as if to codify his point. "They're actors, for god damn sake. You can't trust a word coming out of their mouths."

"I'm not an actor," said Robert.

"You're a writer...that's even worse."

"Take photos," Robert said to the reporters, "of John James body. Send them to England and let my cousin identify him. And those cufflinks. Get a picture...for they belonged to my uncle and he gave them to John James."

CHAPTER 74

COLONEL TEARWOOD'S AMERICAN THEATRE COMPANY made its newsworthy return to New York. The Bowery Theatre, rebuilt and grander than before, would stage the New York premiere of *The Treadmill* to be followed up by the first national showing of the American adaption of *Wuthering Heights*.

They stood on the stage of the empty theatre with its cavernous walls of private boxes and scaling rows of finely clothed seats up to a deep and darkened balcony.

"I was in this theatre as a little girl," said Genevieve. "With my father. I saw the *Elephant of Siam and the Fire Fiend...The Wild Horse of Ukraine*. They were the only decent things he ever did for me."

"Then he up and sold you off as a maid," said Jeremiah.

"Yes..." She went slowly to her knees and ran her fingers across the wooden stage floor. She looked out at the theatre. She was a portrait of private victory and vain, beautiful, thrilling success.

"Four thousand seats," said Robert. "One of the largest playhouses in the world." He glanced at Nathaniel. "And we're back." The words came out in a deep, sweet breath.

The theatre catered to the more well to do now, but the gallery was the domain of the Irish and German immigrants who'd taken over the lower east side neighborhoods that harbored The Bowery. The theatre managers were all about sensational melodrama and heightened tragedy.

The Bowery already had boys on the streets passing out fliers for the play and shouting, "Come see the Pickwick Papers murderer."

• • •

Stories came back from England about John James Beaufort that contradicted each other, that eddied and curtained from povertied quarters to the prestigious house of Beaufort. Even the Colonel himself, approached by reporters, indulged them in taverns where they paid for his brew with tales of John James. "I'll tell you this. His English was too good for a pauper or orphan. I think the closest we'll ever get to the truth was when he was on stage disguised as a prince."

One night in Manhattan, Jeremiah sat alone with Robert, drinking away the moon, and said to the playwright, "Do you think it a lie? That he might well have been married and murdered his wife and abandoned his daughter?"

That scarred face was all a question. "You don't live with people as they were, but as they are." He then shared with the youth a secret. "I'm working on a play about all of this. About all of us."

• • •

A dinner was held for the company at the Knickerbocker Ballroom on Fifth Avenue. It was a formal affair with a full orchestra. The dance floor had been imported from Barcelona with paneled art for the walls showing scenes one would not speak of in polite company.

Nathaniel and Genevieve were asked to take the ceremonial opening dance. They were a touchstone of elegance and beauty. She was glamour personified. Being stared at and envied were about as close to heaven as she could get. But she saw something else in Nathaniel's eyes.

"What is it?" she said.

"For what I've done, I feel guilt," he said. "And for bringing it down on you and the others."

"I'm black," she whispered. "Remember. I would barely be a servant here if any of these creatures knew. It's all a fraud, make peace with that."

And there was truth there. Millicent had, for example, sent an invitation to John Jacob Astor, viewing it as socially correct, and a means of assuaging old wounds. He had a servant bring his response — the invitation torn to shreds.

Nathaniel, sharing a toast with the others, thought back to years upon years of nights on stage and in prison and on the streets of New York to those last weeks in England, seeing Lucretia the evening they met on the roof and her warning him not to respond to her father, not to audition for his troupe.

Never had poison looked so beautiful and necessary to one's being. Now Lucretia was nothingness and dust. Juliet had died, while Romeo waited in the wings.

• • •

Robert sent the family coach away without him and walked home that night, alone. He had turned down any number of parties because he was consumed by an agonizing jealousy. Watching the full display of their beauty and passion, their almost otherworldly presence inflamed his profound personal loneliness.

His desire for her played havoc with his need for love, and those dark Manhattan streets he walked gave him time and mood and backdrop to reach down into the turmoil that was his soul.

Then there he was suddenly, in formal wear and top hat, sitting on a curb feeling the most vile sentiments of such emotional poison. Because the emotional poison that cuts your heart out is nothing more than the emotional poison that cuts your heart out, until you turn it into art.

So, beneath a street lamp, there he sat, a lost figure, lonely in all his elegance, sketching out agonies for his adaption of Wuthering Heights, pouring all that black pain and jealousy into the voices that would become Nathaniel and Genevieve…and even himself. For it was only on paper that he was master of his pain.

ACT V

CHAPTER 75

ROSINA SWAIN WAS BARELY OLD ENOUGH TO PLAY JULIET, let alone be Juliet. She had been born and raised and orphaned in England and was chaperoned to America by the sister of a man who worked at the British Embassy in New York. The embassy had seen to a place for her to live at a decorous woman's rooming house across from The Church of the Holy Angels. She was there, allegedly, to study acting and see if she could start a life. She carried the truth in a small silk pouch that was always on her person.

The Treadmill had played at the Bowery Theatre for a record seventy-nine performances the night Rosina Swain took a seat close to the stage. This was the world of her memory and dreams. The place between everything she knew, and everything she didn't. She quietly sat there trembling, knowing he was somewhere in the darkness beyond the lights.

When the curtain began to rise she grasped the seat handles, a clammy sweat began about her throat, her heart raced, it hurt so. Applause rose from that vast theatre.

Then there was the treadmill and the cells and a shadow figure lying on a cot rose and stepped from the edges of the stage dramatically. "He don't look like a murderer," someone shouted from the balcony. There was a surge of feet stomping on the floor and whistling, and more shouting and applause that she could feel through the very bones of the building in the boards beneath her feet.

He came forward and Rosina pressed back. He was there above her, his face in stark contrast, thanks to the lights beneath him.

This...this was the man who had stalked her life through all the years of rage and loneliness, of wondering and need, who lived within her beyond all natural law.

• • •

What was worse was that he was thrilling to watch, and being that he might be her father exhausted her anger. After the play, she crowded into the alley along with others there to steal a look or hustle a signing.

She hung back in conspiratorial silence, where she could watch and not be seen. He had a forgiving smile and a face that looked to have suffered and she was disarmed momentarily. People were so close around him, it would be easy to take the gun from her silk pouch and walk right up and shoot him.

Her life became his life. She followed him ceaselessly. She meant to know before she killed him, her grievance was grounded in truth. She watched the hotel where he lived with Genevieve in a third floor suite that faced the street, the elegant home on Lafayette Place where the playwright lived with his mother, when he was not keeping time at a brothel. And the nice looking black youth, the stage manager, he didn't live with other blacks, but stayed at the house of the playwright's mother.

Theirs was the life of theatre people, successful people, people who went to parties, who thrived on attention, who slept late, who ate well, who drank a lot and yet——

On certain nights, long after the moon had gone, in those witching hours when there was a nervous stillness about the city, a handful of blacks would be brought to the house on Lafayette. Four, five, in number, often with small children. They would be led out back to the stables where they would be loaded into a freight wagon with huge wooden sides. The wagon would then wend its slow way to the docks and a small steam powered launch.

There the wagon would be unloaded, but there were no blacks. There was just a handful of crates or barrels, sometimes a few long boxes. And these would be placed on the launch that would then make its slow chugging way up the Hudson River. She did not understand at first, but over time, when she learned about America and the underground railroad, she understood.

There were always two of the four with the wagon when it made its sojourn to the river. She spent many a solitary hour in her small room adding this to the inventory of information she collected, so she would not become a bloodthirsty creature without a reason.

What made it all worse, Nathaniel Luck, her alleged father and her mother's killer was charming, and he was handsome, and he seemed goodhearted, even daring, and it made her cry. She desperately needed to hate him, and if he was not all the vile things she had been taught, she wanted him to see her face to face and know she was his daughter.

. . .

"I'd like to talk to the stage manager, please."

Jeremiah turned. There was a girl standing in the actors' entry. She was backlit in perfect stillness.

"I'm the stage manager," said Jeremiah.

Rosina came forward a few steps. Her hands were folded. Jeremiah could make out the girl had short black curly hair, but her face was still in shadow. "I'm trying to find out about the auditions for *Wuthering Heights*. You're still putting on the play?"

Another voice came sweeping in from the dressing rooms, "The woman's part is cast. And besides...You're too young."

Rosina recognized the figure striding toward her as one of the performers in *The Treadmill*.

"There's a part in the book. The heroine's younger sister."

"How old are you?" said the actor.

"Eighteen."

"Fifteen is more like it."

"Which," said Jeremiah, "was about the age of the younger sister in the book. Wasn't it?"

Rosina looked to him now. "That's right," she said.

The actor took umbrage at being upstaged, so to speak. He started off toward the exit and told Jeremiah, "Make sure my boots are shined for tonight's performance."

Jeremiah motioned for Rosina to follow him. They entered a small office of dusty ledgers. There was a window high up in the wall and the sun came down in a long hard block of light. Closing the door, he could see her now. She had a long delicate nose and deep dark eyes to match her hair, made all the darker because of her eggshell skin. She was like the other end of the world.

"How old *are* you?" said Jeremiah.

"How old *are* you?" she answered.

He grinned, and he pointed to where she should sit. He took up his place behind the desk. He set one ledger aside and placed another before him.

"What's your name?" he said.

"Rosina Swain."

"You English?" he said as he wrote.

"I was born there."

"You sound kinda English. But not exactly."

"The people that raised me were in a religious group from Pennsylvania."

"Where are your folks?"

"Dead."

"You're alone here then."

"Alone as can be."

"Where do you live?"

"The Excelsior…it's a ladies boarding house down on Twelfth Street. Very nice, very proper."

She gave him the exact address and he wrote it down.

"You been in any plays in New York? Know any of the theatre managers?"

"No plays here…no theatre managers. I performed in England. Musical parts, children's parts."

"He wrote a date and a time on a scrap of paper. "You come back then. We'll be arranging for auditions."

She stood and thanked him and slipped the scrap of paper into the silk pouch she carried. "That actor," she said, "from a minute ago."

"What about him?"

"I saw the play…his performance…too much brass, as they say, and too little thought."

He understood, and he thanked her with a nod.

He followed her to the door. She had to cross backstage to leave. That's when she saw him. He was in conference with Genevieve and Robert Harrison by the dressing rooms.

She passed along in the shadow, moving among the theatre crew to steal time to study him, to imagine him with her mother. A mother she only knew now like drops of memory from rainy dreams and a lone photo marred and flaking with time.

The moment swam with emotions as something drove her to be seen, or at the very least to be acknowledged with his eyes.

• • •

She was just a girl stepping out of the busy clutter of noisy stage hands shuttling props and scenery. A girl in a simple smock in the light of the huge shipping doors and he felt suddenly this change of expression come over him, as if something inside him had buckled, or he had lost his footing as he climbed a flight of stairs. Looking at her, he could feel the silence of years peel away. She turned, she waved at someone. He saw…it was Jeremiah.

Jeremiah joined Nathaniel and the others. The others who had noticed nothing. "Who was that?" said Nathaniel.

"The girl?"

"Yes."

"Actress…wants to read for the part of the younger sister in *Wuthering Heights*."

Nathaniel watched her and watched her until she walked into the day and was no more.

"She's English," said Jeremiah. "Is here all alone. Parents are dead."

"Are they?" said Nathaniel.

CHAPTER 76

ROSINA WAS HAVING DINNER with other women at the boarding house when a matron entered who appeared none too pleased and addressed her. "Miss Swain…you have a visitor."

She'd had no visitors, and any visitor aroused the curiosity of the other women. Rosina stood and excused herself and started for the parlor. "Not that way," the matron said, which clearly meant there was someone outside of low station.

Jeremiah was waiting down a few steps in the yard with its sheds and privy's.

"What brings you here?" said Rosina.

The matron was watching out a window with a decided stare. And she was not alone, there were other windows with vague images of the curious who deigned to inspect the situation.

"How would you like to go somewhere to practice your acting with others like yourself?"

"Why…yes."

"Now…I mean…tonight."

Rosina returned to the house to retrieve her coat and purse. The matron was anything, if not dictatorial, about her not going out at night, unchaperoned, with a young Negro.

"He's stage manager of the American Theatre Company," she said. "They have that hit play at the Bowery Theatre. I'm being invited to meet other actors…like myself."

One of the boarders huffed at such a preposterous notion. Another said, "There is foolish, and there is disgusting."

Their looks of concern bordered on outright hostility. "I managed to get across the Atlantic," said Rosina. "I believe I can get across Manhattan."

"Manhattan is a lot tougher to cross than the Atlantic," the matron warned her.

• • •

"They were against you coming out with me," said Jeremiah.

"I'm sure you could hear. So, I won't lie to you."

She followed him to the streetcar line. The first car to come along, pulled by a couple of thick bodied draft horses, was for whites only. The next car coming up through the dark had a sign: COLOREDS ALLOWED.

They waited their turn to board when they did, the driver became adamant. "Not you two," he said.

"The sign," said Jeremiah.

"We let niggers on. But not ones with their prostitutes. What do you think this is?"

At first Rosina had no idea the driver meant her. They were already halfway up the car steps when the driver reached for a truncheon he kept wedged up in the seat beneath him. "You hear me, Jade? You and that tramp get off now. Or do I have to persuade you?"

Jeremiah was face to face with a club that looked like it had been in a few scrapes. "It's not what you think, sir."

Rosina tugged at the back of his coat. "Let's just get off."

As the streetcar pulled away, the driver clanged the bell long and hard. They stood there now in the street, degraded. A woman yelled to Rosina as she passed. "You should go home and scrub your heart, girl."

Rage filled Jeremiah's guts, but what could he do about it? Rosina stared down at the street, waiting for sweet distance to be put between themselves and the streetcar.

"I'm sorry," he said.

She looked up. She wanted to tell him it didn't matter, but she knew that it did.

He started up the street. "This is one of my most humiliating moments," he said.

His voice spilled out with pain. She knew that much emotional distress was the child of long time suffering. A river of deep and wide tears her own empty passage of life had taught her. Hopes trampled, she'd heard, are the predecessor of death and death but a mere reckoning.

It had not dawned on her that this scheme to get at the truth would have to be served by climbing into the lives of those she meant to coerce the truth from.

They walked along quietly down through the Sixth Ward with its busy streets of shanty immigrants that blacks lived among. They were not an outlaw couple suddenly, just part of the honest human pittance on those streets, as unlikely and unrewarded as the rest.

From out of nowhere, Jeremiah said, "You never asked."

"What?"

"Usually they can't ask fast enough."

"I don't understand."

"Not five minutes they know me, and they ask...Is Nathaniel Luck a murderer?"

Surprised, she looked as if he had caught her thinking. "Oh...everyone asks?"

He nodded.

"Maybe I will...sometime. But would you tell me the truth?"

CHAPTER 77

No one had ever turned the question like that. He tried to read her expression. You might call it a smile, you couldn't be sure. The eyes were so dark and deep they gave every expression of hers a kind of edge.

Jeremiah turned into a rough looking alley of deep shadows and brick walls. Rosina was frightened and kept close beside him. He saw how she bore her fear silently, and it impressed him. He could have told her to not be afraid, but he worried that would demean her somehow.

Partway down, they reached a high wooden fence with lights on the other side. They came to a scrapwood gate with a sign on it——**Actors Paradise**. He swung the gate open and a whole world spread out before her.

It was a fenced off yard framed on three sides by tenements. There were half a dozen makeshift stages with small groups of actors practicing their craft, performing, playing out scenes from plays, some she recognized, others she did not. They were fresh faced artists, weathered artists, white and black artists, some had accents, some were pre-occupied with finessing makeup or how to express themselves with body language. There were no social borders there, no class structure, it was a raw and itinerant free for all.

And the apartment dwellers, many were watching from their windowsills after a long, hard day. Others sat on the back stoops or homemade benches, some had parked themselves on blankets. It was like a vast outdoor theatre slum on a hot night and the air smelled of cooked foods and tobacco.

It was, she thought, a rehearsal for paradise.

• • •

For Nathaniel Luck, the scene in the empty lot was the future of the theatre. He sat in the second story window of a brothel Robert frequented. He liked to come here, drink, watch the players perform, to feed on their energy, to sometimes go down there and act himself and experiment with the unknown. He understood, you see, that the theatre as he knew it, as he had experienced it, had not long to live. A new level of life and death realism was out there moving among the shadows. A lot of theatre people disagreed with him. Maybe having committed a murder made him acutely sensitive to change. Change being unfed hungers and unrelieved rage.

The theatre one day would be what was going on in that empty lot. Whites would perform side by side with blacks. That black faced minstrel nonsense would be gone with the wind. Plays would be about the poor, the hated, the desperate, the racist, the gangs that marauded the streets of lower Manhattan. They would be about the lives of the immigrant souls in the windows of the tenements around him.

He thought that was why *The Treadmill* attracted the public——seeing a convicted felon and possible murderer brought a striking level of reality to the stage that melodrama and conceits could not. A new audience was being born before his very eyes out of a tortured American landscape. And playwrights of the future would capitalize on that proactive fact to feed the public's imagination.

But that's not why Nathaniel Luck was there that night. To look at her down there, enjoining with the other actors swept him back into his youth when life was an incandescent present. And everything you longed for, longed for you. She was Lucretia, Lucretia's windswept hair and the snowy skin, that shouldery walk, and the striking downward angle to her head as she listened and smiled and expressed herself with a gesture. Everything from that time in London had left just one vast scar, and to see her there, the scar was torn open and he bled memories. Can you bleed to death from memories, he wondered. Maybe that is the most fitting way to go, if not the easiest. Of course, he could be wrong about her. Her look and manner being just accidental rustlings.

But if he were right, as he believed, she had come into their world under a cloak. The waif starting a new life in a new country. A story anyone opens their arms to. This told him she was graced with a plan. And a plan is begot from a reason. And what could that reason be? Dear God... if she were there to avenge, or revenge, what would it do to her? "Walk the pastures of plenty in a lifetime of poison..." A line from a play he could not remember, from somewhere in London.

• • •

When Jeremiah arrived at the hotel in the morning, you could hear screaming all the way down the hall. Guests stood in their doorways, and he realized the violent drama was coming from Nathaniel and Genevieve's suite.
It was Genevieve's voice Jeremiah heard so decidedly. "I want you out of
my life…I want my freedom…I want a chance to live the life that my
relationship with you is stealing from me…Do you understand? I won't be
held back anymore."

Something shattered. Jeremiah made his way down the corridor,
excusing himself. He knocked on the door. He dare not look back for fear
of the looks he was getting, never mind the low threats and insults. He had
to knock again before the shouting stopped. He heard the door unlock
then it swung open… And there was Genevieve, barefoot, in a sleeping
smock, seemingly alone, with a manuscript in one hand and a bottle of
wine in the other.

"What are you doing here?" she said to her cousin. She then noticed all
the people in the hallway. "What's going on? Is there a fire or something?"

He understood now. He pointed to the manuscript in her hand, which
was a draft of *Wuthering Heights*. It took a moment, but she realized. She
stood in the doorway and in a half dressed declaration of selfhood she held
up the bottle, smiled, "I'm rehearsing."

She motioned for her cousin to get the hell into the suite and swung
the door shut.

"When you show up unannounced like this in the morning, I know
something is amiss…Well?"

"It's afternoon," he said.

He dropped down in a soft chair. He looked like a young man with a
burden. His cousin bore in on his silence. "I'm listening."

"Don't laugh," he said. "But I met someone."

Well, this got her attention. She tossed the manuscript on the bed.
"From your look of joyous misery that's not the whole story."

"The girl…yesterday…at the theatre."

"The actress?"

He nodded.

"She's god damn white."

"You're white."

"I pass for white."

She grabbed her cousin's face by the chin. Looked him over like only someone can who has done time in every kind of human misery there is. "Ahhh," she said.

She walked over to the open window and sat on the sill. She brought her bared leg up and pressed her foot against the joist. She took a drink of wine. "That possessed need when you're young isn't all it's cracked up to be…in case you ask."

He turned to her. "They can see you down in the street."

She glanced out the window. "I hope they think of it as a moment of providence."

"I took her down to the Sixth Ward last night."

"That's certainly the way to an actress's heart."

"Nathaniel was there."

"Really?"

"He thinks the girl has potential."

Her cheeks got like iron. She took a drink of wine. "Potential…is that what they call it now?"

CHAPTER 78

WHEN WE MADE OUR WAY THROUGH THE HOTEL for the theatre, it was as if nothing had taken place. Word had gotten around, you could tell that from the blessed sneers you get when people think you aren't looking. Yet the guests in the lobby, and desk clerk and concierge, were all characters of good cheer as we passed on. If they knew Genevieve was my cousin, and half black to boot, she'd be dragged out of the hotel, and burned like Joan of Arc on the sidewalk...even in liberal New York. Don't kid yourself. There's still a lot of Southern porches in all that quaint Northern neighborhood.

Rosina did not come to the theatre that night, nor was she there afterwards. I was despondent. My grandfather would tell us, "I had dreamed the magic circle. And in it I had drawn your grandmother. Maybe because she was there all the time, waiting in my soul for me to find her."

I saw in my heart an America where that girl and I could exist. I saw it down there in the Sixth Ward. Maybe the stage creates a make believe where such notions as tolerance can thrive, can show us a way. Maybe it will take actors performing a truth, for a truth to come true. The next day I waited for lonely hours across from her boarding house with its gloomy matron, hoping, and when she emerged, I was someone again. But who?

• • •

Just watching her go along seemed to cure everything. He could not have guessed she wished she'd never met him, not any of them. It filled her with dismay and consternation. The unfolding of a soul is never easy, the hardening of one more difficult yet. But murder is a stubborn master. And death is the ultimate subtle prompting.

There was a gunshot on that New York street and from up the block came screaming. You could see the crowd begin to part, carriages take off at a dash, carriage horses turning or veering wildly.

There was a couple, a black couple. He was holding her hand and pulling her along. They were running so hard their mouths were open trying to get in air. He kept looking back. There was a riffle of smoke, then the rolling chord of a rifle shot.

The woman's legs gave way and she went to the earth violently. She tumbled along like a broken crate. He'd lost her hand at that moment and stopped and looked back. His eyes became huge and white with desperation and he screamed out her name, his arms a stark black, rising in the sunlight, and he was dead just like that. A second shot a moment later and he was sitting in the road as if he had taken a needed rest. His rest would be eternity.

Rosina didn't want to see more. They were runaways brought down on the streets of New York by slave catchers in their rough suits who now stood over the killed as if they were game. She clenched her jaw and her eyes welled with tears.

Violence had chartered her life. She had been shown newspapers as a child of the murders, she had been questioned, pointed out, derided, made a spectacle of. The bodies there in the street that people crowded around, bodies the police worked their way to get to, bodies prodded by the slave catchers' rifle barrels to be sure they were dead, bodies ready for the meal sack and the dragging away. This is the shocking truth that awaits violence.

She needed to be alone, to face her trial in silence. Up the street the gothic framework of the Famine Church, built by the poor, for the poor, suffering famine of body or soul. She was partway up the church steps when a hand grabbed hold of her arm.

"What you doing here?" she said, seeing it was Jeremiah.

"I was..." He pointed down the street to that bloody scene. "You saw?"

"I saw too much."

"You're crying."

"Go," she said. "Leave me to my own thoughts."

He followed her into the subdued light of the nave. In a few pews were people who'd come to pray. Isolated figures bearing their rosaries and suffering in silence. She sat alone far from all, but Jeremiah followed and sat beside her.

"Please," she said.

"Is it me?"

"You?"

He held up his hand and whispered, "Is it this?" he said, meaning his blackness.

He looked to be suffering. He had no idea. She took his hand and quietly held it in her lap. She did not want to lie, but she had no intention of telling him the truth about herself, and there was little space for anything else in between. "No," she said. "It's not that at all."

He leaned toward her. "I have feelings for you," he said.

It was neither a shock nor a surprise. "Put them aside," she said. "We'd bring each other hurt."

He sat back. They stared up at the altar and its carved reredos with mosaics and niches for statues. A foreboding beauty.

"I used to go to a church that looked like this when I was a child."

"I would take the chance even knowing I'd be hurt," he said.

She leaned toward him. "I'm going to ask you the question."

"What question?"

"The question…do you think Nathaniel killed them? The truth now."

To be asked here, and now, felt like the answer carried tremendous weight and authority. She looked at him with a beseeching stare.

"I think he did," said Jeremiah.

• • •

Nathaniel was sitting on the edge of the bed, a disheveled, naked, drunken mess.

Genevieve stood over him, wearing nothing but one of his shirts. Not quite as drunk and disheveled a mess as Nathaniel, with a wine bottle clasped in one hand. "Jeremiah tells me you think the girl has promise…I don't like the sound of that word. It has too many…" and she made this swimmy move with the hand holding the bottle and managed to spill some wine on him. "You know what I mean."

"She looks like Lucretia," said Nathaniel.

For the first time in Genevieve's presence, he had said the girl's name in a way Genevieve never heard him say her own name. It carried with it the gravity of time and loss.

She took the bottle and she flung it at the wall. "I had a whole drama worked up in my head to rain down on you. And then you tell me this."

She pressed up against him, his head upon the flesh beneath her stomach. He could hear the raised beating of her heart.

"Forgiveness doesn't come easy, does it?" she said.

"No," he said.

"It won't be taken from us."

"What?"

"The freedom…we have on stage. They can't take that from us."

CHAPTER 79

How would you like to see the ruination of
Colonel Tearwood's American Theatre Company?

THIS WAS SCRIBBLED ON A BUSINESS CARD that had been handed to John Jacob Astor via one of his personal secretaries. The name printed on the card was...Lawrence Scarth.

Mister Scarth had waited most of the day for entre before he was ushered into Astor's private lair. The palladium windows made the decorous office seem more like a cathedral. The Church of Easy Money, Scarth told himself.

Mister Scarth did not cut an overwhelming presence. His suit was of inferior material and the design seemed decidedly common. If a man's shoes told his story, Mister Scarth's were of long hours on the sidewalk.

Astor held up the business card. "You have two minutes to impress me."

"I have information, private information, that if made public would bring down the company."

Astor looked the man over, sitting there with his top hat in his lap. The hat, a little too sun weathered, and his fingernails...they needed proper care. He didn't look totally untrustworthy, thought Astor, he looked utterly untrustworthy.

"What's your line of work?" said Astor.

"I've had many entrepreneurial adventures."

"Jack of all failures."

"Not all of us are blessed with your foresight and skill."

Astor sat there and considered. "I would invest handsomely in a business proposal that showed potential. And if the entrepreneur had information that you suggest... all the better. But how would someone come upon such information?"

"I have a connection within the troupe...Genevieve Wells."

"If you'll excuse me, but you don't look the...theatrical type."

"I'm not. Genevieve Wells happens to be my daughter."

. . .

Mister Scarth now waited for the opportune time to line his pockets with a hard fall. The auditions for *Wuthering Heights* began in earnest. Rosina Swain arrived to begin to put an answer to her past. She bore her beauty as only someone can who cares not, and who is living with a private cause.

The play's director, Robert sat in the front row, handing out sugges-tions…highlighting points of drama as Nathaniel and Genevieve filled in the emotions with the actors.

What people see in a performance, or even in something as rudimen-tary as an audition, is as much about the viewer's world as the world itself being viewed.

What Robert saw was a well versed young girl at the tempting edge of womanhood, who had been in a number of plays, child parts all, who could recite the classics and scenes from the burlesques and parodies, and who seemed to have some other province of focus in those icy dark eyes.

What Jeremiah saw from that darkened backstage was this shining, beautiful presence that bled innocence. That made him want to reach across any darkness, take on any test, confront any curse, to empty his soul and gain her affection.

As for Nathaniel, he could neither hide nor escape from what he saw. His past was alive like some strange part of oneself returned from wander-ing or banishment. Terrifying in its simplicity, haunting with omens of destruction that flooded him with aching remembrance and love. And those eyes that were as far as a lifetime away or as close as a tear.

As for being the only other woman there, what Genevieve saw was the future. The untamed youth who would ultimately replace any actress as they get old. But she could also see Rosina through Nathaniel's eyes, his actions, his subtle movements and inflections of speech as they read dialogue. She saw what he had either refused or failed to say. How care-ful he was, how tender. He seemed alive to every nuance, and he did not look at Rosina as a woman who in the play he would marry, or even as an actress he was rehearsing with, but as an heir to his deepest feelings. And Genevieve, like any good actress, could read the text beneath the text… this could be his daughter.

When there was a pause, Genevieve said, "I heard from Jeremiah that both your parents died when you were young."

"Yes," Rosina said.

"Tell the imaginary audience a story about them. Make it up if you wish. But move us."

Rosina looked as if there were suddenly no room left on earth where she might move.

"My memory," Rosina said, "is too cloudy. But one night…my birthday…my third I think. There were woods behind our little house. And on my birthday, my parents dressed up in costume and makeup like forest sprites or good hearted witchly types. They sang and danced, and they brought me a drink in a silver cup and served me cake on a silver plate, and we searched the woods for my presents and the stars were like pearls." She quieted. "And there was magic in my heart." She had been looking from one to the other until her feeling eyes fell upon Nathaniel standing there in the shadows of the treadmill and prison cell.

"But the woods are empty now," she said, her voice choking up. "There is no silver cup to drink from and there is no silver plate to eat cake from and there are no sprites or witches to share my joy with…and my mother is only an old photograph I have of her…and my father…he is a shadow I can't remember." Her voice was shaken, and maybe even a bit angry, sinking in her throat as it was made it impossible to tell.

To Nathaniel, she said, "Would it hurt you to not remember? Or to have a daughter not remember?"

When done Rosina realized without warning, she had said things on stage in a way she would never have been capable of in life. This environment, this unreality, had freed her from herself. It allowed her to step through her uncertainty, and if chance favored her, she could confront him during readings and rehearsals, driving indirect nails into his being and see what effect they would have, if any. Could she force him from a lair of lies and, so righteously, murder him. She also came to feel she was crying.

"Quite a performance, young lady," said Genevieve. "You held the audience silent…By the way, did you make that story up?"

"It's from a play I read for in London," she said, and then ran off stage.

It was not from a play she'd read for. It was not from a play at all. It was one of the last vestiges she could recall of a life stolen from her. And there would be only one other living person in the world who would know that, and he was following her with his eyes, watching Jeremiah cross backstage to walk together with her toward the open alleyway doors.

Robert got up and walked to the edge of the stage and slammed his hand down flat and hard on the boards. This got Nathaniel's and Genevieve's attention.

"What the hell is going on here?" said Robert.

"An audition," said Genevieve.

Robert glared at her. "Lady, your reading of that line...had about as much color as salt."

Later, Rosina was sitting outside on the stairs with Jeremiah, a little afraid. There she and he were. Two strangers and their one shared world, when Nathaniel walked up behind them.

"My old friend," said Nathaniel, "the Colonel...Robert's uncle...the actor who thought up this company, once said to me, *"What would happen if the Red Sea parted, and there was no one there to cross it?"*

"Is that supposed to mean something to me?" said Rosina.

"Yes," said Nathaniel. "It means the woods are never empty. Even if you believe they're empty."

CHAPTER 80

As THE REHEARSALS FOR *Wuthering Heights* began in earnest, the constellation of life was moving against them all. Rehearsals barely masked the brooding urgencies that silently existed. Private demons gave the scenes an added human edge. The worse the players suffered, the better their work stood out.

Rosina maintained this picture of innocence, perfect for the part she played in the play, and just as well for the part she played in life. She was a smooth animal of hard work and aspiration. She did everything she could to will this man——her father——from the shadows of his true identity. She made him her mentor. But Nathaniel Luck was not just slyly versed as an actor, he was subtly trying to influence her, to soften her, to change what he believed was her path, which would end with his death.

He knew, because she was him. He knew because he could feel the rage beneath the calm in a person like none of the others. Because he had killed, he could sense and measure that secret monster as he had acted upon it. Although the word "acted," barely fit.

At night Jeremiah would walk Rosina back to her boarding house. Sometimes they would go by way of the Sixth Ward and Actor's Paradise. But even there, they would have to stay alive and alert to street realities.

It had rained, and this one particular night a soft mist bedded the streets that were wet and quiet but for a few lonely carriages.

"Hey...you there..."

A man's voice from a rig window called out, "You...You're the stage manager at the Bowery Theatre for that acting troupe, aren't you?"

It was odd to say the least, to be recognized and called out in the blackish evening like that. Jeremiah slowed his walk. With the mist it was hard to discern the face within that dark coach.

"Yes...I am."

"You've done pretty well for a colored boy, I would say."

Their walking had slowed, the carriage had slowed. Rosina reached out and tugged at the back of Jeremiah's coat. He started across the muddy street with her following, angling so as to cut behind the carriage.

The man must have slid over in the seat, because his dark visage squared up through the mist in that window. "Walkin' a white girl home… Damn gentlemanly of you."

They paid him no attention. Jeremiah picked up his pace.

"Like to be a white yourself, wouldn't you, *Jeremiah*?"

He stopped now in the street. Rosina alongside him. "Who are you?"

The man ordered the carriage to halt. The wheels made a sloppy business of it. The door opened, and a figure stepped out into the evening. Haze from a streetlamp was just enough to put a few highlights on that singular shadow by the coach.

"Uncle Lawrence," said Jeremiah.

"Surprised to see me, boy?"

Jeremiah was beyond speaking.

"Surprised to see me alive is more like it."

He came toward Jeremiah. He was like something from the dark shores of a bad dream. He was looking the girl over. She already knew that look. She felt the discomfort that led to trembling.

"You don't worry about walking with a colored boy at night?"

"I think I know who to worry about walking with."

"That's how you white girls end up bearing a black baby. Of course, you're an actress. That says it all."

"What do you want, Uncle Lawrence?"

"Be careful who you get right to the point with, child. Tolerance is a hard commodity to come by." His mood lightened. "I saw my baby girl in that play… *The Treadmill*. She sure does shine."

"Yes," said Jeremiah.

"She's living a fine white life."

Jeremiah said nothing.

"Yeah. God sure did give that girl a favor letting her be a fine white, like me. She wouldn't be up on that stage, basking in all that applause, if she were black as her mama."

Rosina looked to Jeremiah to see if this were true.

Lawrence Scarth took out a business card and politely forced it into Jeremiah's pocket. "Want to see her. Let her bathe in my goodwill and affection over her success."

CHAPTER 81

JEREMIAH HAILED DOWN A CARRIAGE. The driver would take the girl, but be damned before he had a black on board. Rosina was to be driven to her boarding house while Jeremiah set off at a dead run for the theatre. Rosina, though, had other plans.

When she arrived at the Bowery it was dark and empty except for Genevieve, who was in a catastrophic state, and the three men who made up Colonel Tearwood's Company. She had by then sobbed out her very soul. She knew her father's sudden appearance would serve the most heartless motives of man.

"Maybe I'm to be the victim of the sins I've committed. Maybe it's a perverse form of——"

She noticed a still and silent apparition among the shadowy sets. "What the hell is she doing there?"

The men turned. They looked to where Genevieve pointed.

"I sent her home," said Jeremiah.

"Does it look like she went home?" said Genevieve.

"Don't blame Jeremiah," Rosina said.

Nathaniel ordered her out of the shadows. The girl came forward reluctantly.

"What were you doing hiding back there?" said Robert.

"I wasn't…hiding. I just didn't want to…I came back because I was concer——"

"Heard everything," Genevieve shouted, "didn't you?"

"I heard…Back there on the street. But you won't ever——"

"Before long," an overwrought Genevieve shouted, "the whole fuckin' city will know."

Genevieve fell into an utter state of panic. "I don't know what to do… What's to become of me?" She screamed, "What do I do?"

Not one of the men had an answer, but Rosina did. "*He* knows what to do." She was looking at Nathaniel. "Better than anyone." And she said it with a cold bluntness they had not heard before from her.

She had brought the uncertain right down upon them. Things became quiet in that unsettled way.

"Jeremiah," said Robert, "take Genevieve home. Go with him, Jennie. And rest. Nathaniel and Rosina will remain here with me. There's knives to be sharpened, and things to be said."

He meant business, and there was no room around it. Jeremiah led his cousin away. She went quietly under the flag of exhaustion. She had to pass Rosina and did. She stopped and looked the girl over. A look of desperation that caused the girl's eyes to quiver and flinch. "I wouldn't say anything, I swear...for Jeremiah's sake, if for nothing else."

"America is full of surprises...isn't it," Genevieve said and walked on.

• • •

"Playwrights can be such bastards," said Robert. "They can start a fight on paper for the most trivial reason with the worst intention and take the character to their own destruction. Then they can throw away the pages and start over. Sealing the character's fate to a totally different set of miseries. And then cast aside scenes and dialogue...mere ghosts.

"Maybe," Robert said, "that's why it's so much harder to be a human being than it is to be a playwright." He focused on Rosina. "We know who you are, and why you are here. Nathaniel has known right from the beginning."

She did not look trapped, or outsmarted. Rather, she looked self-contained.

"Well? What might you have to say?" said Robert.

She did not answer. The two men glanced at each other. What to make of this...presence.

"How do I write you?" said Robert.

"Any way you want."

"That silk pouch you always carry," said Nathaniel. "You wouldn't have a revolver tucked away in there?"

She came forward. She opened the pouch. Her hand reached in and out came a pocket revolver. Robert tensed. Nathaniel had lived this moment in his mind endless times. It was more a relief than anything else. She dropped the weapon on the worktable between them. Nathaniel saw Rosina was surprised at his guessing about the weapon.

"Actors," said Nathaniel. "Our business is props. You should know that by now, being an actor yourself."

"It's no prop. It's not all I carry." She reached into the purse. Neither man had any idea what might be next.

She presented what looked like two photographs. The first she threw on the table. It was part of the original flier Genevieve had made up of COLONEL TEARWOOD'S AMERICAN THEATRE COMPANY with Nathaniel's image. But it was the second that she set gently down and touched.

It was a worn, frayed thing the tyranny of years had exacted its pitilessness upon. There in the faded shading was the image of the girl lost to him all those years ago. Yet more real than everything real about him. The youth, the grace, the beauty, the something wild, hopeful, and tender amid the spider cracks. He wondered, would anyone see all that besides himself?

"You remember that woman," said Rosina, "don't you?"

"How can I remember," he said, "what I never forgot?"

"That is all I have of my life," she said, waving a hand over the two images and the weapon. "There is that, and this endless stretch of loss that is my life afterward. And you created that," she said. There was little charity in her voice, or heart.

She pressed on. "You created that...Just as you created me. And then you destroyed it. Your mark is upon those deaths as much as God's mark is upon the earth. Now...call me a liar. Look into my eyes...Father...and tell me it isn't so."

He looked into her eyes, hands clenched, a fated moment finally come to pass. "I killed your grandfather," he said. "He had strangled your mother, and she died in my arms. I killed him because he was a monster, and I loved that girl. He'd defiled his own, and I did him an end for it. I ask for no pity. I ask for no compassion or mercy. Let it be written in my soul all the year round. You have the gun, the hand, and the will. I am not afraid to die. I have died many times. I curse my own blindness every day, and that is the worst thing in the world you have to curse...so, beware."

He went silent. He unclenched his hand and he sat back. Rosina stared at him unsatisfied, and starkly wounded.

"You haven't answered her question," said Robert.

Nathaniel glanced at the playwright.

"No...he hasn't," said Rosina.

"You made her an orphan...You can't leave her *an orphan*. Unless it is so."

"You son of a bitch," said Nathaniel.

"That sometimes is a friend's duty."

"And a playwright's———" Nathaniel spoke with careful quiet. The theatre was achingly still. "I…" he said, "am your father. Her having a baby was kept secret. Your grandfather used the situation to keep your mother under his control. And my leaving you as I did…is shameful and true."

That was it.

Rosina stood there, this wounded woman child, gathering her emotions, lost but proud, clinging to whatever it was that gave her the resolve to cross half the world to come face to face with that salient answer.

She was the picture of dignity as she picked up the revolver and put it back in her silk pouch. And then she took the photos, not just the one of her mother, and tucked them away with the weapon. She walked out, leaving not a single word behind, and it wasn't until she was out in the alley that the two men heard a faint succession of sobs.

"You lied to her," said Robert.

"That's the playwright in you talking."

"You're not her father."

"Aren't I?"

CHAPTER 82

If it was a lie, why had he lied? Why *that* lie? Was it somehow in *his* mind meant to ease Rosina's suffering? Did he think it would temper her from committing a catastrophic act? It was something Nathaniel certainly knew about, how in a few striking minutes of uncertainty one creates their certain destruction. And it was not because he was afraid to die. That would be proven in two weeks on one of the most infamous evenings in the history of the American theatre.

If only we could live our lives in retrospect, instead of thinking and writing in retrospect. I could not imagine Rosina committing a murder any more than I could imagine myself committing one, as much as that black desire came over me when I was called down and humiliated for not being born white.

During that critical two weeks, another thought crept in, and when I was alone with Robert I felt compelled to ask, "What if...Nathaniel was telling Rosina the truth?"

• • •

Genevieve was well past being drunk when there came this polite knocking at her suite door. Nothing worse than polite knocking in the middle of the goddamn night.

"Once upon a midnight dreary...while I walked around drunk and weary...there came this pain in the ass knocking...knocking, at my hotel door..."

She swung it open. And there was a cried out Rosina.

"You aren't the Raven!"

"I didn't mean to show up at this hour. But I needed you to know I would never...never...say a word. I swear it! I have a great deal of respect for you. And now, even——"

Genevieve gave a scythe with one arm to shut the girl the hell up. "Rosina...do you drink?"

"No, ma'am."

"Well come on in and watch me...Maybe you can at least pick up a few pointers for later. Cause you're gonna need 'em."

They commiserated about the world and the state of the world and their place in that convoluted state of the world. And they covered subjects from adultery all the way to the worst disasters during a play they'd ever heard of or witnessed.

By the time Nathaniel returned in the wee hours the suite was dark and as he came in quietly, carrying his shoes, Genevieve was tiptoeing out of the bedroom with a candle in hand, and as she closed the door behind her Nathaniel caught sight of someone sleeping in the bed.

"Who is that?"

"Your daughter," said Genevieve.

"Where are we gonna sleep?"

"We?" She handed him the candle. "You mean...you."

• • •

Genevieve was to meet her father at Delmonico's Restaurant down on William Street. She was the epitome of confidence and decorum. She sat across from her father and listened with cool politeness to his self-serving and sorry ramblings, and put up with his quiet remonstrations. "You don't visit your mother. I understand you can't afford to be seen with her under your new circumstances. Of course, you do send her money...through Jeremiah. How intelligently cautious."

He took then a folded up document from his coat pocket, "I might never have gotten wind of you and of your success, if not for an article I read about that theatrical business in Buffalo exhuming a body. Your desire for notoriety is my good fortune. He set the document on the table before her. "I see a grand future," he said. "Scarth and Wells. Our own theatrical company. After you make *Wuthering Heights* the success I suspect you will."

She glanced at the document. She could have spit in his face.

"Have your attorney review it."

• • •

Mister Scarth was requested to come to the Lafayette Place house. Nathaniel and Millicent waited there for him, alone. That's when she said, "I have an idea."

"About?"

"Why don't we get married? I'm not too old to have a baby. I could go to Europe like all the other rich matrons and come back with an adopted child. We'd never say a word. You could go on with Genevieve."

He tried to keep from looking stunned by the statement. He held her gently by the wrist. She turned her hand so she could take his. Some feelings are just never bound by the clock.

There was a knock at the door. Scarth had arrived.

Not a word more was spoken.

Scarth tried not to look or act suspicious of being brought there. He had no such skills. Millicent offered him a seat. Nathaniel offered a drink, a smoke.

He was no sooner comfortable, than she bluntly said, "I will pay you to sign a document that Genevieve is not your daughter. That you know nothing about her lineage, her past."

"Why would I agree to what is not so?"

"To sleep well…and in comfort," said Millicent.

"I didn't come here alone," said Scarth. "I'm not a fool like that Mister Jonah who travelled all the way from England to this doorstep and soon after was never seen or heard from again. Mister Halsey is outside…to see I leave here safely."

"And you can leave here safely…and wealthy, if you wish."

He looked from Millicent to Nathaniel. Their calm and gratuitous good manners set him on edge. Civilized types walking the dark side of the street always filled him with distress. The shanks they stuck in you were always smooth and sleek and securely pointed.

"Why do I feel this threat in the air?" said Scarth.

"That's not a threat," said Nathaniel. "That's just one's better angels trying to get your attention."

• • •

Robert and Jeremiah arrived with Genevieve long after her father had gone. The news was not good. Genevieve's father had turned down the offer.

Genevieve put on a brave face. "I'm past the weeping and tearing at my clothes stage," she said. "Or spending whole days locked away drunk. I think I'll have a nice quiet dinner and decide which river to jump into."

"Why did he turn it down?" said Robert.

Someone just then tapped on the door knocker. Genevieve made a showy motion with her hand. "The answer...here it is now."

Sarah went to the door. She returned a few moments later and called for Missus Harrison. Rosina stood in the entry.

"I'm sorry to just show up like this. My name is——"

"I know who you are. Come in."

Rosina followed Millicent into the parlor. She immediately turned to Jeremiah. "Thank you for not telling me where you all were going."

"I told him," said Nathaniel, "not to."

"No one asked me not to tell you," said Genevieve. "Why don't you come over and sit next to me." She tapped the couch seat beside her. "You can help me decide which river to jump into after we have dinner."

"Don't be talkin' like that," her cousin said. "It only makes me more angry."

"I'm trying to put a little base humor into a bleak situation. If you don't...goddamn mind."

The parlor became painfully somber. The players lost in their own uncertainty. "Maybe it's best," said Genevieve, "if I just sign up for the slave ship and be done with it."

It was an ugly passage of moments that followed, with everyone voicing their own harsh narrative of what should happen next.

"He'll let us get the play on its feet...then you replace me," she said, looking from Nathaniel to Robert.

"It won't matter," said Nathaniel. "This is not what he is planning. He turned the money down because he has better money somewhere else. He is using us to better his situation somewhere else."

"How do you know?" said Millicent.

"In prison they had a saying, *'Don't try to be too smart... Just remember...blood always flows downhill.'*"

No one knew what to say. Answers were in short supply. And there was Robert, thinking he'd had the set designers recreate this room on stage for

Wuthering Heights. And here they were on the real set for a living drama that could burn their lives down.

"I could hire people," said Millicent, "who are experts at looking into these matters."

"Scarth," said Nathaniel, "is shifty enough to be thinking about all that already."

"I might be able to find out," said Rosina. She looked about the room at a current of faces that were well beyond downright skeptical. "I would try," she said. Then to her father, "But not for you."

CHAPTER 83

LORD HALSEY HAD A SMALL OFFICE down a slight alleyway from the British Embassy. It was up a flight of rotten stairs and looked like a roach infested attic, which, in fact, is what it was. There was a second office further down the hallway where men laughed and told filthy stories.

Rosina's grandfather had been a successful theatrical producer, despite his flaws, and his murder left Rosina with a very ample estate. The family attorney had been responsible for hiring Mister Jonah to find John James Beaufort and return him to England to take his rightful place on the gallows.

Upon his disappearance, an offer of financial remuneration was made to Lord Halsey. He was, of course, no more a Lord than the first mule you passed on the street. He was also caught short when the demure and polite young lady who was, in effect, his employer, said she was writing her attorney in England to sever their financial relationship with Halsey.

There Halsey was in this cramped office with a slanted roof and blotched water stains, standing, hands in pockets, shoulders stooped, while Rosina sat across the desk from him, politely rattling on about this menace, Mister Scarth.

"For months," she said, "I have worked to ingratiate myself with that troupe. Befriending that ridiculous and vile Negro boy, having people stare at me, insult me, defame me for my association with that black creature. And now…the whole troupe is coming apart thanks to this Scarth fellow. I'll never find out what I came here for."

She stood. "I'm sorry, but if you can't be of assistance any longer, I am forced to look elsewhere."

She started to leave. Here he was, having to plead his case to some——

"I know very little. Mister Scarth doesn't confide in me. He only hired me to be outside the Harrison residence when he went there."

She shrugged. "The worse for both of us."

"There is one thing I did pick up. A detail. It might be worth my… looking into."

She stopped and looked back at Halsey over her shoulder. "And what might that be?"

. . .

Rosina came out of the alley and past the embassy walking along unhappily as a coach glided up alongside her and a voice called out, "Get in."

She saw it was Nathaniel and his tone was not a suggestion or a polite offer.

"What are you doing here?" she said, sitting across from him. "Not suddenly playing the interested father role, are you?"

As the coach started away, she took off her white gloves and threw them on the seat.

"What's wrong?" said Nathaniel.

"I had to say some terrible things that I believed would gain his confidence. Horrible, degrading, inhuman things that I am ashamed came out of my mouth."

She looked out the coach window. It was her mother's profile there in the lacey sunlight. A wisp of a past that could never be.

"Aren't you going to tell me," she said, "it was just a performance? Meaningless words. A means to an end."

"I wouldn't insult or demean your emotions that way."

She hurt to be living this out like this. She tried to smile through the disquiet. "Listen to you," she said. "Acting the concerned father. Next you will come up with some familiar old chestnut of wisdom like...blood is thicker than water."

"Blood is thicker than water...And it's a lot more costly."

He looked out the window now. All the years and the loss so sharply drawn within him.

"I think about killing you...still," she said. "But I'm not sure what you told me back at the theatre is true. Which only makes it worse. But you knew that."

He glanced at her. "Did I?"

"I want very much to help Jeremiah. To make him happy and well and successful. I want to help Robert...And Genevieve..."

She stopped there. She stared at him now. She was searching out something in the man. What she could not see, or know. He was that other person at that moment. The one who played a *Romeo and Juliet* scene with her mother in an old auditorium with street children for an audience watching through broken windows, when they were little more than children themselves.

Rosina leaned forward. "It hurts, doesn't it? Having me this close."

"What did you find out?" he said. "From the lord."

She sat back. "You are as good at changing the subject as you are at changing your life."

"Well?"

"Mister Halsey had one thing to offer…But I don't know if it'll mean anything."

CHAPTER 84

"Astor," said Rosina.

The others were all at the theatre putting together a few last flourishes for the opening of *Wuthering Heights*. Robert had dismissed the cast and the understudies upon Rosina's return.

"That was all Halsey had to offer," Rosina said. "He admitted he'd paid a carriage driver for information and learned that Mister Scarth had gone to see Astor at his office."

On the stage was the parlor set, of all sets. It was like being back at Millicent's the night before. Robert just stared as he listened. It was as if the world were closing in around them.

Rosina looked over that mural of troubled expressions. The dramatic awareness of what she'd learned completely escaped her.

Jeremiah quietly explained, "Astor has it in for the boys. Robert made claims of corruption about an Astor like character in their first play... *The Monster*. Astor basically had them run out. Now they're back as successes."

"The bastard will wait a week," said Genevieve. "Maybe two. He'll want to see us pulling an audience. The better we do the more he can extort from Astor. That's why he turned down your deal. He goes to the press...Negro actress who passes for white secretly onstage with whites, won't go over well...Even in New York. They'll riot in this place."

Robert and Nathaniel were looking to each other. "Different scenery...same stage," said Robert.

Nathaniel laughed at the irony of it. The others didn't understand, except for Millicent, who had been there since before the beginning.

"It got political, again," said Robert.

"Was it ever anything but?" said Nathaniel.

"Cut me loose," said Genevieve. "Fire me. Bring in the understudy. Get a name actress. That will chop the head off that poisonous father of mine."

"Then what?" said Jeremiah.

Genevieve looked out into an empty theatre. All those seats, as if waiting there in judgment.

"I'll go over to England. I'll start over."

"You can start over," said Jeremiah. "But you can't get younger."

There was a blistering honesty to what he'd said.

"You think I don't know." She walked to the edge of the stage. "I hoped I could lie my way through to a life. Foolish Genevieve. Foolish, foolish, Genevieve. They can't strip you of your talent, but they can undress you of everything else."

"Your daddy isn't gonna let you loose after," said Jeremiah. "You know the man. He'll play Old Corn Meal, and he'll have you shingle dancing and doing Negro burlesques like Julius Sneezer...Come see Negro star who passed for white. He'll grind you down till everything about you be black."

"Why don't you cut her heart out while you're at it," said Millicent.

"I'm just thinking out loud, ma'am, hoping someone catches an idea."

"You are...or you aren't," said Nathaniel.

Robert nodded. This was straight out of a talk they'd had on many a bad night. "It is...or it isn't."

Nathaniel nodded.

"We could be ahead of the times...and that would be bad," said Robert. "We could be on the cusp of the times...that would be better. It would at least give us a chance. Or, we could be right on time...that, of course, would be best. But least likely."

No one understood their ramblings. "Where are you going, son?" said Millicent.

"We're going on, Mother."

"What?" said Genevieve. "I have lied and connived and cheated to get here. And I've dreamed of taking the world by storm. But this——"

"Maybe the world is ready. Maybe," said Robert, "they are on the cusp of being ready. And only need——"

"A hundred more years," said Genevieve. "That is what they need."

"We go on as we planned. Let your father go to the press. We live out whatever happens. After all," said Nathaniel, "we survived an alleged murderer in the troupe." He looked to Rosina.

"Being black is a lot worse than being a murderer," said Genevieve. "And we all know it. Remember...They hang murderers after they try them...Blacks go before the trial."

Genevieve looked out upon the waiting empty theatre. That was the white world with all its gratitude's and ingratitude's intact. "You can play anyone on stage," she said. "But they won't let you play you. If you are someone like me."

"Aldridge went to England," said Nathaniel. "He was black. He played Othello before a white audience and became a star."

"He is a black man playing a black character in a foreign country. I am a black woman trying to pass for white in lower Manhattan."

She clasped her hands together and wrung them. "Will the rule of absolute bigotry apply? Is it wrong to want to be thought of by others as great?"

"Wrong," said Robert. "It's absolute blasphemy not to want to."

"Whatever I do, I'll have it taken from me."

"What good is the theatre," said Robert, "if not this? What is the purpose of the stage, if not this? Look around you. This scene, on this set, with these players, is the heart of the theatre…This space gives any man or woman a fighting chance to affect the world with nothing more than a slingshot of thoughts and emotions."

To watch Robert, Rosina thought, one forgot how deeply scarred he was. How physically damaged. The ruined flesh seemed nothing more than blemishes caught at a certain angle of light. The being of the man so overpowered the physical reality. She was caught by this fact because a whole other reality was unfolding before her. She was being swept up in something vaster than herself, and it frightened her, even as it excited her.

"I would give anything," Rosina heard Genevieve say, "to have that moment. On stage. With everyone knowing."

The actress then glanced at Rosina. "Where are you in all this, young lady?"

She sat there with everyone staring at her, her father especially. "I've never seen anyone choose, knowing they'd be hurt so bad."

"Really? Take a look at yourself in the dark one night," said Genevieve. "And then let's have this talk."

CHAPTER 85

Rosina was moved into Millicent's house on the chance of trouble. Nathaniel and Robert worried certain actors would bail out, so they made sure there were enough understudies. Rosina was moody and distant the night we brought her luggage to Lafayette Place. She refused to explain why until I berated it out of her. She told me what she'd said to gain Halsey's confidence. She apologized. It was a terrible blow, even though it was something that Genevieve or myself would have done under the circumstances.

I was cruel to Rosina that night and I made her cry. Never have I felt how unfair the world was as then. I did not know that wanting could cause such agony. I saw my cousin Genevieve for the first time in that light. I thought about the insults I threw at her about shingle dancing and performing in that burlesque, Julius Sneezer. Of all plays... God forgive me.

• • •

Lower Manhattan was, for the most part, a madhouse of cheap entertainment. The closer to the guttural of the streets, the better. The serious and the meaningful were to be as avoided as raw sewage, unless it touched the immigrant workman or seamstress where they lived. But white was still the order of the day where people went for excitement and pleasure. A sign at the entrance to the New York Zoological Society about summed it up:

**People of Color are not permitted to enter,
except when in attendance of children and families.**

This was the political stage as it was set on opening night. Millicent dressed as a simple working woman and sat in the balcony. She was to

286

be the eyes and ears of the troupe. The play had been advertised by the Bowery Theatre as…**A Tragic Romance of America…The Desperate Love Story of a Common Workman and a Lady.**

Millicent noted the unusual number of single women in the audience. More and more immigrant young ladies looking to start a life were moving into lower Manhattan. And as everyone knows——where single women go, men will follow.

Backstage there was an unerring and unnerving intensity unusual even for opening night. To prove the point, Genevieve threw up in a waiting bucket outside her dressing room which inspired two of the understudies to follow suit. To kill off the gagging stench affecting the cast and crew, Jeremiah had them burn incense that left a streamy haze about the roofbeams.

As the time for the curtain grew near, Jeremiah managed a few moments alone with Rosina in her dressing stall. They held hands, and he told her how wonderful she'd be, but they were both scared. Scarth could be out in the audience already poised to commit human misery. Together in that tiny space, he leaned over and kissed her. They rested their heads against the other's, trying to contend with an all too human condition. The scar of love was upon them already.

Nathaniel called out, entered, then asked Jeremiah if he could speak with "his daughter" alone.

"Well," she said.

"If you get lost out there, or drop a line, you can lean on me."

She nodded.

"And be careful," he said.

"Of?"

"If he's out there. If something happens. If people get ugly…or violent. Get off stage."

He started out.

"Is that what my mother would do?"

"No," he said. "She was an actress to the last."

• • •

They came out after the curtain rose, like thunder. Performing was a cakewalk compared to the stress of the waiting. All the pent up fears, the private agonies, the threat that hung over the American Theatre Company drove them, carried them, lifted them, transported them to where only the actor can go. Where they are one with each other and the stage that they inhabit, where they become a living organism of emotion and art with a single soul.

They received reviews that would help fuel a hit. Add to that the number of young women who filled the alley after the show, their handkerchiefs and soggy eyes a giveaway. One night not long after, a letter was given to Jeremiah backstage by the guard at the alley door to whom it had been handed. It was the contract, the long awaited contract. In a moment of theatrical bravery, tormented as Genevieve was by doubt, she tore up the contract in front of the others and put the bits of paper in a cloth sack, then had it defiantly hand delivered to the rooms that her father rented and that he could never have before afforded. That second floor suite of apartments with its private entry that said his deal, most probably with Astor, had already been made.

Their small kingdom was about to come crashing down.

CHAPTER 86

Lawrence Scarth had strategically planned. He'd bought a ticket for an aisle seat near the stage. He'd invited a reporter for the *New York Herald*, having made an exclusive deal with the newspaper for the rights to his story.

The performers were well into the first act. The scene being where Genevieve, as the youthful heroine, confesses to the audience her dreams and private love for the commoner played by Nathaniel Luck. Her desire is her entrapment in a world not of her making, but whose rules are rigidly upheld.

It was then, in the heart of a defining and revelatory monologue, that Scarth stood up, and pointing at Genevieve, shouted, "You are not white…You are a colored woman passing for white. You have been conniving audiences from the beginning. Get off the stage!"

Caught there like that, seeing it was her father trying to cut the heart out of her, the actress within the defiant woman bore down and performed.

But Scarth was not to be outdone, not even over the catcalls and demands for him to shut up and sit down. He went on. "I'm telling you the truth here, people…I know…because I am her father…and her mother is black."

•   •   •

Millicent watched from the balcony as Scarth was escorted out. But she knew, they were all cast upon the waters now.

Offstage, a drained Genevieve clung to Nathaniel before she had to go back on. He would have taken on all her misery if he could, but the tide of love can only rise so high. "The years of being someone else are over now," she whispered.

When she walked back on she was met by this low unsettling ripple of voices, and then came this scattering of applause. She went on as if nothing had transpired. She was free up there on the boards, to live as her character was moved.

After the play, the alley was packed all the way to the street. There was no escaping the theatre that night. They had to press through to their waiting carriage with Nathaniel and Robert leading the way.

Genevieve was being hunted down by one single question. People clung to the carriage as she tried to board, they held the reins, they mobbed the windows. She gave them the answer. It had been thought out and rehearsed, but it came out of her as if born that moment. "I am colored…I am white. And I am an actress."

• • •

Nathaniel and Genevieve were thrown out of the hotel as soon as the newspapers hit the street. Their clothes and belongings tossed into the gutter by management. The headlines were piercing…COLORED ACTRESS PASSES FOR WHITE AND SCAMS AMERICAN PUBLIC…NEGRO ACTRESS PASSES FOR WHITE IN MOCKERY OF GOOD TASTE. *The Emancipator*, an abolitionist newspaper, enjoined the fray and offered the actors a place to stay and a coterie of bodyguards to ensure their safety.

Wuthering Heights became the perfect measure of the times. The characters in the play were transformed into the actors playing the characters. It was now an interracial love story and when they entered, kissed, vowed their love, when they finally died and became the couple they never could in life, it aroused hatred and disgust amidst the audience as much as it did a heightened desire for social change.

Scarth himself was there again the following evening and would be every evening until the American Theatre Company was taken down. The Bowery was packed, people paid to stand in the aisles and watch this living drama play out for good or ill. *Wuthering Heights* was now a riven extension of life. For all the applause and cheers, there was fruit thrown and eggs, dead rats, and liquor bottles and demands that "black bitch" be gone from the stage.

Outside it was a festival of protestors and abolitionists, haters and true believers, and tradesmen selling beer and liquor, candies and oysters, and cooked sausage, chestnuts and soda pop. It was America in all its glorious and unconscionable madness. And the only country that seemed capable of going full speed in two directions at the same time. It was also a country on the verge of an assassination.

CHAPTER 87

THEY GATHERED AT MILLICENT'S HOUSE on what would be their last night together. None of them had a premonition it would be so. Others claimed they knew. That a note had been delivered to the Lafayette Place house warning of an attempted murder. Another claimed that Nathaniel had been told by a stranger in the alley outside the theatre, someone who claimed to be an abolitionist and had gotten wind of the plot. There are always such stories. Why people feed on such rumors is a complete mystery. You would think the killing itself would be enough. Maybe these wild and unsubstantiated tales make bearable the instant and violent hush of blackness.

The theatre was beyond legal capacity. The Bowery had hired attendants to stand at the head of the aisles by the stage. Before the show, it was made clear by the theatre manager that anyone throwing objects at the actors during the performance would be promptly removed and jailed. This garnered a flood of items that came raining down upon the manager and a rush of attendants charging the passageways between rows to get at and remove the guilty parties.

That night was excessively hot, the air heavy as engine oil. The curtain rose, and there came the usual rousing applause and wretched jeers since the news broke about Genevieve Wells. Voices shouting down those who opposed their view of the world, voices echoing from the balcony in response. The atmosphere had more in common with a political event than it did a place of entertainment.

At one point on stage were Nathaniel and Genevieve in a long dialogue living out the tensions that drive men and women together and then apart, tensions about class and money and trying to capture happiness outside the worldly order. They usually played the scene stage center, but on these most recent nights they pressed farther and farther towards the edge of the proscenium as if relentlessly unafraid of the dark reasonings of the audience, or as if art itself could override the obvious hatred.

From where Millicent sat watching, she thought their actions fueled unnecessary danger. People across the audience stood and cheered, women had taken to waving white handkerchiefs.

Rosina watched through a slit in the curtain, waiting for her entry which came in moments, afraid that harm would come to the man, not the actor, but the man who was her father.

They stood with the footlights just below them, their shadows rising black and stark toward a grand coffered ceiling, their voices orchestrating over the cries for Genevieve to get off the stage and the vile verbal assaults about sex and race flung at her, when Rosina saw her father make this sudden and out of place rush toward Genevieve as there came what could only be a gunshot. He had tried to place himself between those standing in the aisle and Genevieve and he grabbed the side of his head, stumbling. There followed a report of repeated pistol fire.

Genevieve had her arm raised at that moment, her hand open, her fingers stretched out, her voice possessed with her lines, when blood shot out from the breast of her white dress. Even in the balcony where Millicent sat they could see what was blood. Genevieve crumpled to the stage floor.

The screaming now and panic, people trying to find who fired the shots, women being trampled by men looking to save their precious hides. Actors and crew members rushed out from the darkened quarters of backstage.

Nathaniel was on his hands and knees, blood dripping down from the wound to his head and onto the boards beneath him. Even dazed, he saw the dying Genevieve. He crawled the few feet toward her to take her hand. He heard his own daughter calling out his name somewhere.

He had seen this kind of dying before. He leaned in close to her. It wasn't a whisper when she spoke to him, it was just there was so little left that was her, as she said… "the woods are never empty…"

He held her hand and looked down into a failing pool of emotions that had carried this woman from nothingness to the New York stage, and then the last of who Genevieve was, was no more. She belonged now to the calmness that was death. An attendant cried out that she'd been murdered.

Nathaniel slipped backward into the arms that were his daughter's. He could hear voices asking he not die as they tried to stanch his wound. Jeremiah stood over his cousin and amidst the chaos, the people running, cast members crying, stricken, keeping back in shock, the blood spreading across her white dress, enraged and wailing, he yelled out at the mob. "You've killed her, you bastards…You have had your way tonight… Tonight…but there's tomorrow…and the tomorrow after that."

CHAPTER 88

THE BULLET HAD SCORED THE SIDE OF NATHANIEL'S SKULL and part of his ear. It had done nerve damage, giving him vertigo. He could not stand or walk for days. He was taken to the Lafayette Place house. It was Rosina who watched over him for many hours. Tragedy had torn them apart, and it was tragedy that would bring them together. They talked of many things, and the light that came through the window and passed between them had a kind of warming love. Nathaniel watched as Rosina took on the subtle shadings of an adult the more he stripped down to the bared essentials of his past. And as he did, he could see the suffering of those long years in her seemed to ease. This new pain had given them different eyes to see with.

• • •

People congregated outside the Lafayette Place house. Abolitionists, true believers, blacks. Haters would sometimes pass along in packs, on horseback or speeding carriages, with their inflammatory detestations in full throat. Sometimes, but not often, they would rail away, firing pistols into the air. Millicent Harrison became the bane of the neighborhood. An ostracized matron receiving anonymous notes on fine stationery asking her to move on.

What Robert Harrison wrote in response and had delivered to the neighbors, he suspected had been reported in the newspapers, leaving out the obligatory execrations.

When reporters from certain newspapers appeared at the front door trying to solicit a comment or news, it was Sarah and her loyal mate, Sam, who ran them off with heartless efficiency. Nothing made the reporters angrier, which was Millicent's heartful intention.

They were, for all practical purposes, at war.

• • •

The theatre was closed for the nights *Wuthering Heights* was to be performed. The rest of the evenings were circuses and bawdy burlesques. As per Robert Harrison, the play would resume as soon as Colonel Tearwood's American Theatre Company recast. With that news, the play sold out for weeks in advance.

"Death," said Nathaniel upon learning this, "is the master salesman."

• • •

Genevieve Wells was not allowed to be buried in a white cemetery. Millicent would have laid her to rest in the family plot, but this was denied her. Genevieve was to be buried in a place for blacks near Collect Pond, which was nothing more than a filled in sump, and where it was not uncommon for the bones of former slaves and freeman to rise up through the muck to take in a little sunlight.

The funeral was to be simple and unassuming, but it took on a life force of its own. A huge number of blacks just seemed to mythically appear at the funeral home to pay their respects and then follow the hearse to the cemetery. Former slaves, freedmen, shop keepers, people of means and position. Somber and respectful. Then came the show people in a sign of solidarity. Actors from across the map of types and ages, many heavily costumed. Some say to stop any revenge against them for being white and at the funeral. They were all part of the cortege. And there were jugglers performing along the way, and gymnasts, there was a fire breather out front cocking his head back and spewing up great shocks of flame, and a snappy, high stepping marching band in full regalia that could be heard blocks and blocks away. It was an eye grabbingly gaudy paean to entertainment and more worthy of Genevieve Wells' unapologetic desire for fame.

Newspapers reported on the exquisite, beaded white silk dress the young actress was to be laid to rest in, and the hand carved coffin. How she was being treated as if she were a princess, or lady, and not the common black that she was.

• • •

They expected to find Robert completely wasted, if not worse. He had been in his brothel suite overlooking Actors Paradise, locked away for days, until Jeremiah kicked the door in. Robert was at his work table writing. He was sickeningly pale, an unfed shell of himself. Pages of drafted dialogue were everywhere, and the floor was decorated with empty bottles of Doctor McMumm's. Robert spoke with a hallucinatory dizziness.

"Remember the play I told you I was writing…About us all… That I didn't have the last act?" He swept an arm across that sea of stage play scenes. "We lived it. I've been getting it all down. And you…" He grabbed Jeremiah. "I need you to write down everything from the moment you met Nathaniel, so I can weave it into the story…for your character. You see… you'll be at the far edge of the stage. At your work desk. And you'll talk directly to——"

Jeremiah nodded, then he glanced at the doorway. Robert made a drifty turn with his shoulders. There was Nathaniel in the doorway, smoking. Sam, there alongside him.

"The woods are never empty," said Robert. "Are they?"

"Never," said Nathaniel.

"That will be the title of the play," said Robert. "We'll perform it right after *Wuthering Heights*."

"Pack up his work papers, will you, Jeremiah?" said Nathaniel.

Robert didn't want to go anywhere. Not really. But he knew the law of numbers and goodwill was against him.

"We both lost the woman we loved, didn't we?" Robert said.

Nathaniel jutted his chin toward Jeremiah. "The three of us."

"Yes, of course," said Robert. He grabbed Jeremiah by the shoulder, and the pages he was gathering up fluttered to the floor. "Forgive me for being…insensitive."

Robert reached for the carte de visite of Genevieve that he kept on his desk. He was so thankful to her vanity for having this made. "There was so much more I wanted to do for her. To love her the only way I could."

"You gave her the play."

"From my heart. Every word I had your character say…was me. Your soul on stage was my soul everywhere else. That was how I told her how I felt…how I feel."

"She knew," said Nathaniel.

"Yes?"

Nathaniel guided Robert to his feet. He was so wobbly, Sam had to take the other shoulder. "I think I spent it all," said Robert. "My emotions."

"Not all."

"The woods are never empty," said Robert. "It means so many things.

You can see that."

"Too well," said Nathaniel.

One sun washed morning soon after they got Robert home, word came to the Harrison home the grave had been defiled, the casket exhumed and destroyed, and the body taken.

That is when a brokenhearted and vengeful Jeremiah, who up to that point had reluctantly kept his powder dry, began to plot the murder of his uncle.

• • •

The night after the body was stolen, Rosina tried to coax Jeremiah into taking her down to the Actors Paradise, that it would help lighten the soul for a little while. Her reason was a lie.

He did not want to go, and Rosina knew why. She had seen the secretive comings and goings at the stable behind the house of a handful of former members of the stage crew. All young hardcases who had an allegiance to Jeremiah.

She faked infuriation and hurt at him and went off alone. She knew he would follow, and he did. She hoped his love for her would outweigh his plan to murder his uncle.

The actors who recognized them at Paradise were flush with condolences, and offered them liquor and food and good cheer. Rosina slipped through the crowd with a silent and distant Jeremiah following until she ended up at a mock stage of trampled grass that was framed in by a dozen lanterns. Actors were crowded around there listening, watching a few of their own doing a read through from copies of a manuscript. It was, Jeremiah came to hear, Robert's version of *Wuthering Heights*.

"Where," he said, "did they get those?"

"Robert had me give them out. For the auditions."

He suspected suddenly. Her tone, manner, threatening to come here alone, guiding him efficiently to this. It was all too neat.

"Jennie should be playing that very scene tonight," he said, looking toward the actors there in the lamplight, shadow players breathing their dreams.

"We're the theatre company now," said Rosina, "You and I… Robert and——"

"He's being invited to table, bought drinks in taverns. My uncle is being interviewed by reporters for what he thinks and feels."

"I know what you're plotting," she said.

He studied her, like one would a stranger you are in desperate need of. "What would you do for love?"

"Love is a verb, not a noun. I know that much."

"You of all people," he said. "Who came halfway around the world to kill a man."

She saw in him the full force of the rage she herself had lived with.

CHAPTER 89

AFTER MIDNIGHT THERE CAME A MIST OF FINE RAIN. Lafayette Place shadowed and emptied, the street lights becoming smoky pots. From her room in the dark, Rosina watched out the window to the stables, the entry door open, a lantern hanging from the ceiling by an iron claw. Jeremiah was listening to one of the stage crew who was intensely animated, then he held up something very small, something he could hold between two fingers that was then placed in Jeremiah's palm. His fingers closed around it. The other youth then upped the collar on his coat and took off out into the rain.

Whatever it was he had been handed, Jeremiah set on the table. He went to a wallrack and removed a slicker and slipped it on and as he returned to the desk there was Rosina in the doorway, bits of rain having streamed down her face.

"Where are you going?"

"I need to walk and think." He approached the desk and picked up what was a key...a house key it looked like.

She took the hand that closed around it. "It'll be all right, if you let it be all right, instead of——"

"I'm bleeding hatred. It's not just him. The whole world brought us to this minute."

"The yelling quiets down, but it takes a while."

He saw that she was suffering, and he could not bear it. Rage and love cannot stand side by side for long and one not fall.

• • •

Rosina Swain ran back to the house. She could piece it all together in her mind. The key was in all probability to Scarth's apartments, passed on through an underground of manservants and housekeepers who were part of the black underclass whose lives went invisibly along in service to the white world.

Rosina screamed from the vestibule across the empty parlor. "Nathaniel...He's going to murder his uncle!"

She had already told Nathaniel of what she suspected. He could well see it might be true, having been carried on a sea of torment to that same end. Nathaniel came from his room and grasped the railing, still weak from having been shot.

"He's gone," a frantic Rosina told him. "To Scarth's…I'm sure of it. He just left now. He has a key."

Millicent had come running from the study, along with her was Sarah.

Rosina had grabbed her coat from the vestibule rack. She knew where Scarth lived, they all knew. He had made a shameless point of letting everyone know. He had even sent a note to Jeremiah inviting him to visit if he ever cared to. It made the youth spew bile because he was sure Scarth meant it to wound, and that he thought he was above retribution…from a black.

• • •

Through the rain, like a wraith she ran, past dwellings of gloomy brick and burning windows, out of breath from running, running, begging Jeremiah in her mind, the sky above a midnight sea shrouding in, pools of rain water where was cast her desperate strobing image.

Jeremiah was already there in an unceremonious alleyway alongside Scarth's apartments, while Nathaniel rode atop the Harrison carriage beside Sam who whipped the horses on to get there in time.

On the first floor was a haberdasher and a stout door that opened to a stale smelling entry with a lightless flight of stairs up to the lone apartment where Lawrence Scarth presided over his poisonous existence. All was still when a rain matted Rosina arrived and climbed the stairs silently. You'd have thought it madness when she knocked on the door and called out, "Mister Scarth…Are you there? Mister Scarth…If you're there, please——"

The door swung open and Jeremiah violently pulled her into a shuttered atrium. "What are you doing here?"

She saw he had a heavy calibre percussion pistol in one hand. All cocked and ready to mete out finality.

"Answer me," he said.

"I came here to stop you."

"By warning him, I suspect."

"If I had to."

"Do you want me to go to jail for even——"

"That's why we should get out. Be gone from here before——"

It was too late.

They heard the lazy clopping of boots on the stairs.

"Can we get out?" Rosina whispered. "Please."

Jeremiah nodded, and he took her by the arm and quietly slipped down through a murky hallway to a door that opened on to an outdoor stairwell. He then pushed her out and pulled the door shut behind him.

Scarth had entered by then, with a couple of drinks and a good dinner under his belt, a thin knotty cigar between his teeth, when this figure emerged from the deep shadows. Shocked, a burst of air came from his throat, the cigar dropped from his lips. He saw it was Jeremiah and he said, "Jeremiah, what are you——"

It was then he spotted the huge revolver being levelled at him. Jeremiah pulled the trigger——but the weapon misfired.

The back door had slammed, but not locked. Rosina could hear the men fighting. By the time she made her way through the apartments, the two were locked in a violent physical struggle.

Jeremiah was a tough youth, but Scarth was a hardcore cracker who had bled and been bled by the best of them. He had a lantern in one hand that he kept beating down on the youth's skull. The lantern glass shattering. Jeremiah went to his knees. Rosina tried to stop Scarth. She screamed at him as she grabbed hold of his shoulders, but he flung her aside with pure animal disregard. The lantern, by then, was a mass of bent and twisted metal.

She had landed just feet from the pistol. When the lantern was a useless mass, Scarth resorted to his bare knuckles and his boots, kicking the downed youth.

Jeremiah was barely conscious when Rosina stood with the revolver centered in both hands. She had cocked the hammer like she had seen done by actors endless times in plays. She yelled at Scarth. He was so bound up in his fury that all she could do then was shoot him.

Blood flew. The pistol recoiled with such force it drove her back against the wall.

• • •

Thank God for the rain. Thank God for the mist and the dark. The coach had just pulled up when there came the report of a gunshot and a voice howling out.

Nathaniel leapt to the street. He looked about for witnesses, for anyone that might have heard. He told Sam to pull the coach into the alley and then come on.

The door at the top of the stairs was open, Nathaniel came upon the scene in bits of shadowy vignette. Scarth was on the floor with his back against the wall. He had hold of his chest between the throat and heart. Blood seeped out from between his grubby fingers. He was trying to call for help. Jeremiah lay motionless by an overturned table. Rosina knelt beside him. Nathaniel saw a huge revolver on the floor.

"Is he dead?"

She looked up shaken and pale. She shook her head no. "I shot his uncle. He was trying to kill———"

Nathaniel stopped her from speaking. Footsteps bounded up the front stairs, Sam whispering Nathaniel's name.

"In here."

"There's a woman in the street," Sam said. "Another in a window. One is calling out for a watchman."

"Is there another way out of here?" said Nathaniel.

Rosina pointed. "Back stairwell. Down the hall."

"Sam...carry Jeremiah out of here. Put him in the coach. Take Rosina. Get away."

Nathaniel picked up the weapon and slipped it into his coat pocket.

"What about you?" said Sam.

Nathaniel looked to Scarth. "I'm not done here."

Sam lifted the boy. Rosina grabbed her father by the arms. "I'm so sorry. I didn't want this to happen. I———"

He leaned down and he took her face tenderly in his hands. All the years ahead of them would be lived out in these few moments. The journey would always come back to this place, and this time. He kissed her as a parent would a child. "Go now," he said, "and take your mother's and Genevieve's souls with you, for both our sakes."

Once alone, Nathaniel turned to Scarth. Whether or not he would survive his wound was of no matter. Nathaniel walked into the parlor. Scarth understood when he saw Nathaniel return with a pillow. He tried to pull himself to the door. His voice rumbled and broke calling out for help. Could he be heard in the street over the rain? Only God knew. Scarth then tried to beg.

"If I help you," said Nathaniel, "you'll have the girl put in prison for shooting you. And the boy…being black, he is as good as hung."

Scarth's pleas were vacant and foolish. Nathaniel knelt down. "It will be easier for you, if you don't fight. Because it will happen anyway."

Nathaniel moved swiftly and forced the pillow over Scarth's face. The words coming out of the man stalled and severed. His bloody hands did not have enough strength to even push away that brocaded nothing of a cushion and his frantic desperation slipped into a weary cry and that weary cry wore down into shallow breaths that grew shallower and fewer and soon after, Scarth urinated in death.

Nathaniel stood and tossed the pillow aside. He looked down at this man who was now no more than some useless artifact of a lost race. Scarth had helped create a venomous headline, tomorrow he would be a headline.

CHAPTER 90

Nathaniel Luck left Manhattan that night never to be seen or heard from publicly again. As for the murder of Lawrence Scarth, that would be officially solved the evening Colonel Tearwood's American Theatre Company premiered *Wuthering Heights* with a new cast headed by Rosina Swain.

The center aisle and box seats were a litany of the city's noted, the balcony its unrewarded nameless. But they both had one thing in common with the unreal number of reporters on the scene. They were there to see what shock might be in store for them.

And who were we to disappoint?

• • •

Robert Harrison staged the whole affair. When the curtain rose, a candle suddenly lit at one end of the stage and there I was, at my worktable and chair and stacks of ledgers, now well placed props where my candle flickered.

I could feel the audience asking themselves—Who is this black youth? What is he doing on stage? When I tried to speak my throat felt narrow as a section of string. "My name is Jeremiah Fields. I am the stage manager." I heard quiet murmurings pass over the audience. After all, there were no black stage managers in New York. "It is my job tonight to introduce you to the members of our company."

On that line, candles across the stage unexpectedly lit, each in the hand of a cast or crew member. The black and white of them. A twinkling ensemble of artists and artisans who stood at the cutting edge of the darkness. That is when Rosina stepped forward. She was wearing a white dress similar to the one Genevieve Wells had worn when shot down. She walked to the edge of the proscenium and set her candle down on the spot where the actress' body had lain murdered. She rose up, a figure that now seemed to burn with light.

"Before the show begins," she said, "There is something I have been asked to read to you."

She was holding a letter. The audience moved a bit in their seats, they were highly anticipatory, as this was not the usual theatre fare. And coming so soon upon the tragedy—

Rosina began to read, "I...Nathaniel Luck... actor ...admit to the murder of Lawrence Scarth on the evening of June nineteenth...eighteen fifty four... in revenge for his responsibility in bringing about the death of Genevieve Wells." She held up the letter. "It is signed by Nathaniel Luck...and by an attorney at law and notary public...H. Hughes of Fifth Avenue."

Before she was done, a scattering of men had left their seats and were rushing up the aisles. Reporters most likely.

Rosina reached down and picked up her candle. Nathaniel was there suddenly, she could feel his ghostly presence in that anxious world of faces.

She waited until the audience had settled back into their seats, had calmed a bit.

"We want to thank you for coming tonight," she said. "And now...Colonel Tearwood's American Theatre Company presents the American version of *Wuthering Heights.*"

On that line, all the candles went out. The stage went black. Moments later in the midst of silence, the glimmer of footlights. And with the parting of shadows, the players stepped forth.